LAMBS TO THE SLAUGHTER

A DCI Monika Paniatowski Mystery

Sally Spencer

severn
House

This first world edition published 2012
in Great Britain and in the USA by
SEVERN HOUSE PUBLISHERS LTD of
9–15 High Street, Sutton, Surrey, England, SM1 1DF.
Trade paperback edition first published
in Great Britain and the USA 2013 by
SEVERN HOUSE PUBLISHERS LTD.

British Library Cataloguing in Publication Data

Spencer, Sally.
    Lambs to the slaughter.
    1. Paniatowski, Monika (Fictitious character) – Fiction.
    2. Police – England – Fiction. 3. Detective and mystery
    stories.
    I. Title
    823.9'2-dc23

ISBN-13: 978-0-7278-8192-2 (cased)
ISBN-13: 978-1-84751-442-4 (trade paper)

All Severn House titles are printed on acid-free paper.

Severn House Publishers support The Forest Stewardship Council [FSC],
the leading international forest certification organisation. All our titles that
are printed on Greenpeace-approved FSC-certified paper carry the FSC logo.

MIX
Paper from
responsible sources
FSC FSC® C018575
www.fsc.org

Typeset by Palimpsest Book Production Ltd.,
Falkirk, Stirlingshire, Scotland.
Printed and bound in Great Britain by
MPG Books Ltd., Bodmin, Cornwall

ONE

The woman was in her middle-to-late twenties. She was wearing a bushy black wig, which was both beautifully constructed and very expensive, and she thought it was most unlikely that there was a single person in Bellingsworth Miners' Institute that night who would even question whether or not it was her real hair. She was heavily made-up, almost theatrically so, but the make-up had been applied with a great deal of skill, so that instead of looking like a slapper – as she so easily could have done – she appeared merely temptingly exotic. She had a slim figure – she had once heard someone call it 'pixieish', and rather liked that – and carried herself like a model. She had never been to a miners' institute before, and as she glanced around it with undisguised curiosity, she decided that she very much liked what she saw.

It was its simplicity and lack of pretension that she appreciated most – its stark, stripped-down functionality. It was a place to drink and to play dominoes or snooker, and if you wanted anything else from your evening out, you'd be well advised to look elsewhere.

Actually, she *had* been wanting something else from her evening – and was still hoping to get it later – but Harry Price, the young miner sitting next to her, had been most insistent that before they got down to the only thing which would ever have drawn them together, they would at least have to show their faces at the Institute.

'We won the cup today, you see,' he had explained to her.

'The cup?' she'd repeated.

Price had looked at her as if she was from another planet, and – in so many ways – that was exactly what she was.

'The Brough Cup!' the miner had explained.

'I still don't . . .'

'We always knew we had the best brass band in the north-west, and now we've got the cup, it's official.'

'Ah, *that* Brough Cup!' she'd exclaimed. 'We'd better go celebrate the famous victory, then, hadn't we?'

And so they had.

* * *

They'd arrived at around half past seven, and it was a little after eight when the main door opened, an old miner walked in, and Harry Price said, 'Oh, I don't like that at all.'

'Don't like what?' she asked.

'The feller who's just come in is called Len Hopkins, and there's nobody in the village who's more against calling a strike than he is.' Price paused. 'You know there's going to be a strike ballot, don't you . . . err . . . err . . .?'

As he turned red, the woman smiled.

'You've forgotten my name, haven't you?' she asked.

'Yes, well, I mean, it's not really a very common one, and . . .'

'It's Zelda.'

'But that's not your real name, is it?'

'It's real enough,' the woman said, enigmatically. 'When we're doing what I came here to do, I will *be* Zelda – although tomorrow morning, of course, I might be someone else entirely.'

Harry Price still seemed uncomfortable.

'Look, even if it isn't your real name, that's still no excuse for me forgetting . . .'

She raised her index finger to his lips, to silence him. The fingernail was long, artificial and the colour of congealed blood.

'Let's not pretend this is a new experience for either of us, Harry,' she said softly. 'I was with someone else last week, and I'll be with a different someone else next week, so it's not exactly going to break my heart if you forget my name, now is it?'

'You . . . you have a different partner every single week?' Harry asked, amazed.

'Well, not *every* single week,' the woman admitted. 'Occasionally, when things get a bit too rough, I need a little healing time between dates, but let's just say it's most weeks.' She smiled again. 'Now what was it you were saying before you got all confused over forgetting who I was?'

'I was asking you if you'd heard about the strike ballot,' Harry said, glad to be back on more conventional ground. 'Have you?'

Oh yes, she'd heard about it, she thought. Everybody in her line of work had heard about it – and a not insignificant number of them were shitting themselves at even the idea of it.

'I think somebody may have mentioned something about a strike to me in passing,' she said aloud.

'You don't pay much attention to current affairs, do you, Zelda?'

Price asked, using the name with both emphasis and confidence this time. 'I bet you know as little about the strike as you do about brass band music.' Then he grinned and added, with a roughish tone to his voice, 'Still, as long as we share one interest, that's all that matters, isn't it?'

He really was rather cute, she thought, and hoped that he wouldn't turn out to be *too* cute – that the hard muscle she'd noted when they first met, an hour earlier, would come into its own later.

'When Hopkins walked in, you said you didn't like it,' she reminded Price. 'Why was that?'

'Do you see that other old man, standing at the bar?' Price asked, by way of an answer.

'Yes?'

'Well, that's Tommy Sanders, and he's as much *for* the strike as Len is *against* it.'

Len Hopkins wasn't looking for trouble, and when he saw Tommy Sanders leaning against the bar, he almost turned around and walked out again. Then he told himself that this was *his* institute as much as it was Tommy's, and that he had as much right to celebrate the victory of the Bellingsworth brass band as the other man did. Besides, as long as they kept out of each other's way, there was no real reason for unpleasantness, and Tommy, he was sure, was as eager not to do anything to spoil the night as he was himself.

He walked up to the long oak bar, carefully selecting a place at it two men down from where Sanders was standing. Then, once he had got his elbows firmly ensconced, he signalled to Ted, the bar steward, that he wanted a drink.

'Your usual?' Ted asked.

'That's right,' Len agreed.

His 'usual' was lemonade, because although record numbers of pints of bitter were being consumed all around him that night, the particular Christian God he subscribed to was known to be dead set against alcohol.

And wasn't it more than a little ironic, he thought whimsically, that of all the men in the bar that night, the two furthest apart in their views should be the only ones who were stone-cold sober – though in Tommy's case, it was doctor's orders, rather than a firmly held belief, which prevented him from getting hammered.

Behind him, he heard a voice call out, 'Phil, Walter, you're on.'

The two men he had chosen as his shield between himself and Tommy turned around, and ambled over to the snooker table. Now, there was only a stretch of empty counter dividing him from Tommy Sanders, but that was more than enough, as long as they behaved themselves.

As it happened, it was Len's hand which misbehaved, knocking over the glass which the steward had placed on the bar. A stream of bubbly liquid cascaded through the air, and then descended again – with enviable accuracy – on to the left sleeve of Tommy Sanders' best sports jacket.

Tommy looked down at the stain, and then across at Len.

'Watch what you're doing, you clumsy old bugger,' he said, though using the kind of light-hearted tone he would have employed if they were still the friends they had once been.

'I'm sorry, lad,' Len replied. 'Can I buy you another drink?'

'It wasn't my drink you spilled,' Tommy pointed out.

'Well, then, let me pay for that nice jacket of yours to be dry-cleaned,' Len suggested.

'It's only lemonade – it won't stain,' Tommy said.

He should have left it at that – a slight accident and an amiable resolution. But those who knew Tommy well – and most of the people in the Institute did – were not in the least surprised that he didn't.

'I'll let you buy me a drink – in fact, I'll buy you one – but only if you're willing to start being more sensible about this strike ballot,' he continued, in a much louder voice.

'Do you think you can buy my soul for the price of a glass of lemonade?' Len asked, and though there was an edge of anger to his tone, it wasn't yet an anger which could not be reined in should he choose to.

Around them, all talking had ceased, and the attention of everyone in the room was focussed on the two old men.

Tommy sighed, in an exaggerated manner, as if he could not believe that Len Hopkins was being so stupid.

'Of course I don't think I can buy your soul for a glass of lemonade,' he said. 'I know that you're a man of principle – as I am myself – but you can't blame me for hoping that, for just once in your life, you'll see reason, now can you?'

'I can see reason well enough,' Len said. 'And my reason tells me that a strike would ruin this industry.'

'It'll be ruined if we *don't* strike,' Tommy countered. 'Don't you realize how many pits have closed down since the war?'

'And don't *you* realize that this Tory government wants to close down even more – and that a second strike in two years will give it just the excuse it's looking for?' Len asked.

'I'll tell you one thing . . .' Tommy began.

But then, instead of telling him anything, he began coughing violently.

'Is that real?' the woman asked Harry Price, as she watched the scene at the bar being played out.

'Is what real?' Price asked.

'The coughing fit. Or is he just stalling, while he comes up with a new argument?'

'Oh, it's real enough,' Harry said. 'He's got what the experts call pneumoconiosis, though to us miners it's just "black lung". It comes from breathing in all that coal dust and silica down the pit.'

'And is it serious?'

'In some cases – like Tommy's – it's very serious. Most people round here don't think he'll live to see next Christmas.'

Tommy was continuing to cough, and Len Hopkins took a couple of steps sideways and laid his hand gently on the other man's heaving shoulder.

'Take it easy, lad,' he advised.

Slowly, the coughing subsided, and Tommy reached out for his glass of lime cordial and took a small sip.

'Better now?' Len asked sympathetically.

'I'll better be when you start thinking straight,' Tommy said. He looked Len straight in the eyes. 'Listen, lad, this strike won't be just about wages – we want compensation for all the miners who've had their health destroyed by working down the pit. That's only right and proper, isn't it?'

'Yes,' Len agreed sombrely. 'It's only right and proper.'

'And the thing is,' Tommy pressed on, sensing he'd gained the advantage, 'your support could be vital in getting us that.'

'I'm only one man,' Len said. 'I can't alter anything.'

'Now you know that's not true,' Tommy said. 'There are certain miners whose word carries more weight than others – and you're one of them. With you backing us . . .'

'That isn't going to happen.'

'. . . we could win the ballot. But without you . . .'

'I'm sorry, Tommy, I really am,' Len said – and he sounded it. 'Now, given your condition, I understand how you feel, and if I was in your shoes, I'd probably feel the same.'

'That was a bit below the belt, wasn't it?' Zelda asked Harry Price. 'It was, the way it came out,' Harry agreed, taking a thoughtful, but generous, slug from his pint of bitter. 'But I don't think it was intended that way. Len's just trying to be honest – like he always is.'

Tommy Sanders swayed a little, then steadied himself.

'And if I was in *your* shoes,' he said, his voice thick with malice, 'if I had no family to follow in my footsteps – then I might feel the same as you do. But I very much doubt it.'

'Now that really *was* below the belt,' Harry whispered.

'What makes you say that?' Zelda wondered.

'Len had two sons – great lads by all accounts – but they were killed, along with Len's wife, in a car crash, twenty years ago now.'

'Jesus!' Zelda said.

Things were turning nasty at the bar.

'You're a bastard, Tommy Sanders!' Len Hopkins hissed.

'You're the bastard,' Tommy shot back at him. 'You're a mean, bitter bastard who wants to stop everybody else having what he can't have himself.'

Later, when the Mid Lancs police had become involved, there were people who would claim that it was Len who launched the attack, though there were others – equal in number – who were prepared to swear that Tommy had started it. But whatever the truth, blows were exchanged before anybody watching really had time to grasp what was happening, Tommy punching Len on the jaw, and Len hitting Tommy hard on the nose.

Several of the miners – Harry Price among them – jumped to their feet and rushed over to the bar, grabbing the two combatants and pulling them apart.

'Now, fellers, we don't want any trouble,' said the bar steward – approximately thirty seconds too late. 'In a minute, I'm going to ask these lads to let go of you, and when they do, I want you to shake hands.'

'I'd rather shake hands with the devil,' Tommy snarled, between gasps for breath.

'And I'll not shake hands with him,' Len said. 'But I didn't come here looking for a fight, and if you let me go, I'll leave quietly.'

The bar steward nodded, and the miners released their grip on Len.

Len walked towards the door, stopping only to exchange a few words with some miners, sitting at a table near the door, who supported his anti-strike stance.

Tommy turned to face the bar steward. 'I'll have a whisky,' he said.

'Are you sure you should, what with your condition and everything?' the barman asked dubiously,

'I'm sure,' Tommy said, 'and while you're at it, make it a double.'

Harry Price smoothed down his jacket and looked across the room to the seat where Zelda, the woman with whom he'd been looking forward to spending an erotic evening, should have been sitting – only to find that her place was empty.

Tommy picked up his whisky and knocked it back in one.

'Another!' he said.

Len Hopkins had finished his conversation with his supporters, and had almost reached the door.

'Somebody should do something about you!' Tommy Sanders called after him. 'Somebody should fix you so you can never betray the working man again – you bloody Judas!'

They were harsh words – many would say *unjustified* words – and almost everyone who heard them that night would remember them the following morning.

TWO

The politicians on the morning radio programme had all had their say – the Conservatives obviously blaming the Labour Party for the crisis, the Labour Party naturally blaming the Conservatives – and now it was the turn of the show's resident pundit to give his own take on the situation.

'The roots of the current problem lie in the miners' strike of 1972,' he said, in a calm, authoritative voice.

'Is that right?' asked DCI Monika Paniatowski, taking the hot bread out of the toaster, and quickly dropping it on to the plate.

'In the aftermath of that strike, the government felt it had been held to ransom by the National Union of Mineworkers, and to avoid ever finding itself in that position again, it decided to build up stocks of coal at both the pithead and the power stations.'

'Must have seemed like a smart move, at the time,' Paniatowski said to herself, as she reached for the butter.

'At the time, it seemed like quite a smart move,' the commentator unwittingly echoed, 'but back then, of course, no one had any idea that the Egyptians and Syrians were planning to invade Israel during the Israelis' Yom Kippur religious holiday.'

'That's not quite true,' Paniatowski said pedantically, 'I imagine the *Egyptians and Syrians* had a pretty good idea it was going to happen.'

She walked into the hallway, stopping at the foot of the stairs.

'Breakfast's nearly ready, Louisa!' she shouted. 'Get yourself down here right now!'

'When the war started to go badly for the Arabs, they sought to put pressure on Israel's Western allies by first curtailing the supply of oil, and then increasing the price,' the commentator told her. 'In early October, it cost $3 a barrel, by mid-October it stood at $5, and would reach $11.63 by Christmas.'

'Or to put it another way,' Paniatowski said, 'it now costs me an arm and a leg to fill my little MGA with petrol.'

'And what effect did the oil price hike have on overall economic planning?' the commentator asked.

'It made using coal suddenly look like a pretty good idea?' Paniatowski suggested.

'It made solid fuel more viable,' the journalist said. 'Indeed, given the precarious state of the British economy, it made it an outright necessity. And the miners, realizing how much stronger their position had become, began to press for a large pay rise by taking industrial action. And that, in a nutshell, is the story of how we reached the point at which we began experiencing selective power cuts and the three-day week.'

'Speaking of which, how long is it to *our* next selective power cut?' Paniatowski asked herself.

She glanced up at the kitchen clock, and strode into the hall again.

'The electricity will be going off in five minutes, Louisa!' she shouted. 'Have you got that? Five minutes!'

'Just coming, Mum,' a sleepy voice replied from upstairs.

'Well, make sure you are,' Paniatowski replied.

As she passed the hall mirror, she noticed the rueful smile that was playing on her lips.

And it might well be rueful, she thought, because after all those years of listening to the way other women talked to their children – and promising herself that, in the highly unlikely event she ever became a parent, she'd never sound like them – she had become a carbon copy of all those mothers. And the worse thing was, she told herself, as the rueful grin widened into a joyous smile, she couldn't possibly have been happier about it.

Becky Sanders had awoken in darkness and dressed by candlelight that morning, but by the time she set off for her grandfather's house, the power for Bellingsworth had been switched back on.

It had become a regular part of Becky's routine to visit the old man before she left for school every morning. She didn't do this on the instructions of her parents – they took little or no interest in any of her activities – nor had anybody else, her grandfather included, even so much as hinted that it might be a good idea. She did it because she *wanted* to do it – she did out of both love and pity.

When she arrived at his house that particular morning, she found her grandfather sitting, as usual, in his favourite battered armchair, with a chipped enamel bowl on his knee.

'How are you feeling today, Granddad?' she asked.

'Not too bad,' Tommy Sanders replied, though evidence of the black and red phlegm at the bottom of the bowl showed he was lying.

'So what's it to be this morning?' Becky asked, with forced cheerfulness. 'The full cooked breakfast? Or would you just like toast and jam?'

'I don't fancy any food at all,' Tommy Sanders replied. 'But a cup of tea would go down a treat.'

'You have to eat, Granddad,' Becky said severely.

'I know,' the old man agreed, then added unconvincingly, 'I'll have something later.'

It was then that Becky noticed that her grandfather's best sports jacket was draped over the back of the chair, and that he was wearing the trousers that went with the jacket.

'Are you planning to go out, Granddad?' she asked.

'No,' the old man replied. 'Why did you ask that?'

'Because of the way you're dressed.'

'Oh, this is just what I put on last night, to go to the Institute.'

'So why are you wearing the same things this morning?'

'To tell you the truth, I haven't been to bed yet.'

'Why not?'

'Because I didn't think I'd sleep, and it seemed pointless to go upstairs and just lie there.'

'You have to look after yourself, Granddad,' the girl said.

'I know, I know,' the old man replied wearily.

'You're the one who persuaded me I was clever enough to go to university. I'd never even have considered it if it hadn't been for your encouragement. And if I *do* get in . . .'

'You will.'

'. . . and I end up walking on to the stage to collect my degree, I want you sitting in the audience.'

'I'll be there,' Tommy promised.

'You'd better be.'

But they both knew it was never going to happen. It would be four years before Becky was accepted by a university and another three years before she graduated – and Tommy would be long dead by then.

Becky put the kettle on, and spooned some tea into the teapot.

'When I was working down the pit, I used to dream of retirement,' Tommy said.

'Did you?' asked Becky, who'd heard this particular refrain many times before.

'But back then, you see, I always pictured retirement as being very different to what it is now. I thought I'd be healthy and vigorous – I thought I'd be able to go for long walks in the hills.'

'Everybody has to grow old, Granddad,' Becky said, reaching into the fridge for the milk.

'And I thought I'd have your grandma by my side,' Tommy continued.

A single tear ran down Becky's cheek.

'We *all* miss Grandma,' she said.

'Well, I've had my time and there's no point in dwelling on it,' the old man continued. 'It's other people I worry about now.'

'If you're worried about me, then there's no need . . .'

'It's these young miners, you see,' her grandfather interrupted her. 'They never had to live through the 1930s, so they've no idea what it was like. Some of them – not all, by any means, but some of them – only care about this week's wage packet, so they can pay off an instalment on their colour televisions and their new sofas. They don't see that if they won't stand and defend their ground, the bastar— the beggars . . . who run the mines will cut that ground right from under them.'

The more he had said, the louder and angrier his voice had become, and suddenly he was coughing again.

'You shouldn't upset yourself, Granddad,' Becky said, laying her hand gently on his shoulder.

The coughing fit subsided, and Tommy looked down into the bowl.

'By gum, lass, there must be half a coal shaft down in them lungs of mine,' he said.

'You need to look after yourself,' Becky cooed again.

'If I can just get these young lads to see sense, then there'll have been some point to this miserable life of mine,' Tommy said. 'And if I can't, then it will all have been a waste.' When he raised his head from the bowl to look at his granddaughter, his eyes were blazing with what might almost have been madness. 'I'll do anything to see this strike succeed, Becky,' he told her.

'Now, Granddad, remember what I said about keeping calm,' Becky said plaintively.

'Anything!' Tommy Sanders repeated.

Paniatowski had just finished lighting the candles when she heard the church clock chime in the distance.

'One, two, three . . .' she counted.

On the fourth stroke, the power went off – just as the local newspaper had announced it would – and Louisa appeared in the doorway.

'You'll be eating your breakfast by candlelight – and it's your own fault,' Paniatowski told her daughter.

As she down at the table, Louisa sighed.

'Breakfast by candlelight,' she said. 'How romantic!'

How romantic!

Paniatowski grinned. A couple of years earlier, the word 'romantic' would not even have been part of Louisa's vocabulary, but now it tripped off her tongue as easily as 'dolly' and 'teddy' would once have done.

She examined her daughter in the flickering candlelight – took in the dark eyes and coal-black hair she had inherited from her real mother, and the pleasantly stubborn line of her jaw, which came from her dead father. There was no doubt about it, she told herself, the girl was growing up.

Paniatowski broke four eggs into a frying pan and added a little milk. She had just begun to stir the mixture when the phone rang in the hallway.

'Get that for me, will you, love?' she said. 'If it's headquarters, ask them if it's urgent – and if it isn't, tell them I'll ring back in ten minutes.'

Louisa stood up again. 'Honestly, Mum, sometimes you work me to death,' she said with a grin.

For Betty Cousins, resentment had become a way of life, and she resented the power cuts more than she could say.

The first reason for this was that *she* knew – though no one else seemed to – that the so-called 'industrial action' was not about pay or conditions at all. No, it was about the fact that the miners – who she'd lived among her entire life – were all lazy devils, and would do anything to get out of doing a decent day's work.

Her own husband had been a case in point, always complaining about how life down the pit was hard, and using any excuse – even the bit of blood he coughed up some mornings – for staying away from the colliery. Well, he was gone now – too lazy to even bother going on living, in her opinion – but the rest of them who were left behind were just as bad.

The second reason for her resentment was that she half-suspected these power cuts to be nothing more than a plot to prevent her fulfilling her sacred mission, which was to watch the weakness of others being played out in the street below her bedroom window. But the plot – if that was what it was – had only partially succeeded. It was true that the street lamps were not switched on even when there was electricity, but the lights from the miners' bedroom windows – as they dressed for work they could no longer avoid – filtered out on to the street and stopped it from being in complete darkness.

It was in the light from the miners' bedrooms that she observed the dumpy woman who was shining her torch in front of her and making her way carefully down the street.

Even though the woman herself was little more than a dark blob, Betty knew it was Susan Danvers, Len Hopkins' housekeeper.

'*Housekeeper!*' she said to herself in disgust.

Well, that was one name for it – though she could easily think of another!

It was over twenty years since Len's son, who'd had ideas above his station, had bought a car and then proceeded to crash it, killing himself, his brother and his mother in the process.

And hadn't Susan Danvers been quick to get her feet under the table after the funeral?

By God, she had!

It was strange there wasn't a light on in Len's front parlour, Betty thought, because although he was as idle as any other man, he usually made an effort to be up and about by the time his 'housekeeper' arrived.

Susan opened the front door without knocking – and that told you all you needed to know – and stepped inside.

Once she'd closed the door behind her, there was nothing more to see, because Len Hopkins – being a secretive, mistrustful man – always closed his parlour curtains at night.

It was just as well, in a way, he did close the curtains, Betty thought, because whatever was going on in there should certainly be shielded from the eyes of ordinary decent people.

And yet she couldn't help wishing that, just once, he'd forget and leave the curtains open.

When Louisa picked up the phone, the voice on the other end of the line said, 'This is Ellie Sutton. Could I speak to Louisa, please?'

Ellie Sutton! Calling her! Louisa felt her heart start to pound just a little bit faster.

'It's for me, Mum,' she called across the hallway.

For me! she repeated in her head. And it's Ellie Sutton!

'Well make it quick, or your food will be completely spoiled,' Paniatowski shouted back.

Louisa didn't care if her food *did* spoil. At the moment, she didn't care if she never ate again.

'Hi Ellie,' she said.

She knew the reply was inadequate. She knew she should say something much smarter and wittier when she was talking to the coolest girl in school. But she just couldn't think of anything else.

'It's my seventeenth birthday on Friday, and Robert says I can have a big party,' Ellie told her.

'Who's Robert?' Louisa asked.

'My dad! You must remember him. He gave a lecture to your year on some boring old subject or other.'

'*Dr* Sutton!' Louisa exclaimed. 'He's brilliant. The talk was all about local history, and—'

'Yes, well, I'm glad you enjoyed it,' Ellie interrupted. 'But I didn't call you to tell you about Robert – I called to tell you about the party!'

But why would Ellie want to tell her about the party? Louisa wondered. Why would this cool girl – who she was surprised even knew that she existed – ring her at all?

'Well?' Ellie asked, a little impatiently.

'Well what?'

'Can you come?'

'Me?' Louisa gasped.

'Of course you!'

It was like a dream. It was better than a dream!

'I'll have to ask my . . .' Louisa began.

'What?'

'Of course I can come – if you really want me to.'

'I wouldn't have asked if didn't,' Ellie replied. 'See you in school.'

As Louisa put down the phone, her hands were trembling. She'd have to handle this carefully, she thought – very, very carefully – or her mum would never let her go.

The miners on the morning shift had started to come out of their houses now, and Betty Cousins shifted her attention from Len Hopkins' unpromising front window to the men on the street.

There was Phil Drummond, whose wife – the poor deluded fool – thought he was giving her his full pay packet every Thursday, whereas the truth was that before it ever reached her hand, he'd already extracted a couple of quid which he would shamelessly waste backing the ponies.

And there was Tony Clarke. *His* wife thought that when he went out on a Saturday it was to race pigeons, but Betty knew that what he was really doing was conducting a secret affair with – appropriately enough – a bus *conductress*.

Betty was following the progress of these men down the street when she heard the scream, which was so loud that she almost dislocated her neck in twisting round to find out where it came from.

And that was when she saw Susan Danvers again, standing outside the front door of Len Hopkins' house – and making as much noise as a scalded cat.

THREE

nstead of wolfing down her omelette, as she would normally have done, Louisa pushed it listlessly around her plate.

'Is there something wrong with your food?' asked her mother.

'Not really.'

'Then why aren't you eating it?'

The truth was that she was too excited to eat, Louisa thought – but she knew instinctively that it would not be a good idea to tell her mother that.

'How much longer do you think these power cuts are going to last, Mum?' she asked.

Paniatowski shrugged. 'Who knows?'

'It's all the miners' fault, isn't it?' Louisa said. 'We're all having to struggle in the dark, just because they're on strike.'

'That's a bit judgemental, isn't it?' Paniatowski asked.

'I don't know what you mean.'

'Well, for a start, the miners aren't *on* strike – they're just not working any overtime. And it's far too simplistic to say that it's all their fault. You're old enough now to stop simply seeing things in black and—'

'Will there be a power cut on Friday?' Louisa interrupted.

'There's a power cut every day. You know that,' Paniatowski replied. 'What's so special about Friday?'

'Nothing really,' Louisa said. Then, deciding this was as good a time as any to make her play, she continued, 'It's just that that's when Ellie Sutton's got this birthday party.'

'Who's Ellie Sutton?'

'She's a friend of mine.'

'I thought I knew the names of all your friends.'

'She hasn't been my friend for long, but she's really cool, and she's invited me to her birthday party.'

'And how old will she be?'

'Fifteen, I think.'

'You *think*?'

'It must be fifteen, mustn't it?' Louisa said hastily. She paused for a second – but *only* for a second, because she didn't want to give her mum the chance to ask any more questions. 'The thing is, you see, her dad's different from most of the dads, but even he might put his foot down if, because of the miners, the party has to be held in the dark.'

Mild alarm bells started to ring in Paniatowski's head.

'What do you mean – he's different from most dads?' she demanded.

Louisa shrugged awkwardly. 'Well, he teaches up at the university, doesn't he?'

'And that makes him different, does it?'

'In a way.'

'In *what* way?'

'Well, he gives Ellie a bit more freedom than the old-fashioned parents give their kids.'

'Am I old-fashioned?' Paniatowski wondered.

'You can be – when you're here,' Louisa said bluntly.

Paniatowski felt as if she'd been hit by a hammer.

'Do you resent me being out of the house so much?' she asked tremulously.

'Not really,' Louisa said, as if she hadn't realized the impact her last comment had made – and maybe, with the callousness of adolescence, she really hadn't. 'There are a lot of latchkey kids in my school. It's the modern way.'

'I could get a transfer,' Paniatowski told her. 'I could move over into administration, and that would mean I'd be home every night.'

'You'd hate working in administration,' Louisa told her. 'You love the horrible, grisly job you have now.'

Yes, she did, Paniatowski agreed silently, but she loved her adopted daughter more.

'Look, if it really bothers you that I'm not around much, I'd be more than willing . . .' she began.

And then the phone rang, and before she even realized it, she was standing in the dark hallway, with the receiver in her hand.

'I've got a murder for you, Monika,' said a heavy voice that she recognized as belonging to her one-time lover, Chief Constable George Baxter, 'and it could be rather a tricky one.'

'A tricky one?' Paniatowski repeated. 'What makes it tricky?'

'For a start, it's in a village. And you know what villages are like in this neck of the woods – they don't like outsiders coming in, even if those outsiders are trying to catch a killer for them.'

'That's true,' Paniatowski agreed.

'And what makes it even worse is that this particular village – Bellingsworth – is already deeply divided over whether or not to vote for the strike.'

'Well, shit!' Paniatowski said.

And then she became aware that her daughter was standing beside her.

'Shit!' Louisa repeated gleefully. 'What kind of language is that for a detective chief inspector to be using?'

Paniatowski covered the mouthpiece. 'I'm on the phone to the chief constable, sweetheart,' she said. 'What is it you want?'

'I just came to tell you that I've washed my plate, and I'm on my way to school,' her daughter replied.

'Are you still there, Monika?' asked George Baxter, from the other end of the line.

Paniatowski took her hand off the mouthpiece.

'I'll be with you in a second, sir,' she said, then covered the mouthpiece again. She turned to her daughter. 'Take care when you're outside,' she warned, 'it's still dark, and there will be no street lights on.'

'I'll be careful,' Louisa promised. 'About the party, Mum – would it be all right to go, if there's proper supervision?'

'Monika?' Baxter said impatiently.

'Yes, as long as the supervision *is* proper,' Paniatowski told her daughter.

'I'm sure it will be,' Louisa said happily. 'Bye, Mum.'

'Bye,' Paniatowski said. She uncovered the mouthpiece again. 'Sorry, sir, what were you saying?'

'The victim's an old miner, and this is just the sort of story that the press love. I can see the headlines now. "Murder in strike-torn village – pit killer on the loose!" That'll be on days one and two. By day three, they'll be suggesting, in their own subtle and inimitable way, that when compared to the Mid Lancs CID, even a stray cat would look like Hercule Poirot. That's what they'll say – and that's why I want this one wrapped up as soon as possible.'

'Understood, sir.'

'If you want extra men, you've got them,' Baxter said. 'If you need them to work overtime, I'll find the money from somewhere. Just bring me a result.'

'I'll do my best, sir,' Paniatowski promised.

'Do *better* than that, Monika,' Baxter said.

There were two police patrol cars parked outside Mr Hopkins' house, and when one of the police constables standing by the front door saw Becky Sanders, he gestured her to come across to him.

'Now then, young Becky, where are you off to at this time of the morning?' he asked.

'I'm going home, Mr Mellors,' the girl replied.

'That's right, you live on Ash Road, don't you?' Mellors said, and without waiting for an answer, he continued, 'I suppose what I should really be asking you is where you've *been*.' He chuckled. 'Let me guess – was it to one of them all-night discotheques?'

She laughed, because she knew that was what was expected of her, but she sensed that though the policeman was putting his questions in a light manner, there was a serious intention behind them.

'I've only been down to me granddad's house,' she said. 'I make his breakfast for him.'

'Well, that is very kind of you,' the policeman said. 'And how is he this morning?'

She sensed, once again, that there was more to the question than first met the eye.

'His chest's not very good today,' she said.

'And was he behaving in any way unusually?' Mellors asked, with deceptive innocence.

'I don't know what you mean,' Becky said.

'Did he seem particularly nervous – or anxious?'

'Like I said, his chest's bad. He'd coughed up enough gob and blood to fill a jam jar.'

The constable sighed. 'How was he dressed? Was he in his pyjamas?'

Becky, picturing her granddad in his best trousers, felt a cold shiver run through her.

'No,' she said, then added hastily, 'I mean, yes.'

'No? Yes? Which one is it?'

Think! Becky's brain ordered her. Come up with a story!

'He doesn't wear pyjamas,' she said aloud, 'he prefers an old-fashioned nightshirt.'

'Must have been a bit cold for him, sitting around in a nightshirt,' the policeman said sceptically.

'He keeps the fire banked up at night, so everywhere is as warm as toast in the morning,' Becky said. 'Anyway, he's got this old overcoat that he uses as a dressing gown.'

'And you're sure there was nothing unusual about him this morning – apart, that is, from the phlegm and blood?'

'The phlegm and blood isn't unusual at all,' Becky said. 'I only wish it was. Can I go now, cos I've got to get ready for school?'

'You can go,' the constable said, 'but just keep in mind that I might want to talk to you again later.'

'Well, you know where to find me,' Becky said. She paused. 'Sorry, that sounded cheeky.'

The constable laughed. 'If you think that's cheeky, you should hear my kids,' he said. 'Off you go, now.'

'Thanks, Mr Mellors,' Becky said, over her shoulder.

Detective Inspector Colin Beresford awoke, in an unfamiliar bed, to the sound of his beeper screaming at him from the bedside table.

He groped in the dark for the lamp he had noticed the night before, and clicked on the switch.

Nothing happened.

'Bloody power cuts!' he said.

Beside him, the woman rolled over and moaned softly to herself.

Beresford climbed out of bed, and flicked on his lighter. With the illumination it provided, he could locate the candle, and in the light of the candle he could read his beeper. He was not the least surprised to find that the call had come from Monika Paniatowski.

His clothes were on the floor, where he had hurriedly discarded them the night before, and now he began to collect them up.

'What's the matter?' the woman asked sleepily.

'I have to go,' Beresford replied.

'Will I see you again?' the woman asked.

Beresford sighed. 'When we met, last night, I thought I made it clear to you that I wasn't looking for a long-term girlfriend,' he said, quickly stepping into his underpants. 'You seemed quite happy about that at the time.'

'I was,' the woman admitted.

'Well, then?'

'It's just that . . . I thought we got on really well together in bed.' The woman paused. 'Didn't I please you?'

'You were great,' Beresford said, putting on his shirt, and mentally ranking her at number five in the chart of the women he'd slept with since his traumatic night with Detective Sergeant Meadows. 'Really great!'

'But you still don't want to see me again.'

'It's not you, it's me,' Beresford said. 'My life's too complicated at the moment to become involved with anybody.'

And besides, he thought, when you don't lose your virginity until you're in your thirties, you've got a lot of catching up to do.

Under normal circumstances, the road Louisa was walking along would have been very busy at that time of the morning. But these were not normal circumstances. The emergency regulations decreed that, in order to save power, industry was only allowed to work for three days a week, and in Whitebridge's case that meant the factories and mills were silent on Monday, Tuesday and Wednesday.

Thus, as she made her way to school, she saw very few cars at all. There weren't many people about, either – or at least, not many grown-ups. The government had, in effect, given most of the adults permission to stay in bed for an extra hour or two, and it was only the poor bloody kids – and, of course, their teachers – who were required to carry on as normal.

I wish the miners would start working properly again, she thought. It wouldn't have to be for long – they can go on strike for ever once Ellie Sutton's party is over.

She felt a little guilty about having lied to her mother, but she knew that Monika would never understand why a much older girl – a girl she hardly knew – would ever invite her to a party. As a matter of fact, she didn't understand it herself – but you didn't need to *understand* it to be over the moon about it!

Wrapped up as she was in her own thoughts, it was some time before she noticed the car behind her.

It was a big, impressive-looking vehicle, but it was travelling at an almost agonizingly slow speed, so slowly, that despite the fact she had passed six lamp posts since she'd first become aware of it, it had still not overtaken her.

Why was he driving so slowly? she wondered.

Was it because of the icy road conditions?

No, it couldn't be that, because the roads weren't *that* slippery, and the few other cars which had passed had been going much faster.

So maybe the poor man was simply lost. It couldn't be that easy to drive around an area you didn't know when all the street lamps were out, and as the car crawled along close to the kerb, the driver was probably struggling with an open map on his knee.

It was time to do her good deed of the day, she thought.

'Beneath the school uniform of mild-mannered Louisa Paniatowski lies a true super hero,' she said aloud – and in a pseudo-American accent. She stopped and turned around. 'This looks like a job for *Navigator Woman*.'

What happened next startled her – and perhaps even frightened her a little.

The car's headlights suddenly switched from being dipped to full beams, and she was instantly enveloped in a circle of blinding yellow light which made her eyes prickle.

She held up her arm to shield herself from the glare, and as she did so, she heard the car's gear crunch and its engine rev.

'Do you mind!' she called out, though she doubted whether the driver would hear her over the noise of his engine.

The car shot forward, and disappeared down the street, leaving her with golden balls of light dancing in front of her eyes.

'Well, that wasn't very successful, was it, Navigator Woman?' she asked herself.

The car continued to accelerate until it had turned the corner, then it slowed down again, though to nothing like its earlier snail's pace.

The driver turned to his passenger and said, 'Well?'

The passenger rubbed his nose with his index finger. He had fine wavy blond hair, which gently caressed his collar, and he could, when he chose to smile awkwardly, look no more than sixteen or seventeen, though when he adopted a more serious troubled air, most people would have taken him for twenty or twenty-one.

'Well?' the driver repeated.

'Well what?' the young man asked.

And now that he had reverted to being his true self – his arrogant, privileged self – he could almost have been in his mid-twenties.

'Did you get a good look at her?' the driver asked.

'A very good look,' the passenger confirmed. 'That was a neat trick, driving so slowly that she was almost bound to turn round, and then switching the headlights on.' He laughed. 'Talk about putting her in the spotlight!'

'None of this should be necessary, you know,' the driver said angrily.

The passenger said nothing.

'You *do* know that, don't you?' the driver persisted.

'Yes, I know,' the passenger said sulkily.

'You'll have no trouble in recognizing her when you see her again, will you?' the driver asked.

'I'm not a fool, you know,' the passenger replied.

'The jury's still out on that,' the driver said cuttingly. 'Will you recognize her, or won't you?'

'I'll recognize her.'

'And you do know exactly what I expect you to do when you see her again, don't you?'

'Will you *ever* stop treating me like a child?' the passenger asked.

'I might – if you get me what I want,' the driver said.

FOUR

Paniatowski had found it a strange experience approaching Whitebridge Police HQ that morning. All around it were buildings illuminated by tiny, flickering lights – storm lanterns, candles and electric torches – yet the HQ itself, which had its own generator, was ablaze with the harsh glare of functional strip lighting.

Now, in her own office, she looked through her window at the team, who were waiting for her outside.

There was Colin Beresford – keen brain, rock-hard muscles and soft heart. She had worked with him since she was a detective sergeant, and he a detective constable still wet behind the ears. She admired him for the conscientious way he had nursed his mother, who had been struck down by Alzheimer's disease, and pitied him for the way in which this had robbed him of his twenties. Now that Charlie Woodend had retired, Colin was her best friend in the whole world, and while it was true he'd been a little difficult in the previous few weeks, she could not wish for a better one.

There was Detective Constable Jack Crane, who looked more like a nineteenth-century romantic poet than a bobby – and sometimes even talked more like one. Jack was destined to be a high-flyer, and if, one day, he ended up as her boss, she thought she could live with that.

And finally there was her new bagman, Kate Meadows, who had cropped brown hair, huge eyes and elfin features, and who dressed with a style – and at an expense – which made her stand out from other female police officers. Kate hadn't been with her long, but she was already starting to regard the young sergeant as solid gold.

Yes, she thought, this was the team – *her* team – and she was both fond of them and proud of them. In fact, she admitted to herself, they were almost the family she'd never had when she was growing up.

She took a deep breath. 'Enough of the sentimental crap, Monika,' she told herself. 'You've got a killer to catch.'

She opened the door, and stepped out of her office.

'We need to hit the ground running on this one,' she said crisply. 'What details have we got on the victim, Kate?'

'Retired miner, widower, living alone, looks like he was killed by a blow to the head,' Meadows said.

'We'll know more about that last part once the police doctor's seen him,' Paniatowski said. 'What about the incident centre, Inspector Beresford? Do you think we should use the HQ basement, like we usually do?'

'No,' Beresford replied. 'I think it would be better if we had an incident room closer to the incident.'

'I agree with you,' Paniatowski said. 'Can I leave it to you to find a suitable building?'

'Yes, boss.'

'And how many men will you be needing to do the legwork and answer the phones, Colin?'

'Hard to say before I get there, but I think that if I had more than ten men in a village that size, they'd be tripping over one another.'

'Ten it is, then, and if you find you need more later, the chief constable has assured me you can have them.' Paniatowski looked around the team. 'Is there anything else anybody wants to say at the moment?' Crane and Meadows shook their heads, and Beresford said, 'It all seems clear enough.'

'Fine,' Paniatowski said. 'DC Crane, you stick with Inspector Beresford until I need you for some other assignment. Sergeant Meadows, we'll be leaving for Bellingsworth as soon as I've had a cosy little chat with the chief constable, who, by the way, expects us to work miracles on this one.'

'He *always* expects us to work miracles,' Beresford said.

'*Plus ça change, plus c'est la même chose,*' Crane muttered, before he could stop himself.

'That's French, isn't it?' Paniatowski asked.

'Yes, boss,' Crane replied, cursing himself for revealing a hint of the education that the others – with the exception of Meadows – didn't even know he had.

'What does it mean?' Paniatowski asked.

'Roughly speaking, it means, "The more things change, the more they remain the same".'

'Nice,' Paniatowski said appreciatively. 'Maybe I could talk Mr Baxter into making that the motto of the Mid Lancs CID.' She walked towards the door. 'I should be about half an hour, Kate,' she called over her shoulder.

Once she'd gone, Meadows turned to Beresford and said, 'Could you spare me a few minutes, sir?'

'I suppose so,' Beresford replied. 'What is it that you want to get off your chest?'

'I rather thought we could talk about it over a cup of tea in the canteen,' Meadows said, flicking her eyes in Crane's direction.

'Oh, I see,' Beresford said. 'Let's go then.'

Tom Mellors had been born and brought up in Bellingsworth, and if his dad had been a miner, it would have been almost inevitable that he would have become a miner too. But Mellors' father – 'Old Tom' as he was known locally – had been the village policeman, and the younger Tom had followed in his footsteps without a second's thought.

'Back when I first got this posting, I was the obvious choice for the job,' PC Mellors told Cadet Officer Briggs, as they stood on guard in front of Len Hopkins' house. 'It wouldn't happen now – not with modern police thinking. Today, they'd look at my record and say, "Hello, this feller knows the area like the back of his hand, so let's post him to somewhere else – a place he knows bugger all about. And while we're at it, we'll send somebody to Bellingsworth who's so pig-ignorant about collieries that if you showed him one picture of a mine shaft, and another one of his own arsehole, he wouldn't know which was which."'

Briggs laughed – because it was always wise to laugh at your instructor's jokes.

'You have a pretty low opinion of headquarters, then,' he said.

'Low is overstating it,' Mellors told him. 'It used to be that if you knew who to arrest and who to just give a clip round the ear and send on his way, you were considered a pretty good bobby. Now it's how neatly you can fill in all the forms that counts. You'll see that for yourself, as soon the hotshot team from Whitebridge gets here.'

'Is that right?' Briggs asked neutrally.

'Yes, it is right,' Mellors replied with conviction. 'You just watch them at work. I'll guarantee you that they'll come up with all kinds of fancy theories – most of which they will have learned from books – when all they really need to do is ask me who the murderer is.'

'You know who the murderer is, do you?'

'I do,' Mellors said. 'And so do you, if you stop to think about it.'

'I'm not sure that I . . .' Briggs began.

'You've been with me for over a month now, haven't you?' Mellors asked.

'That's right,' Briggs confirmed.

'And so, though you don't know the village anything like as well as I do, you've a pretty fair idea of how it ticks. So let me ask you this – what's the main topic of discussion in Bellingsworth at the moment?'

'The strike ballot,' Briggs said.

'And who is – or was – most strongly opposed to a strike?'

'The dead man.'

'And who is most strongly in favour of it?'

'I see what you mean,' Briggs said.

'Of course you do,' Mellors replied. 'But them buggers from Whitebridge won't.'

*   *   *

The Whitebridge police canteen was where officers went at the beginning of shifts, at the end of shifts, and sometimes – if they thought they could get away with it – in the middle of shifts. Over its fried breakfasts – each one a heart attack in the making – case strategies were discussed, and adulterous assignations planned. If it was not quite the heart of police headquarters, it was definitely the stomach, and when Beresford and Meadows arrived there that morning, it was already doing a thriving business.

'You get the table, and I'll buy the brew,' Beresford said.

He went over to the counter and ordered the teas. When he turned around again – a thick pottery mug of industrial-strength tea in each hand – he noted that the table Meadows had chosen was as far away from any other officers as conditions allowed, which definitely seemed ominous.

'So what's all the mystery about?' he asked, as he sat down. 'And why did you keep signalling that we needed to get away from young Crane?'

'I thought it better not to get Jack involved,' Meadows replied.

'Involved in what?'

Meadows hesitated for no more than a split second, then said, 'I'd rather the boss didn't know this, but I saw the victim last night.'

'You saw *what*?' Beresford exploded.

'I was in the Bellingsworth Miner's Institute, and I saw the victim,' Meadows said.

'And what exactly were you doing there?'

'I was out on a date.'

'A date!' Beresford snorted. 'Is that what you call it?'

'As a matter of fact, I do,' Meadows said coldly.

'And how did you meet this date of yours?'

'I met him through an advertisement that he'd placed in one of the contact magazines.'

'"Man with whip wants to meet woman with back that needs whipping. Handcuffs optional"?' Beresford asked.

'If you go on like this, you'll make me sorry I ever came to you,' Meadows told him.

'And why *did* you come to me?' Beresford asked aggressively. 'Is it because you want me to pull you out of the shit?'

'I'm not in the shit,' Meadows said.

'Of course you're not! Why would I ever think you were? Why would I even imagine there was a problem about you going into a village as a detective sergeant that you'd visited as a masochist only a few hours earlier?'

'A fetishist,' Meadows said firmly. 'I'm not a masochist, I'm a fetishist.'

'All right, why would I even imagine there was a problem about you going into a village as a detective sergeant that you'd visited as a *fetishist* only a few hours earlier?'

'I wasn't there,' Meadows said.

'But I thought you just said—'

'Zelda was.'

'And who the bloody hell is Zelda, when she's at home?'

'She's the person I become when I'm out having fun – and don't you dare sneer at me for calling it "fun".'

'I wasn't going to,' Beresford lied. 'But surely, even you must see that just changing your name—'

'I don't just change my name. I'm a completely different person. When I'm Zelda, even you wouldn't recognize me. Now can we get back to the point?'

'What *is* the point?'

'I saw Len Hopkins get into a fight with another old miner called Tommy Sanders – quite a violent one, given their age – and, a few hours later, Hopkins was dead.'

'Jesus!' Beresford said.

'I think the boss needs to know about it,' Meadows told him.

'So do I.'

'But given how I acquired the information, it can't come from me, so you need to discover it yourself, and pass it on to her.'

'And how do I *discover* it?'

'You'll find a way.'

'Yes,' Beresford agreed, 'I probably will.' He thought for a moment. 'You really need to get a grip on yourself, you know, Kate.'

'And what's that's supposed to mean?'

'All this meeting men through contact magazines – having one-night stands all over the place – it's not good.'

'From what I've been hearing around headquarters, you've been doing exactly the same thing,' Meadows countered.

Beresford looked uncomfortable.

'That's different,' he said.

'How is it different?'

'Well, what I do is normal.'

'I like you, Colin, I really do,' Meadows said. 'But sometimes you make me want to throw up.'

Becky Sanders had had the whole weekend to prepare for the Monday morning history test, but when she left school on Friday afternoon, she'd decided that, rather than leave it to the last minute, she'd get stuck in as soon as she'd eaten her tea. Then television had got in the way – as television sometimes does – and before she knew it, it was time for bed. Saturday had somehow slipped by unnoticed, and Sunday had been the day of the brass band competition.

Now, on Monday morning, as she sat on the bouncing bus which was taking her on the six-mile journey to school, she was desperately trying to make up for her earlier lack of self-discipline.

But it was no good – with all that had been happening in the village, she found it impossible to commit to memory why Henry VII had a claim to the throne of England, and why Richard III had lost the Battle of Bosworth Field.

The bus pulled up in front of the school, and Becky felt her sense of dread – which was not only connected with the history test – increasing by the second.

And then she saw him!

He was leaning against the railings, with an unlit cigarette in his hand. He didn't wave at her when she got off the bus. He didn't even seem to look at her as she walked towards him. But she didn't mind. She knew as well as he did how tongues wagged – how gossip spread – and understood that it was far too soon for word of what was going on between them to get back to her family and everyone else in the village.

So it didn't matter that he probably wouldn't speak to her – it mattered that he was *there*, giving her his silent support.

And then, as she drew level with him, he *did* speak.

'Excuse me, Miss, have you got a light?' he asked.

She stopped and looked at him.

'Of course I haven't got a light,' she said, trying to sound offended. 'Can't you see I'm only a schoolgirl?'

'Sorry, Miss, my mistake,' he replied.

And somehow, without anyone else noticing, he managed to slip a folded piece of paper into her hand.

She walked on, feeling the paper pressing against her skin, bursting to read it. They played these games through necessity, she thought – but there was no disputing that they were also quite thrilling.

And suddenly, she felt all her worries melt away, and she could see quite clearly how Henry Tudor – who was not, strictly speaking, even of royal blood – should have had the right to wear the crown.

FIVE

I t was an ancient highway, connecting towns and villages which had once been a day's journey apart, but now, because of the internal combustion engine, were practically sitting in each other's laps. On the maps, it was listed as the B something-or-other, but the people who used the road which ran across the high moors simply referred to it as the 'Top Road'.

There was little traffic on the Top Road that morning – there was little traffic anywhere, thanks to the three-day week – but Paniatowski restrained herself, and pushed her small red MGA only slightly over the speed that most people would consider prudent.

'I adore these moors,' she said to her passenger, DS Meadows.

Meadows looked out of the side window at the object of this adoration. The moors, it seemed to her, were always harsh and always unforgiving, though they could, when the heather was in bloom, at least give the impression of being welcoming. But there was no welcome now – not in the dead of winter. Now, they were hard and cracked and frozen.

'What is it, *exactly*, that you like about them?' Meadows asked.

'I don't know,' Paniatowski replied.

But she did. It was on the moors that she and Bob Rutter – Louisa's father – had conducted their adulterous affair. It was there that she had experienced true love for a man for the first and last time. The moors *always* reminded her of Bob, and it was only rarely that she wished they didn't.

The road began its descent into the valley, and down below, Bellingsworth was suddenly spread out before them.

The village consisted of no more than eight or nine streets, some running north–south parallel to each other, the others running east–west and intersecting the north–south streets at right angles. All the houses were in squat stone terraces, and the only building which stood out from them was the church. A railway line bounded one side of Bellingsworth, and this came to an abrupt halt half a mile beyond the village, when it reached the colliery. The colliery itself – with its skeletal winding gear and smoking chimneys – was stark enough to make even the village which serviced it look attractive.

'Is this your first visit to a mining village, Kate?' Paniatowski asked.

'Sort of,' Meadows replied, ambiguously.

'It's only there at all because of the coal,' Paniatowski said. 'It's not exactly ugly by design, it's just that the men who planned it never bothered to make it anything else.'

It couldn't have been called a shock to find that Dr Shastri's Land Rover was not parked outside Len Hopkins' house – Paniatowski had known, on a conscious level, that it wouldn't be there – but it was still, nevertheless, a disappointment.

Shastri had been the police surgeon for years, and Paniatowski had pretty much taken it for granted that, just as winter always followed autumn, she herself would always arrive at a crime scene to find the doctor – her delicate sari just peeping out from under the heavy sheepskin jacket she wore for most of the year – bending over the deceased.

But Shastri had gone – at least for a while.

'I am taking a sabbatical and returning to my native India, my dear Monika,' she had said before she left. 'I am looking forward to it immensely, but I shall certainly miss my favourite chief inspector and her almost-daily demands that I perform the impossible.'

And I miss you, Doctor, Paniatowski thought, looking at the Jaguar XJ6 – parked between an ambulance and patrol car – which had usurped the space that rightfully belonged to Shastri's vehicle.

A uniformed constable, heavy-set and middle-aged, strode over to the MGA and said, with some gravity and self-importance, 'You can't park here, love – and if you had any sense, you'd already have worked that out for yourself.'

'Worked it out for myself?' Paniatowski asked innocently. 'I don't know what you mean.'

'It must be true what they say about blondes,' the constable told her. 'Do you see that police car and that ambulance?'

'Yes. Has somebody been taken ill?'

The constable shook his head, as if finding it hard to believe that even a dizzy blonde could be *quite* so stupid.

'No, love,' he said indulgently. 'Nobody's been taken ill – there's been a murder.'

'Now that is a happy coincidence,' Paniatowski replied, pulling out her warrant card and showing it to him. 'Because, you see, investigating murders is what I do for a living.'

The constable's mouth dropped open, then he pulled himself together and saluted.

'Sorry, ma'am,' he said. 'You must be DCI Pany . . . Pany . . .'

'Paniatowski?' Monika suggested.

'That's right,' the constable confirmed. 'I've seen your picture in the paper dozens of times, but you look different in the flesh.'

A mistake, his expression said. A big mistake! You're only making matters worse.

'I'm PC Mellors, ma'am, the local bobby,' he said hastily, 'and that lad over there is PC Briggs, my trainee.'

'I imagine that PC Mellors is teaching you quite a lot, PC Briggs,' Paniatowski said. 'Particularly in the area of how to deal diplomatically with members of the general public.'

Briggs grinned, then wondered if that was appropriate, and instantly assumed a bland expression.

'Yes, ma'am,' he said.

Paniatowski turned her attention back to Mellors. 'We'd like to see the body now,' she said. 'That is, if it's not too much trouble.'

'No trouble at all, ma'am,' Mellors said, completely missing the irony.

He led Paniatowski and Meadows through the front parlour of the house – a room that, as in most of the terraced dwellings, was only used on special occasions – and into the only other room on the ground floor, the kitchen, which had a coal-fired range on which the cooking was done, and was where the people who lived in these houses spent most of their time.

'Mr Hopkins is in the lavvy, at the bottom of the yard, ma'am,' Mellors said, opening the back door.

The yard was perhaps twenty feet long. It was bounded by party walls with the neighbours on each side, and a back wall which separated it from the alley. The wash house, containing a coal-fired boiler, a mangle, and the house's only tap, was close to the back door, and the toilet – as Mellors had promised – was at the far end of the yard.

The 'outside lavvy' was a small windowless brick shed. It was around eight feet tall at the front, three feet wide and five feet deep. It had a sloping roof, and was whitewashed. The door was open, but their view of what was inside was blocked by a large grey-haired man.

The man turned.

'Ah, the constabulary have arrived,' he said. 'You're DCI Paniatowski, aren't you?'

'That's right.'

'Thought you were. I'm Taylor, Dr Shastri's temporary replacement. Taylor's the name, and cutting's the game.' He stepped to one side. 'Behold, Chief Inspector – the stiff!'

The victim was sitting on the toilet at the back of the lavatory, his head slumped forward. His trousers and underpants had been pulled down to his knees, and the naked legs above them were pale, veined and mottled. The legs, trousers, and much of the floor, were stained with blood.

The doctor took hold of the legs, and lifted them, thus rocking the corpse backwards.

'It's rather macabre, but I have to do it this way,' he explained. 'Rigor's set in, you see.'

The middle of Len Hopkins' forehead had been smashed in – but *only* the middle.

'The way I see it,' the doctor said, 'he was sitting there, minding his own business – if you know what I mean – when the door was flung open. Now what would you do in that situation?'

'Try to close the door again?' Paniatowski suggested.

'And that would be easy for you to do, being a woman,' the doctor said. 'All you'd have to do is stand up and take a couple of paces forward, but if *he'd* stood up, he'd probably have fallen over – because his trousers would have been round his ankles.'

'Are you sure of that?'

'Nothing's sure in this life, but most men like to get their clothes as far away from the "operations centre" as possible. We're as careless about performing our bodily functions as we are about most of the other things we do, you see, and certain stains can be very embarrassing.'

'So what do you think he *actually* did?' Paniatowski asked.

'My guess is that he would have lifted his backside slightly and tried to pull the trousers up again, which would have both given him more freedom of movement and done something to alleviate his embarrassment. But all the time he was doing that, he would be looking at the intruder – not that he could have seen much of the man.'

'What makes you say that?'

'This was the only lighting,' Taylor said, pointing to a burnt-down candle on a small shelf. 'It was bright enough for him to see by, but it wouldn't have cast any light outside the shithouse. In other words, while the candle would have allowed the killer to see him, it wouldn't work the other way.'

'You're probably right,' Paniatowski agreed.

'Anyway, even though he couldn't *see*, he was probably still *looking*. And that was a big mistake, because it presented the murderer with a perfect target.'

The doctor lowered the legs, and the body returned to its former position.

'How many blows were delivered?' Paniatowski asked.

'As far as I can tell without slicing the top of his head off, there was just the one.'

'And do you have any idea what type of instrument the murder weapon might have been?'

'Could have been anything with a tapered end,' the doctor said. 'But, as it happens, I know for a fact that it *wasn't* just anything.' He turned, and took a few steps towards the wash house. 'Follow me.'

Lying against the side of the wash house, almost at the party wall, was a small pickaxe. The pointed end of it was stained with what was probably blood.

'If that's not what he used for the dirty deed, I'll eat my own scrotum,' the doctor said.

'Have you touched it?' Paniatowski asked.

The doctor laughed. 'My scrotum?'

'The pickaxe.'

'I most certainly have not. It's lying exactly where it was when I first noticed it.'

Paniatowski studied the pickaxe again. It didn't look like any she'd seen before.

'It's a short-handled pick, ma'am,' PC Mellors explained, seeing the puzzled look on her face. 'Miners used to use them in seams which were too narrow to swing a normal pickaxe in.'

'But they don't use them any more?' Paniatowski asked.

'Not really,' Mellors said. 'The brute force days of mining are all but over – it's nearly all done mechanically now.'

'But the fact that it *is* a short-handled pick makes it the ideal weapon for murdering somebody in an enclosed space, you see,' Dr Taylor said.

It had once been a working tool, Paniatowski thought – from the scars on the wooden haft, there was no doubt about that. On the other hand, the haft itself had been recently polished, and the cord which was looped through the hole at the bottom of it was clean, so someone had been taking care of it since it had been retired from the mine.

She opened the wash house door, and stepped inside. Hanging on the wall were a spade, a yard brush, a hammer and a saw, and between the hammer and the saw there was a strong hook with nothing on it.

She returned to the yard.

'Would the assailant have to have been strong to deliver the blow he did?' she asked the doctor.

'It would certainly have been an advantage, as strength is an advantage in most situations,' Taylor said, 'though I suspect that even a comparatively weak man could have done the damage if he'd been angry enough. But again, I won't know for sure until I've taken a closer look inside his noggin.'

Paniatowski tried to picture the scene in her mind – tried to reconstruct the event which had only been witnessed by two men, one of whom was now dead.

The killer, pickaxe in hand, flings open the toilet door, and sees an old man with his trousers round his ankles, looking up at him.

And what is the expression on the old man's face?

Is it anger?

Is it fear?

He cannot see the man in the doorway, but does he know who he is and why he is there? Does he know, in fact, why he is about to die?

And what about the killer?
What is he feeling?

He was feeling rage, Paniatowski told herself. She could sense that rage, still in the air hours after the murder. She could almost smell it. So what happened next?

The killer swings the pickaxe, and feels it jar as it connects with the middle of the old man's skull.

The axe has done its work, it is of no further use to him, yet instead of dropping it then and there, he keeps hold of it as he turns to make his escape.

And what route does he choose for that escape? Not the alley – which would be the sensible course – but through the house!

He still has the pickaxe in his hand as he draws level with the wash house.

Has he always been intending to throw it against the wash house wall?

No! There would be no point – absolutely no advantage – in doing that.

So why is it still in his hand?

It's still in his hand because he doesn't realize it's there!

He has been grasping it tightly during his murderous attack, and he had been so caught up in his own passion that he has simply forgotten to let go.

But now, as he reaches the wash house – perhaps four or five seconds after he has taken a life – he finally becomes aware of it.

And it disgusts him. It horrifies him.

He flings it away – not caring where it lands!

He was no cold-blooded murderer, this man, Paniatowski thought. A cold-blooded murderer would not have been so disoriented by the act that he would have forgotten to let go of the murder weapon. He had killed because he felt he must – because there were forces inside him driving him to do it.

She sensed the rage again, and wondered just what Len Hopkins could have done to engender it.

SIX

I t had been light for over an hour when Beresford and Crane passed the chipped enamel sign which said, 'You are now entering Bellingsworth. Please drive carefully', but because of the heavy grey clouds hanging over the village, it was that dismal sort of light which made even the darkness which preceded it look good.

Beresford parked at the end of the main street, which was distinguished from all the other streets in the village only by the fact that it contained two or three buildings which were not part of a row of terraced houses.

'You might sometimes catch yourself thinking that Whitebridge is a bit of a dump, but compared to this place, it's bloody Las Vegas,' he said sourly, as they climbed out of the car.

They had only walked a few paces when they reached the Miners' Institute. The building, like most of the miners who used it, seemed both squat and powerful. It was constructed mainly of large blocks of roughly dressed stone that must once have been pale – almost golden – but, over the years, had turned deepest industrial black. It had big double doors – which were painted emerald green, and provided the place with its only real splash of colour – and very small windows, which suggested that once they were inside the institute, the miners wanted to leave thoughts of the outside world behind them.

In front of the Institute there was a large free-standing noticeboard, which informed anyone who cared to look at it that – among other things – the next darts' match was on Thursday, the racing pigeon society would be meeting the day after that in the committee room, Eddie Brown had a second-hand motorcycle (in very good condition) he was willing to sell, and the membership secretary would very much like to remind all members that their yearly subscriptions were due.

But it was the poster in the centre of the board which drew Beresford and Crane's attention.

It was crude, and obviously hastily printed, but its message was more than clear.

Why we must strike!
We are fighting for our lives and our industry.
Voting 'yes' on the strike ballot will ensure our victory.
Come to the public meeting at the Miners' Institute on
Monday night, and make your voice heard.

The poster did not invite comments, but several had been added at the bottom of it anyway.

'Don't vote yourself out of a job,' someone had written.

'Smash the capitalist system,' a second writer had countered.

And a third had scrawled, somewhat incongruously, 'Jenny Talbot will do it with anybody.'

The two detectives carried on up the street, passing a mini-market – which had formerly been two miners' cottages, and was offering big savings on five-pound bags of potatoes and tins of pineapple chunks – a small post office, an even smaller library (which only opened on Mondays, Wednesdays and Fridays) and what appeared to be the village's only pub. They looked at the parish church, which was capped with an unambitious spire, at the graveyard beyond it, and at the single-storey brick-built church hall which lay beyond that.

When they reached the far end of the village, no more than five or six minutes after they had set out, Crane said, 'They're worried.'

'Who's worried?' Beresford asked.

'The miners who want to have a strike. Since we saw that poster on the noticeboard outside the Miners' Institute, I've counted another fifty-six just like it.'

'I don't see where you're going with this,' Beresford admitted.

'In terms of spreading the news, there was no real need to put up the posters in the first place. This isn't a big city, it's a village of no more than a couple of thousand people. And I'm willing to bet that everyone in it knew about the meeting before a single poster was pasted to a single lamp post.'

'Yes, they probably did,' Colin Beresford agreed. 'But I'm still not entirely on your wavelength.'

'At the start of the Russian Revolution, the Bolsheviks did exactly the same thing,' Crane said. 'They practically inundated St Petersburg – or Petrograd, as it was in those days – with posters.'

'So?'

'The point is that it was a small party which was trying to give the impression that it was a big one which was in total control of the situation.'

'You're saying that if you really are in control of something, there's no need to make a big song and dance about it,' Beresford asked.

'Exactly, sir.' Crane agreed.

And if you really weren't in control of things, you might resort to even *more* desperate measures, Beresford thought – like bumping off your opponents.

'We'd better start thinking about setting up our incident centre, Jack,' he said. 'Where – in this vast metropolis – would you choose?'

'There's only really the Miners' Institute and the church hall,' Crane replied, 'and since our killer may well be a miner himself, using the Institute would be a little bit like setting up camp in the middle of enemy territory.'

'So you'd favour the church hall?'

'Yes, but only by default.'

'We'd better go and find the bloody vicar then, hadn't we?' Beresford said.

Chief Constable George Baxter gazed out of his office window at the sky above Whitebridge, where the weak winter sun was making a valiant – though probably doomed – effort to free itself of the clouds which had been masking it.

Baxter shifted his gaze onto the man sitting opposite him. The man's name was Forsyth – or, at least, he said that was what it was. He was probably in his late fifties or early sixties, but his skin was almost as smooth as a baby's. He was wearing an expensive suit and sporting an expensive manicure. He worked for a government department which he refused to put a name to, and though Baxter knew that Monika Paniatowski had clashed with him three times in the past, this was only the second time that the chief constable himself had had to deal with him.

'Do you always have such dismal weather in this godforsaken part of the country?' the visitor asked.

'Yes, we do,' Baxter said. 'It can be a bit depressing at times, but as long as it keeps you poncey southerners out of our hair, we're more than prepared to put up with it.'

Forsyth chuckled, though there was no hint of amusement in it.

'Ah, that wonderful dry northern humour,' he said. 'I can't tell you how little I've missed it.'

'So, if you don't like the weather and you don't like the humour, maybe you should just stay away,' Baxter suggested.

'Believe me, I'd like to,' Forsyth admitted, 'but there's a job up here which needs to be done, and I'm here to do it.'

'And what job might that be?'

'I'm here to compile a report on industrial relations in the north of England, with particular emphasis on the proposed miners' strike,' Forsyth said.

'You're here to do everything you possibly can to prevent that strike from ever happening,' Baxter translated.

'And what patriotic Englishman would not wish to see it prevented?' Forsyth asked. 'If it does go ahead, it will do great damage to our already-struggling economy.'

Baxter glanced down at his watch. 'Well, thank you for dropping in, Mr Forsyth, and now – if you'll excuse me – I've got work to do,' he said.

But Forsyth showed no signs of leaving.

'It is at pits like the one in Bellingsworth that we stand the best chance of turning the tide,' he said.

'Bellingsworth!' Baxter repeated.

'That's right – the very place to which you have recently dispatched the admirable DCI Paniatowski and her team.'

'Stop playing games,' Baxter growled.

'Bellingsworth, you see, is not so strongly in the grip of the communist conspiracy as some of the other collieries,' Forsyth said. 'There are positive forces at work there, and one of them – an old man called Len Hopkins, who was a very positive force indeed – was, much to my annoyance, murdered last night.'

'So are you saying that he was killed because he opposed the strike?' Baxter asked.

'You surely don't expect me to do Monika's job, as well as my own, do you, Mr Baxter?'

'Answer the question.'

'I don't think he was taken out by some professional assassin, working on Moscow's instructions, if that's what you're wondering. It is far more likely that he was murdered by a local hothead, inspired by the Kremlin, but acting entirely independently of it.'

'If you're asking me to pull my people off the case, and let yours take over, then you're wasting your time,' Baxter told him.

'I'm not asking that at all. I have every confidence that Monika will find the killer, though she may need a little help from me.'

'If I get even a whiff of you sticking your nose into police business, I'll have you arrested,' Baxter said.

'The point you seem to be failing to grasp is that the miners of Bellingsworth – on both sides of the divide – will reach the same conclusion about Hopkins' death as I have, and at the meeting tonight—'

'*What* meeting tonight?'

'What meeting!' Forsyth repeated, with just a hint of contempt in his voice. 'You fondly imagine you have no need of my help – yet you don't even know about the meeting in the Miners' Institute to discuss the strike!'

'I've only been on the case for a few hours,' Baxter said, suddenly feeling rather uncomfortable.

'And I have been studying Bellingsworth *for weeks*,' Forsyth countered. 'In the light of the murder, and based on the intelligence I have received, I expect there to be trouble at the meeting – and if it is allowed to get out of hand, it could seriously impede Monika's investigation.'

'In what way?'

'In all sorts of ways, not the least of which is that the miners would be less willing to talk to the police after an incident of that nature.'

He was right, Baxter thought. The bastard was spot on.

'So you're advising me to send in reinforcements for the meeting, are you?' he asked.

Forsyth laughed. 'Of course not. Sending in hooligans in uniform would only make matters worse. It is for that reason that I have asked the head of Scotland Yard's Special Branch – which occasionally runs little errands for us – if he would be so kind as to send a couple of his men up to Bellingsworth.'

'So that's why you're really here, is it?' Baxter asked. 'You want permission to send your men on to my patch.'

'They are not *my* men, and I don't need *your* permission,' Forsyth said in a chilling voice. 'You have no power over me, though I – if I seriously put my mind to it – could probably have you out of your job within a week.'

'Threaten me like that again, and you'll leave my office head first,' Baxter said.

'If you did decide to eject me in that manner, I'd have you out of your job in a *day*,' Forsyth said, unperturbed. 'But there's no real need for antagonism on either side, Chief Constable. My only aim is to ensure that Monika comes out of this investigation covered in glory. I have a great deal of affection for her, you know, and she, for her part, is fond of me . . .'

'She despises you,' Baxter said.

'You're wrong about that. She is *very* fond of me – even if she doesn't quite realize it herself. We have now worked together on several investigations, and—'

'You've never worked *together*,' Baxter interrupted him. 'You don't *work* with anybody – all you ever do is *use* them.'

'And doesn't it reflect well on Monika that I consider her worthy of using?' Forsyth asked.

'When will these goons of yours from Special Branch be arriving?' Baxter asked.

'They should be in Bellingsworth sometime this afternoon.'

Baxter smiled, as a new thought – and one which he was sure would get right under Forsyth's skin – occurred to him.

'They should be in Bellingsworth this afternoon,' he repeated. 'Isn't that a bit like closing the stable door after the horse has bolted?'

'I have no idea what you mean,' Forsyth said, though from the uncharacteristically defensive look which had come to his face, it was fairly plain that he did.

'I mean that you're a day too late,' Baxter said, starting to enjoy himself. 'If you'd sent them up *yesterday*, they would have been able to protect Len Hopkins, your ally in the battle against the Red Menace – then none of us would have been faced with the problems we have now.'

Anger blazed in Forsyth's eyes for a split second, and then was gone.

'You're quite right, of course,' he agreed, as smoothly as ever. 'Given the depth of feeling over this strike, it would have been advisable to give Mr Hopkins some protection. I made a mistake – but then we're all only human, aren't we?'

'I am, certainly,' Baxter said. 'But I've got serious doubts about you.'

SEVEN

L en Hopkins' body, bent at the knees and still frozen in rigor, had presented a challenge to the ambulance men attempting to balance him on the stretcher, and the problem had been further compounded by the fact that the doors on his terraced cottage had not been designed with awkwardly shaped corpses in mind. Eventually, however, they managed to slot the dead man into the back of the ambulance, and drive away.

Dr Taylor stood on the pavement, watching the ambulance make its slow – almost stately – progress down the street.

'Just you wait until they've turned the corner,' the doctor told Paniatowski and Meadows. 'It'll be a different story. Oh yes, indeed – then you'll smell the burning rubber.'

'I seem to be missing the point,' Paniatowski said.

'They'll race me back to the mortuary,' Taylor explained, climbing into his car. 'You might consider that childish – and you'd be quite right – but that's what they'll do.'

'How do you know they'll race you?' Paniatowski wondered.

'Because since I've caught on to their little game, I've been really hammering the Jag, but so far they've still managed to get back first,' the doctor said, firing up the engine. 'But today – because the journey's a little longer than usual – they just might have met their match.'

'About the post-mortem report . . .' Paniatowski began.

'You'll have it as soon as is humanly possible,' Taylor promised, 'and don't you worry, I'll stay within the speed limits until I leave the village, because unlike those two reprobates, I'm *responsible*.'

He closed the car door, slid the Jaguar into gear, and pulled gently away from the kerb.

'So what do you think of the new doctor, boss?' Meadows asked.

'I like him,' Paniatowski admitted. 'He's no Shastri, but he has a certain style that I think I can work with.' She lit up a cigarette. 'We need to interview the woman who found the body – Susan Danvers. Where is she?'

'She's at home. Her doctor's with her.'

'Go and talk to the doctor,' Paniatowski said. 'Ask him if she's in any state to be questioned.'

'And where will you be when I've got an answer, boss?' Meadows asked.

'I'll be here – trying to make some sense of what happened,' Paniatowski said.

She turned around and walked back into the house – through the parlour, through the kitchen and into the yard. She looked down the yard at the lavatory in which Len Hopkins had met his end.

The back gate had blown open, and a cold wind which had been roaring down the alley had taken advantage of the fact to conquer the yard. Paniatowski shivered as she felt its icy fingers reaching for her, but even with the wind, the stink of the killer's rage still hovered in the air.

The church hall was about ten times the length of an average car garage, and roughly five times as wide, Crane estimated. There was a small stage at one end of the room, on which hung a heavy purple mock-velvet curtain, and there were a number of tables and chairs stacked up along the wall.

Two women, well past pensionable age, were mopping the floor near the stage, and a tall thin man in a clerical collar stood a little distance from them, watching them work, and occasionally popping something into his mouth from the paper bag he held in his hand.

The vicar noticed he had visitors, though from the expression on his face, it was more likely that he considered them intruders.

'I'm not interested in buying anything, so you're simply wasting both your time and mine,' he called across the hall.

'Blessed are the meek,' Beresford said.

'Should we go over and tell him . . .?' Crane began, taking a step forward.

'No,' Beresford said, grabbing his arm to restrain him, 'let the bugger come to us.'

Crane noticed the dark edge that was creeping into his inspector's voice. It was quite a new thing – this edge – but it always spelled trouble.

The vicar, seeing that they were making no effort to move, strode towards them.

'Treat him gently, sir,' Crane advised.

'I've had quite enough of you travelling salesmen,' he said. 'This church hall is private property, and you are only allowed to be here with my permission – which I do not grant. So either leave now, or I will call the police.'

'But we are the police,' Beresford said, producing his warrant card.

'Oh!' the vicar replied, somewhat taken aback. 'I took you for—'

'You made it quite clear what you took us for,' Beresford interrupted him.

'It's just we've had such a plague of travelling salesmen in this village recently. And they're so forward and pushy, aren't they? They hardly ever show the proper respect.'

'I suppose they've got their job to do, just like everybody else,' Beresford said. 'You don't mind if we have a look around, do you?'

'No . . . uh . . . I suppose not,' the vicar said, dipping his hand in his paper bag, and pulling out a peppermint. 'It is not much, as you can see for yourselves, but it serves our humble purposes.'

'Hmm,' Beresford said, striding off towards the stage and leaving Crane with the vicar.

Though not a believer himself, Crane's view of religion was, on the whole, a rather positive one – he would for ever be grateful to the priest who had comforted his father in his last agonized days – but that did not mean he granted his blanket approval to all members of the clergy, and this one had definitely got up his nose almost as much as he seemed to have got up Beresford's.

It irritated him that the vicar spoke with such oily humility – 'it serves our humble purposes' – while at the same time acting as if he were the most important person in the room, if not in the county. It bothered him that the man should have been watching the two old ladies work, yet made no effort himself. And it annoyed him both that the vicar should greedily crunch his endless supply of peppermints instead of sucking them, and that he hadn't thought to offer one to either his cleaning ladies or his visitors.

Beresford returned.

'This place isn't perfect, but it will have to do,' Beresford told Crane.

'It will have to do what?' the vicar asked.

'It will have to do as our incident centre,' Beresford said.
The vicar shook his head. 'Oh, dear me, no, I'm afraid it won't
"do" at all. This building does not have the same sanctity as the
church, of course, but it is a vital part of village life, and I'm afraid
I could not possibly allow—'

Beresford sighed heavily. 'You do know a man's been murdered,
don't you?' he asked.

'Indeed I do, but since that man was not one of my parishioners,
I feel under no obligation to—'

'If you make me go to all the trouble of sending to Whitebridge
for a court order which will compel you to let me use this little
shack of yours, I shall be most pissed off,' Beresford interrupted
him.

He was handling it all wrong, Crane thought, but that came as
no surprise, because he had been handling *most* things all wrong
for the past month or so.

'Could I have a quiet word, sir?' he asked.

'A quiet word?' Beresford repeated.

'Won't take a minute,' Crane promised.

They walked to the other corner of the room, and Beresford said,
'What's this all about?'

'We could get a court order, but that would take time, and –
according to the boss – time is just what we don't have,' Crane
said. 'Besides, the rest of the team is already on its way from
Whitebridge, and it'll need a base ready for it when it gets here.'

'Do you think I don't know that?' Beresford demanded. 'I don't
want to go through all the rigmarole of getting an order, but if this
pompous little shit won't cooperate, what choice do we have?'

'I think I can persuade him to agree,' Crane said.

'Now this I've *got* to see,' Beresford told him.

'I think I can persuade him *if you're not here*,' Crane said firmly.

'You've no chance,' Beresford scoffed.

'Just give me ten minutes alone with him,' Crane suggested.

Beresford thought about it. 'All right, I'll do it, Jack,' he agreed,
'but only to show you that while you're a smart lad, you're nowhere
near as smart as you think you are.'

'I appreciate it, sir,' Crane said.

Beresford left the church hall, and Crane sauntered over to the
vicar.

'I don't much like your superior's attitude,' the vicar said.

'I don't much like it myself,' Crane said.

But even on his worst day, he's probably better than you on your best, he added mentally.

'And you do see my point, do you not?' the vicar asked. 'I simply cannot allow the church hall to be used for the purpose your colleague suggested. So much of village life is focussed on this place – the Sunday School, the Mother's Union, the Christian Fellowship . . .'

'And no doubt you foster local talent by allowing the village rock bands to practise in here,' Crane suggested.

The vicar sniffed.

'Certainly not,' he said.

Crane sighed, philosophically. 'I'll do my best to get the inspector to drop the idea,' he promised.

'I would appreciate it,' the vicar told him.

'I mean to say, when all's said and done, sir, you're a simple country priest, and it would be most unfair to foist all that unwelcome publicity on you,' Crane continued.

If the vicar had objected to the phrase 'simple country priest', Crane would have immediately apologized and tried another tack. But, in fact, those were not the words that the other man chose to pick up on.

'Unwelcome publicity?' the vicar said.

'If you allowed this hall to become our incident centre, it would be one of the focuses of attention for the media,' Crane explained. 'That's not too bad in a way, but that attention would also spill out into other areas connected with you. Since it *is* your church hall, the television people would constantly be pestering you for your views on what's happening to the village.'

'I see,' the vicar said thoughtfully.

'And it wouldn't stop there,' Crane continued. 'Once we'd packed up and gone, the sightseers would arrive – taking pictures of the hall and tramping through your lovely church. You'd find yourself treated like some sort of celebrity – and you wouldn't want that, would you?'

'No,' the vicar said, unconvincingly. 'No, I wouldn't. But perhaps we need to look beyond our own selfish needs, and consider the general good.'

'How do you mean?' Crane asked, suppressing a grin.

'It is true that the dead man was not an active member of the church – I believe he belonged to some kind of wild Methodist sect

in the next valley,' the vicar continued, in the voice he probably
normally reserved for sermons, 'but he was, when all is said and
done, as much one of God's children as any of us, and we should
all do all we can to help see his killer brought to justice.'

'So we can use the hall?' Crane asked.

'I think it would be only right and proper,' the vicar said solemnly.

When Louisa Paniatowski saw Ellie Sutton walking across the
playground towards her, she thought she would just burst with
happiness.

There was no one else in the whole world quite like Ellie, she
decided. Ellie was intelligent. Ellie was sophisticated. And now Ellie
was coming to talk to *her* – and all her other friends would see it
happening.

'Robert says he'll hire DJ Dee for the party, Louie,' Ellie gushed.

Louisa didn't really like being called 'Louie', but if that was the
name that Ellie would be using, she supposed she could get used
to it. She wasn't sure, either, that she'd like to call her mum 'Monika',
as Ellie called her dad 'Robert', but maybe if Ellie insisted – and
Mum would allow it – she could get used to that, too.

'Did you hear what I said! DJ Dee!' Ellie repeated, as if expecting
more of a response.

'I don't know . . .' Louisa confessed.

'The disc jockey on "Radio Whitebridge Late Night",' Ellie said.
'You *must* listen to him! Everybody does!'

'Oh yes, course I do,' Louisa said weakly, though she was sure
that by the time 'Radio Whitebridge Late Night' came on the air,
she was already safely tucked up in bed.

'He's the best DJ in Lancashire,' Ellie bubbled, 'and he'll be
playing at *my* party.'

'Great!' Louisa said, because if Ellie thought he was so good,
then he simply had to be.

'The only problem is, we've had to change the date,' Ellie said.
'It's tonight, instead of Friday.'

'Tonight,' Louisa repeated. 'But we have school tomorrow.'

'To hell with school,' Ellie said. 'If I don't feel like coming in,
I'll get Robert to write me a note – and you can get your mother to
do the same.'

'That might be difficult,' Louisa mumbled. 'My mum doesn't
like me missing school.'

'A bright girl like you could soon talk her round,' Ellie said airily.

'And I'm not even sure I'll see her, because she's working on this new murder case, and—'

'Boring!' Ellie interrupted her dismissively. 'Murder is so really, really boring!' She paused. 'Can you come, Louie – or can't you? Because I'd like to know right now!'

It was an ultimatum, Louisa recognized. Say yes, and Ellie would continue to be her friend. Say no, and the older girl would want nothing more to do with her.

It would be wrong to go to the party – she knew it would be wrong – but somehow she couldn't bring herself to say that to Ellie.

'I don't know how I'd get to your house,' she said, hoping to yet find a way to steer through the two disastrous choices which lay ahead of her. 'You see, Mum probably won't be home, and Lily Perkins, our housekeeper, doesn't drive, so though I'd really like to come . . .'

'I'll get Robert to pick you up,' Ellie said.

And with those few words, any chance of doing the right thing completely melted away.

The Lower School had to go to the office if they wanted to make a phone call, but the Upper School were regarded as having earned the privilege of bypassing the secretary, so a payphone had been installed for their exclusive use – and it was to this phone that Ellie Sutton went immediately she had finished her conversation with Louisa Paniatowski.

The number she dialled connected her to the university switchboard, and the switchboard put her through to her father's office.

'I've done it, Robert,' she said, when her father picked up the phone.

'Good girl!' Dr Sutton replied.

'But it wasn't easy,' Ellie told him.

'I'm sure it wasn't.'

'In fact, it was very hard work, and I shall expect some suitable reward.'

'What kind of reward are we talking about here?' Dr Sutton asked cautiously.

'You know that ring I showed you in the jeweller's window . . .'

'Yes?'

'That's what I want.'

'But . . . but it costs hundreds of pounds!' Sutton protested.

'You're right – it's far too expensive,' Ellie said. 'So I'll just go and tell that grotty little girl that the party's off, shall I?'

Sutton sighed resignedly.

'You'll get your ring,' he said.

EIGHT

The two civilian Scenes of Crimes Officers – or SOCOs for short – were called Bill and Eddie, and though they must have had surnames as well, no one in Whitebridge HQ knew what those names were, nor felt any need to find out. Bill was tall and thin, Eddie was small and round, and together, in Paniatowski's opinion, they were a formidable team.

It was Eddie who usually acted as the spokesman for the team, and looking round Len Hopkins' kitchen, it was Eddie who spoke now.

'The dead feller wasn't much of a one for what you might call popular entertainment, was he?' he asked. 'No television, no hi-fi system, nothing like that.'

'No, nothing like that,' Paniatowski agreed.

'Books, though,' Eddie said. 'A *lot* of books.'

Yes, Paniatowski thought, a lot of books.

So many books crammed on to the bookshelves in the parlour that the shelves were bending under their weight.

Books in the kitchen, books in the bedroom, and books in the spare bedroom that looked on to the yard.

Books on Marxism and capitalism, sociology and the history of the working class, a Bible and a set of religious commentaries.

And pamphlets, too – stacks of them. National Coal Board bulletins, reports issued by the Fabians, briefings from *The Economist* . . .

A forest of information!

Len Hopkins, it appeared, had not only been a voracious reader, but a *serious* one.

'I'd like you to get an inventory to my sergeant as soon as you can put one together, Eddie,' Paniatowski said.

'No problem,' the SOCO replied. 'Anything else?'

'I'd also like you to look at the lock on the front door, and see
if it's been tampered with.'

'Locks are Bill's forte, aren't they, Bill?' Eddie said.

'Locks are my forte,' Bill agreed.

'I'll leave you to it, then,' Paniatowski said.

She opened the back door, stepped into the yard, and walked all
the way down to the lavatory.

This was where the killer had been standing, she told herself.
And then he had gone back towards the house – and she knew
that for certain, because he had abandoned his weapon by the wash
house.

But *why* had he gone back to the house? Why risk making his escape
down the street, where he might have been spotted from any of the
windows of the other houses, when he could have simply disappeared
into the back alley, where he would be protected by the high walls?

'If you knew that, Monika, you'd probably be half way to knowing
who killed him and why he was killed,' she told herself.

She went back into the house, to find lanky Bill squatting down
next to the front door, examining the lock.

'Was it forced, Bill?' she asked.

'It was not,' the SOCO said. 'This lock's never been treated with
anything but loving care.'

'Is there a chance it was picked, then?'

'I suppose anything's possible,' Bill conceded, 'but if it was, the
feller who did it had more skill than any burglar I've ever come
across.'

'There doesn't seem to be a latch on this door,' Paniatowski said.

'There isn't. This is a very old-fashioned lock. If you're inside,
and the door is locked, you'll not get out without a key.'

Did the killer *have* a key? Paniatowski wondered.

And if he didn't have one, had he tried to open the door when
making his escape, failed to, gone back into the yard, and left via
the alley?

Of course, it was always possible he didn't need a key at all,
because the door hadn't been locked.

Her head hurt!

'If you could step aside for a minute, I'd like to go outside and
get a breath of coal-filled air,' she said to the SOCO.

'No sooner said than done,' Bill replied, springing to his feet like
an eager grasshopper.

Paniatowski stepped out on to the street and saw that Meadows was approaching.

'I've just been talking to Susan Danvers' doctor,' the sergeant told her. 'He says that as long as we're not too rough on her, we can talk to Susan whenever we want to.'

Colin Beresford had been striding around the village for over half an hour. For the first ten minutes or so, he had been telling himself that all he was doing was following the advice of his old boss 'Cloggin'-it' Charlie Woodend, and getting a feel for the place. Then he realized that if anyone had asked him exactly where he'd been – and exactly what he'd seen – he would have had no idea.

He should never have handled the vicar in the way that he had, he told himself for perhaps the fiftieth time.

He could see that now.

And he *wouldn't* have handled him that way even a few weeks earlier.

But somehow, without him even noticing it was happening, he had become a new man. And this new man wasn't about to take crap from anybody. This new man wanted to be in control of each and every situation.

This new man was even starting to resent Monika – and to think that he could do a better job than she could.

It wasn't true, of course. It wasn't just that Monika had more experience than he did – she also had a certain flair which he was not sure he would ever be able to emulate.

Yes, he could see *that* now, too.

At this moment.

But at this moment he was the 'old' Colin Beresford, and he didn't know when the new one would take control of him again.

There were ways in which he reminded himself of his mother, in the early stages of her Alzheimer's. He had been shocked when she'd been diagnosed with the disease in her fifties, because he had always thought of it as an old person's illness, but the doctor had told him that while it was rare to contract it before the age of sixty-five, it did sometimes happen, even to someone in their thirties.

In their thirties!

It was worrying! It was definitely worrying!

*   *   *

Stepping into Susan Danvers' front parlour was like entering a time warp, Paniatowski thought. The sofa and armchairs were at least thirty years old, and the mirror on the wall – which had a stylized painting of a lady occupying half its surface – had ceased to be in fashion sometime in the thirties. The parlour was clean – scrupulously so – but it seemed cared *for*, rather than cared *about*, and if the room was a shrine to the past, then it was a past which was not filled with golden memories.

Susan herself was in her late fifties. She was short and stocky, and had a broad face and slightly bulbous nose. She looked like a kind woman – a sensitive woman – but it was quite obvious that, even when she was much younger, she had never been a pretty one.

'Would you like a cup of tea?' she asked, after Paniatowski and Meadows had sat down.

'No, thank you, we're fine,' Paniatowski replied.

'I could do with one myself, and it'll not take a minute,' Susan insisted.

'My sergeant will make it, won't you, Kate?' Paniatowski said.

'Be glad to,' Meadows confirmed.

Susan shrugged. 'Well, I'm not really used to being waited on, but if you're sure . . .'

'I'm sure.'

'Then the tea caddy's on the shelf, the kettle's on the hob, and the tap's in the backyard. If you can't manage . . .'

'I'll manage,' Meadows said, standing up and walking into the kitchen.

'Why don't you tell me about Len Hopkins,' Paniatowski asked Susan Danvers.

'I wouldn't know where to start.'

Paniatowski smiled. 'Why don't you start at the beginning?'

'All right then. I started working for Mr Hopkins a couple of months after his wife and two sons were so tragically taken from him. They died in a car crash, you know.'

'Yes, I did know that. How did you get the job? Did he ask you personally, or did you see an advertisement?'

'Neither. It was my idea.'

'Your idea?'

Susan shrugged again. 'Well, it was obvious he had no clue of how to look after himself, wasn't it. What miner does? It's their job to hack coal – which is dirty and dangerous work – and to bring home a pay packet every Thursday. And then, as far as they're concerned, they've done all they need to do – and quite right, too.'

Women's lib didn't seem to have made much impact on this village, Paniatowski thought, but then that was hardly surprising, because mining communities were a world of their own – close-knit and traditional.

'Go on,' she encouraged.

'The pay wasn't much,' Susan Danvers continued, 'but I needed something to keep me occupied after Mother died . . .'

'You looked after your mother, did you?'

'She was an invalid for many years. I'd like to be able to tell you that she bore her suffering with fortitude, but I've never been one for sugar-coating the pill, and the truth is that she was the most cantankerous and ungrateful old bugger – and that's swearing – that you could ever hope to meet. Anyway, she did finally die, and, like I said, I needed something to fill my time. And as you can probably imagine, there aren't that many opportunities for gainful employment in a place like this.'

Meadows returned with the tea, and Susan Danvers took a sip.

'Is it all right?' Meadows asked.

Susan Danvers nodded. 'You make a good strong cuppa, lass,' she said. 'Are you from a mining family yourself?'

'No,' Meadows said, although that was not quite true, because her family had once *owned* a coal mine.

'What exactly *was* your relationship with Mr Hopkins?' Paniatowski asked Susan.

'I've just told you, I was his cleaner,' the other woman replied sharply. 'Well, more like his housekeeper, if truth be told.'

There was much more to it than that, Paniatowski sensed.

She patted the pocket where she kept her cigarettes, and felt her fingers drum against the packet of Benson and Hedges.

'Damn, I seem to have left my ciggies in the car,' she said. 'Could you go and get them for me, please, Sergeant.'

'Sure thing, boss,' Meadows said, reading the message in her eyes.

Paniatowski waited until Meadows had closed the front door firmly behind her, then said, 'I can see that you're an intelligent woman, Miss Danvers.'

'Flattery will get you nowhere,' Susan Danvers said, pretending to take it as a good-natured joke, but clearly decidedly uncomfortable with the comment.

'You are intelligent,' Paniatowski insisted. 'You know you are, don't you?'

Susan nodded, almost imperceptibly. 'I was all set to go to the teacher training college when Mother got taken ill,' she said. 'Now that was quite a coincidence, wasn't it – Mother getting ill just as I was about to leave home?' She sighed, heavily. 'I think I would have made a good teacher, if I'd been given the chance.'

'I'm sure you're right,' Paniatowski replied. 'So we're agreed that you're a clever woman, are we?'

'Well, I'm not stupid,' Susan Danvers conceded.

'Then you'll understand that what I'm trying to do now is to build up a picture of Mr Hopkins and the life he led – and the reason I'm doing that is because it may help me to find his killer. You *do* understand that, don't you?'

'Yes.'

'So you'll also understand that when I ask you a question, there's a purpose behind it, and however awkward you might find it to answer that question, I'd appreciate it if you were honest with me.'

Susan Danvers sighed. 'Len was a good-looking man when he was younger,' she said, 'but, more importantly than that, he was a *nice* man.'

'So when you started working for him, you hoped it might lead to something else?' Paniatowski guessed.

Susan looked at the floor. 'Yes.'

'And did it?'

'He first took me to bed a couple of years after I started working for him,' Susan said. She paused. 'Have you ever read any of those romantic novels about handsome young doctors and beautiful young nurses?'

'No, I can't say I have,' Paniatowski admitted.

'A good-looking girl like you wouldn't need to,' Susan Danvers told her, with only the merest hint of bitterness. 'But I'd read hundreds of them by the time I went to work for Len, so though I was still a virgin when we first went upstairs, I thought I had a vague idea of what to expect.'

Paniatowski smiled. 'And what *were* you expecting?'

'A wave of pleasure which would sweep me off my feet – a real river of passion,' Susan smiled sadly. 'It wasn't like that at all. It was more like a tiny, tiny stream. Sex isn't supposed to be like that, is it? I'm only asking *you* because, apart from what I did with Len, *I* don't have any experience in the matter.'

A brief memory of her time with Louisa's father flashed across Paniatowski's mind.

'No, sex isn't supposed to be like that,' she agreed.

Susan nodded sadly. 'That's what I thought,' she said. 'I don't think it was my fault – I was willing to do whatever Len wanted me to do. But I don't think it was his fault, either. The simple truth is that he missed his wife too much to ever give me and him a real chance.' She took a handkerchief out of her handbag and dabbed her eyes. 'Anyway, what started out as a trickle soon dried up completely, but I didn't mind – or, at least, I told myself that I didn't mind. He did still *need* me, you see, and that has to count for something, doesn't it?'

'Yes, it does,' Paniatowski agreed. 'What can you tell me about his movements yesterday?'

'Not a great deal,' Susan admitted. 'I made him his breakfast, and then I didn't see him again until . . . until I found him this morning.'

'You didn't make his tea?' Paniatowski asked.

'No,' Susan said, suddenly evasive.

'Wouldn't you normally do that?'

'Yes.'

'But you didn't yesterday?'

'No.'

'And why was that?'

Susan sighed again. 'He went to see the brass band championship in Accrington.'

'And you didn't go with him?'

'No.'

'Was there any particular reason you didn't go?'

'No.'

'Wouldn't he normally ask you to go with him to something like that? Wouldn't he *want* you to go with him?'

'Yes.'

'But he didn't ask you this time?'

'No.'

'Why not?'

'I don't know.'

She could ask as many questions as she wished to on this particular subject, and the answer would never be much more than a monosyllable, Paniatowski decided.

'Let's move on to this morning, then,' she suggested. 'What exactly happened?'

Susan took a deep breath. 'I arrived at his house at my usual time,' she said. 'Len is normally . . . Len *was* . . . normally up by then. When he came downstairs, the first thing he'd do would be to switch on the parlour light and unlock the front door. Then he'd go into the kitchen to wait for me to arrive. But the parlour light wasn't on this morning, and the door was locked, so I had to use my key.'

'Did you normally enter the house through the front door?'

'Yes.'

'I thought most people round here used the back door.'

'Len didn't like me walking down the back alley in the dark. I told him nothing was going to happen to me in this village, but he said it was better to be safe than sorry. He . . . he could be quite protective – quite caring – sometimes.'

'What happened next?'

'I went through to the kitchen. Len's cocoa mug was there on the table – he always made himself a cup of cocoa before he went to bed – so I boiled up a kettle and made a pot of tea, and while I was waiting for it to brew, I washed out the mug with the hot water that was left.'

'Go on.'

'There was still no sign of Len, and I didn't want the tea stewing, so I went to the foot of the stairs, and called out, "Your tea's ready!" And when he didn't answer, I started to get worried, because he's normally such a light sleeper.'

'So you went upstairs?'

'Yes, I did. And that's when I really started to get worried.'

'Why?'

'His bed didn't look slept in, and he hadn't touched his water jug. But it was the fact that his clothes weren't there that really scared me.'

'Where should they have been?'

'On the chair. When he got undressed at night, he always folded his clothes – well, sort of folded them, anyway – and left them on one of the bedroom chairs. Then, in the morning, I'd decide what needed washing, and what could be hung back up in the wardrobe. But, you see, the clothes weren't on the chair.'

'You didn't think he might simply have put them on again when he got up?'

'No, because I always laid out a fresh set of clothes on the second chair before I went home, and those were the ones he put on in the morning.' Susan smiled sadly. 'He always used to say I bullied him, but I think he rather liked it.'

'The fresh set of clothes were still on the second chair, were they?'

'Yes, and that had to mean that he'd never been to bed. So I rushed downstairs again, and went straight down to the lavvy – because that was the only place he could have been.'

'If you thought that was where he was, why didn't you just wait until he came back into the house?'

'Because I knew by then that something was wrong.' Susan paused. 'I screamed when I found him in the lavvy – with his trousers round his ankles – but there was part of me that was already expecting it.'

And then, as Paniatowski had been anticipating for some time, she burst into tears.

NINE

The van from Whitebridge had arrived ten minutes earlier. It had already been unloaded, and now the driver and his mate were positioning the desks in the approved horseshoe pattern, while two engineers from the Post Office were laying the cabling necessary to ensure that each desk had a phone. The room still looked more like a church hall than an incident centre – but it was getting there.

'You've done well to talk the vicar round so quickly,' Beresford told Crane, and then added candidly, 'I left you with a bit of a bloody mess to deal with, didn't I, Jack?'

'Yes, that was a clever move on your part, sir.'

'What do you mean?'

'Well, what you pulled was the classic good-cop bad-cop routine, wasn't it? The vicar was so pleased you'd gone that he'd have been prepared to give me pretty much anything I wanted.'

'I don't need you finding ways to excuse my screw-ups, Jack,' Beresford said sternly.

'Sorry, sir.' Crane replied contritely.

Beresford smiled. 'But thanks for trying, anyway.' He checked his watch. 'Can I leave you in charge here?'

'I should think so.'

'Then I'll go and see about fixing us up with some lunch,' Beresford said.

He had done no more than glance at the village's only pub when he and Crane had made their tour of the High Street, but now Beresford gave it a more leisurely examination.

It was not the sort of pub you would ever expect to find in a mining village, he thought.

For a start, it should have been called something like the Pit Pony or the Miners' Rest, instead of the Green Dragon. And the incongruity continued inside. The walls were covered with rich flock wallpaper, the fitted carpet had a thick pile and a subdued pattern, and there were even horse brasses on the wall. The whole pub looked as if it belonged in one of those pleasant, shady villages, so beloved by the moderately prosperous, chunky-sweater-wearing middle class, and the fact that it existed in this grimy industrial setting was distinctly odd.

A man appeared behind the bar. He was wearing cavalry twill trousers, a check shirt and a cravat, and looked as if he, too, would have been comfortable in the company of country doctors, senior clerks and teachers with posts of responsibility.

'What can I get you, sir?' he asked, with the assumed joviality that some landlords – and dressed like this, he could *only* be a landlord – have turned into an art form.

'A pint,' Beresford told him. 'No, better make it a half for now.'

'Ah, a wise man to hold himself in reserve, especially when you're probably due for a heavy session later with your boss, DCI Paniatowski,' the landlord said.

'What!' Beresford said.

The other man laughed. 'Most people think that landlords are a bit like their beer pumps – permanently stuck behind the bar,' he said. 'But the fact is that we have a life of our own outside these four walls, though when we *do* go outside, we tend not to mix with civilians.'

'You're a member of the Licensed Victuallers' Association,' Beresford guessed.

'Just so,' the landlord agreed. 'We like to get together now and again – us landlords – and when we do, we swap stories about what goes on in our establishments. Not that we reveal anything confidential,' he added hastily, 'we're a bit like doctors and lawyers in that way. But we do allow ourselves the luxury of painting affectionate word portraits of some of our more colourful customers.'

'Or to put it another way, you've been gossiping with the landlord of the Drum and Monkey in Whitebridge,' Beresford said.

'Exactly,' the landlord replied. 'He's very proud – some might say overly proud – of the fact that what he calls one of the finest teams of detectives in the whole of Lancashire uses his pub as a base.'

What he *calls* one of the finest teams of detectives in the whole of Lancashire? Beresford thought, feeling a prickle of irritation. We *are* one of the finest teams of detectives in the whole of Lancashire.

'Anyway,' the landlord continued, 'when I learned that the bobby leading this investigation had lovely blonde hair and a big conk, I knew it had to be DCI Paniatowski.'

Beresford's feeling of irritation cranked up a notch or two. It was true that Monika's nose was larger than the average Lancashire issue – she was Polish, for God's sake! – but she was still one of the most attractive women he had ever met.

'Is it always as quiet as this?' he asked, looking around the empty bar.

'At this time of day, yes,' the landlord replied.

'Yes, I imagine it must be tough, competing with the Miners' Institute,' Beresford said, and realized – as soon as the words were out of his mouth – that he was punishing the landlord for his comment about Monika.

What was it with him? he wondered. One moment he was resenting the fact that it was Monika – and not himself – who was leading the investigation, and the next he was leaping to her defence.

Maybe it wasn't Alzheimer's he was suffering from at all – maybe he was developing schizophrenia!

'I'm not in competition with the Miners' Institute,' the landlord said, stung by the comment. 'The Institute is a bit rough and ready, so that's where most of the coalface workers go when they're out with their mates. But when they take their wives or girlfriends out, this is where they come. We also cater for the pit managers and the clerks,' he continued, counting them off on his fingers and watching Beresford's reaction closely, 'the commercial travellers . . . and then, of course, we've started getting a lot of the miners who are opposed to the strike.'

'And why's that?' Beresford asked.

'They come here because they don't feel welcome in the Miners' Institute any more.'

It was the perfect opportunity to 'discover' the information which Kate Meadows had given him and which he needed to pass on to Paniatowski, Beresford thought.

'I hear there was a bit of trouble in the Institute only last night,' he said casually.

'You are well informed,' the landlord said, impressed.

'I'm part of what some people think is one of the finest teams of detectives in the whole of Lancashire,' Beresford said. 'You wouldn't like to give me a few details of the trouble, would you?'

'There was a punch-up between two retired miners who are on opposite sides of the fence when it comes to the strike,' the landlord said.

That was good enough, Beresford decided.

'We'll be needing food while we're here in Bellingsworth – hot lunches if possible, and sandwiches otherwise,' he said. 'Can you handle that?'

'I most certainly can,' the man behind the bar confirmed. He paused for a moment. 'Does the landlord of the Drum and Monkey lay on hot meals and sandwiches?'

'No,' Beresford replied.

The landlord rubbed his hands together.

'Excellent!' he said.

It had taken some time to calm Susan Danvers down, but now she looked just about ready to start talking again.

'I've just a couple more questions, and then we'll be done,' Paniatowski said. 'All right?'

Susan nodded. 'All right.'

'As far as you know, did Len Hopkins have any enemies?'

'Do you mind if I tell you a bit more about Len as a person?'
Susan Danvers asked.

'Not at all,' Paniatowski said – although she could spot an evasion
when she heard one.

'Len got religion after his family died. Well, nobody can blame
him for that, can they? He grew very serious about this religion of
his, but he never let that spill over into his normal life,' Susan
paused, 'at least, not until recently.'

'Not until recently?' Paniatowski repeated.

'Anyway, he was a very well-read and a very thoughtful man,'
Susan said, hastily, as if she was now regretting that last qualification.
'All sorts of people would ask him for advice on all sorts of subjects.
They'd just turn up at his door, and whatever the hour of day or night,
he'd never turn them away.'

'So he was a sort of village wise man?' Paniatowski suggested.

'That's exactly what he was,' Susan agreed. 'There was nobody
in this village who was treated with more respect – and nobody
who had more right to it.'

'So you're saying that he *didn't* have any enemies?' Paniatowski
asked innocently.

Susan paused again. 'He didn't have any enemies *as such*,' she
said finally.

'What do you mean by that?'

'He got into quite a lot of arguments recently over whether or
not there should be a strike,' Susan admitted.

'Did he argue with anyone in particular?'

'I'd rather not say.'

'If you don't tell me, someone else will,' Paniatowski pointed
out.

Susan sighed. 'I suppose you're right. The man he argued with
the most was another old miner called Tommy Sanders – but Tommy
would never have harmed him.'

'How can you be so sure of that?'

'Tommy's a man of principle, just like Len.' Susan paused again.
'And I wouldn't like you to get the wrong impression about those
arguments. They were passionate – because they both cared about
the issues – but they never got personal.'

'Never got personal,' Paniatowski repeated sceptically. 'I find
that very surprising, considering the importance of the issues they
were arguing about.'

'You wouldn't find it the least surprising if you'd known Len,' Susan Danvers said. '*I've* known him all my life – and been looking after him for nearly twenty years – and I've never once seen him really lose his temper.' She suddenly fell silent, and a deep frown came to her brow. 'I'm making a liar of myself,' she said, after a few seconds had passed. 'I did hear him really lose his temper once – and there's no excuse for me forgetting that, because it was only last week.'

'Tell me about it,' Paniatowski suggested.

'Len's been doing a bit of what you might call research into his family history, and he asked me to help him with it.'

'He asked you to help him with it, did he? So I'm not the only one who thinks you're clever,' Paniatowski said.

'Get on with you,' Susan told her, blushing. 'Anyway, checking back on the last four generations of the Hopkins' family was easy, because they'd all lived in this village. But then we hit a snag. Len's great-great-great-great grandfather . . .' She paused. 'If it's four generations, have I got that right?'

'Close enough,' Paniatowski told her.

'Anyway, he was apparently working on one of the ships that took coal from here to London when he met Len's great-great . . . whatever . . . grandmother, and after they got married, he moved up here – which meant that in order to take the research any further back, Len would have to go down to London. And he couldn't do that, could he?'

'Why not? Wasn't he well enough to travel?'

'Oh, he was well enough – he was very fit for a man of his age – but he couldn't afford it. He was never a big saver, you see – if he had any money in his pocket, and somebody came to him with a sob story, that money would be gone in the blink of an eye. And on a miner's pension, you can't go very far. Then I had an idea.' Susan smiled. 'A *clever* idea, if you like.'

Paniatowski returned the smile. 'And what was this clever idea of yours?'

'I said, "Why don't you apply for one of them grants?" "They'll never give a grant to somebody like me, lass – I've had no proper education," he said. "Well, they certainly won't give you one if you don't apply for it," I told him. And I went to the library and copied down the addresses of some government bodies that might be willing to give him a few pounds . . .'

'You were going to tell me about the only time you ever heard him lose his temper,' Paniatowski pointed out.

'And so I will, lass, if you'll be patient for a minute or two,' Susan Danvers said, with a hint of reproach in her voice.

'Sorry,' Paniatowski said meekly.

'He sent off the letter to the Department of Education and Science, and they wrote back straight away. They said that they were very interested, and that there should be no problem with a grant.'

'And you're sure this letter came from the Department of Education and Science?' asked Paniatowski, who was surprised by the willingness of the department to fund what was no more than a hobby, and couldn't imagine *any* government department writing back straight away.

'Yes, it was from them,' Susan said firmly. 'Len showed me the letter.'

'Did it say anything else?'

'It said they'd be sending somebody round to interview him, and sure enough, last Thursday, a young man did turn up.'

And three days later, Len Hopkins was dead, Paniatowski thought.

'Did you meet this young man?' she asked.

'In a manner of speaking.'

'What do you mean by that?'

'It was about half past four in the afternoon when I went to Len's house to make his tea, and when I reached the front door, I could see the two of them – Len and the young man – in the front parlour. Well, I didn't want to disturb them – not when they both looked so serious – so I stayed out on the street. And it was while I was standing there that the shouting started.'

'Were they both shouting?'

'No, the young man seemed quite calm. It was Len that was making all the fuss.'

'Did you hear what he was shouting?'

'Some of it. He was bellowing so loudly, that it would have been hard not to have.'

'Tell me as much as you can remember of what he said.'

'He said something like, "You might call it a bursary . . ." That's a grant, isn't it?'

'Yes,' Paniatowski agreed, 'it's a grant.'

'He said, "You might call it a bursary, but I call it a bloody bribe!" Then the young man said something very softly. "These are my people," Len told him, "and if you think I'll betray them for a mess of pottage, you're off your bloody head." That's from the Bible, that bit about the mess of pottage.'

'I know,' Paniatowski said. 'When he was talking about betraying his people, do you think he was referring to his own family?'

'No, I don't, because he didn't have any family left, to speak of,' Susan said. 'And anyway, the next thing he said was, "I've grown up with these people. They're my neighbours. And even when they're wrong, they're a bloody sight righter than you'll ever be, you fancy piece of shit." And you have to remember that Len never swore – so that shows just how upset he was.'

'What happened next?'

'The young man left. He came out of the front door, and walked quickly up the street. I don't think he even noticed me.'

'He didn't have a car?'

'He must have done, unless he came by bus – and he didn't look like the kind of person who'd even know how to use a bus – but he hadn't parked it anywhere near Len's house.'

'Could you describe him?'

'He was quite tall, and had fairly long blond hair. He looked a bit young to be working for the government, but he was wearing a nice suit – quite an expensive one, if you ask me – so I suppose he must have been what he said he was.'

'What did Mr Hopkins tell you about him?'

'Not a thing. He refused to discuss it. But while I was making his tea, he kept muttering the same thing over and over to himself.'

'And what was it?'

'He kept saying, "It's all true. You read about it, and you think it's an exaggeration – but it's all true."'

'And you have no idea what he meant by that?'

'Not a clue.'

'Do you think the young man might have been responsible for Len's death?' Paniatowski asked.

'Good heavens, no,' Susan said, completely taken aback.

'Why not?'

'Because if he'd killed Len – and I'm not saying he ever would have, but *if* he had – he'd have shot him, or maybe strangled him. I didn't see much of him, but I saw enough to know that he'd have thought it far too messy to smash his head in with a short-handled pickaxe.'

'So you know he was killed with a pickaxe, do you?' Paniatowski asked sharply.

The question seemed to take Susan Danvers by surprise.

'Of course I know,' she said. 'Probably everybody in the village knows by now. It was the one Len used himself, when he was working down the mine. He kept it in the wash house, and every week, he'd polish the handle.' Susan gave another sad little smile. 'Men are funny creatures, don't you think?'

'Very strange,' Paniatowski agreed. 'So if the young man wouldn't have thought of killing him with the pickaxe, who do you think would have?'

'I can't think of anybody,' Susan told her. 'Like I said, he had no enemies.'

'But somebody *did* kill him,' Paniatowski said firmly, 'and I'd still like to know what kind of person you think *would* use a pick.'

'It could be anybody,' Susan said – conveniently ignoring the fact that there was no great leap from turning a miner's tool into a miner's *weapon*.

TEN

The detective sergeant who would be in charge of coordination was the first to arrive at the church hall. He was a middle-aged man with white hair, and he went by the improbable name of Eddie Orchard.

'The name's been a burden to me my whole life, sir,' he told Beresford, who he hadn't met before.

It must have been, thought the inspector, who could well imagine the younger Orchard having to endure nicknames like Apple, Pear and – perhaps worst of all – Cherry.

'Yes, it's been a real curse on me,' the sergeant continued, with a grin. 'I could never understand why I wasn't called something more sensible – like Frank!'

The detective constables who Orchard would be coordinating arrived in a bunch. They were all young, mostly newly promoted, and clearly very enthusiastic, and as Beresford watched DS Orchard assign them to their places on the horseshoe, he felt an unexpected pang of envy.

Once the constables were seated, Beresford climbed on to the small stage at the end of room, and, aware that all eyes were on him, began his address to the troops.

'Those of you who are working your first murder inquiry are probably almost bursting with excitement,' he said to them, 'so here's a bit of advice – get rid of that feeling of excitement now.' He paused, to let the remark sink in. 'There's nothing thrilling about this kind of investigation,' he continued. 'It's hard work and it's tedious work. But it has to be *careful* work, too, because one of those tedious little details may be just the one that cracks the case wide open.'

He had them in the palm of his hand, he thought, looking down at their faces. At this stage of their careers, he was the man they looked up to – the man they one day wanted to be. And he'd earned their respect, he told himself, because he was very good at his job, and played a vital part in a well-oiled machine.

So why wasn't that enough for him?

Why did he want more?

He realized he had been silent for several seconds.

'You're probably asking yourselves how you'll feel when we get a result,' he said, picking up where he had left off. 'Well, get rid of that feeling, as well, because a result is by no means guaranteed, and the more you're sure it will all eventually come together, the less the likelihood that it will. Assume nothing. Check everything. And then check it again.' He paused, and smiled. 'But if you *do* get a result, lads, it's a great feeling. It's not better than sex, because *nothing's* better than sex,' he paused again, to allow for the expected laughter which followed the remark, then added, as a kicker, 'but, let me tell you, it comes pretty bloody close.'

He saw that Paniatowski had entered the hall and was standing at the back with Meadows, and he felt suddenly self-conscious.

'That's about it, lads,' he said. 'Sergeant Orchard will assign the streets he wants each of you to cover on the door-to-door, and remember, when you're out there, that though your individual contribution is crucial to the success of the investigation, the most important thing is that you're part of a team.'

He walked down the steps, and made his way to the back of the hall.

'Lunch?' he asked his boss.

'Lunch,' Paniatowski agreed.

The landlord of the Green Dragon had spotted the team's approach, and was waiting for them at the door.

'Welcome, welcome, welcome,' he said effusively, already beginning to compose in his mind the heavily embellished stories of this visit that he would soon be telling to his – until recently much-envied – colleague at the Drum and Monkey in Whitebridge. 'I've reserved a table in the corner for you.'

'Thank you,' Beresford said.

'It's for your *exclusive* use,' the landlord said as they entered the pub, in case Beresford had missed the point. 'As long as you're here conducting your investigation, there'll be no one else allowed to use it.'

'Thank you again,' Beresford said – though he couldn't help thinking that since there was no one else in the pub at the time, it was less of a singular honour than it might have been.

'If there's anything you want – anything at all – then you only have to ask,' the landlord said.

'There's such a thing as being shown *too* much hospitality, you know,' Beresford said gruffly. 'In fact, it gets rather wearing after a while.'

The landlord looked puzzled for a second, then smiled and said, 'Oh, I see, it's your little joke.'

'That's right,' Beresford agreed. 'What's for lunch?'

'You could have Lancashire Hotpot,' the landlord suggested. 'It's made to my wife's special recipe, and I can thoroughly recommend it.'

'Sounds a bit fattening,' Meadows said. 'What else have you got?'

The landlord shrugged. 'Well, nothing really,' he admitted.

And so the whole team decided that, taking all factors into consideration, they'd have the hotpot.

The landlord's wife's special recipe Lancashire Hotpot turned out to be not that special after all, but it was undoubtedly food, and as they ate it, Paniatowski told Beresford and Crane what the doctor and Susan Danvers had said, and Beresford told Paniatowski about the fight in the Miners' Institute.

When the plates had been cleared away, Paniatowski lit up a

cigarette, turned to Crane, and said, 'Why don't you summarize what you think we've learned so far, Jack?'

'We know that Len Hopkins went to Accrington to see the regional final of the brass band competition, and that – for some reason – he didn't take Susan Danvers with him,' Crane said. 'We know that when he got back to Bellingsworth, he paid a visit to the Miners' Institute and got into a fight with Tommy Sanders.'

'Do we have a time for that fight?' Paniatowski asked.

'It was at about a quarter past eight, boss,' Meadows said.

'Who told you that?' Paniatowski wondered.

'Can't remember, boss – somebody I talked to,' Meadows said vaguely. 'It's in my notes.'

Or, at least, it will be in my notes, when I can find someone to confirm what I already know from seeing it with my own eyes, she thought.

'Len leaves the Institute shortly after that,' Crane continued 'He goes back home . . .'

'We don't know that for a fact,' Beresford interrupted.

'No, we don't, sir, but all his mates were still at the Institute – celebrating the victory – and there's nowhere else *to* go in this village.'

'When did they have their daily power cut?' Paniatowski asked.

'It started at ten o'clock,' Crane told her.

'So the village is plunged into darkness at ten. And then, at some time in the night, Len pays a visit to the lavatory,' Paniatowski said. 'We know it *was* in the night, rather than early morning, because by the time the body was discovered, full rigor had set in. But until we get the post-mortem report, we can't pin it down any more accurately than that.'

'Have we got an inventory yet, Sergeant?' Beresford asked Meadows.

'Yes, sir. The SOCOs gave it to me a few minutes ago.'

'And is there a chamber pot on it?'

Meadows reached down into her bag, pulled out the thick wad of paper, and flicked through it.

'Yes, it was under the bed, just as you might expect.'

'So why would he go outside, on a cold night, when he could have used the pot in his bedroom instead?' Beresford wondered.

'And more to the point, how could the killer have possibly known he would do that?' Crane asked.

'Perhaps he didn't,' Paniatowski said. 'Maybe he entered the house, saw that Len wasn't there, and worked out that the lavatory was the only place he could possibly be.' She paused for a second, as she saw the flaw in her own logic. 'For that to be true, the killer would have had to have a key, wouldn't he? And as it's unlikely that he did . . .'

'Len Hopkins could have left the front door unlocked,' Beresford said.

'He could have,' Paniatowski agreed, 'but he didn't, because when Susan Danvers got there this morning, the door was locked.'

'She could be mistaken about that,' Beresford said.

'She seems quite certain,' Paniatowski countered.

Beresford shrugged. 'She's an old woman, and old women are always making mistakes.'

'She's not *that* old.'

'She's old enough to have forgotten the door wasn't locked when she got there this morning.'

Why was Colin so keen to establish that the front door was unlocked when the evidence clearly suggested that it wasn't? Paniatowski wondered. Did he have his own agenda that he wasn't telling anyone else about?

'But while it's highly unlikely that his entry point was through the front door, we can be almost certain that he did go into the house after he'd killed Len,' she said, moving on, and leaving the bone of contention behind her. 'And how do we know that, DC Crane?'

'He was on his way to the house when he threw the pickaxe away,' Crane replied.

'Exactly,' Paniatowski agreed. 'Now it's possible he went into the house because he was planning to make his escape down the street – though why he should decide to do that, when the alley was much safer, I've no idea – but it's much more plausible that there was something inside the house that he needed to take away. The only question is – what could it be?'

'Something that could connect him with Len in some way – something that would point us in his direction, when we were looking for the killer,' Meadows suggested.

'Like what, for example?'

'I haven't a clue.'

'Then let's try thinking about something else – let's consider motive,' Paniatowski suggested.

'What's to consider?' Beresford asked. 'Hopkins was killed because of his opposition to the strike. That's what everybody in this village probably thinks – and that's what I think too.'

'It's a bit early in the investigation to be making that sort of judgement,' Paniatowski said mildly.

She was slapping him down, Beresford realized. She was doing it gently – for the moment – but she was definitely slapping him down. And she had every right to, because she was the boss, so his best plan – by far – would be just to sit back and take it.

'I disagree,' he heard himself say. 'There's an obvious motive for the murder of Len Hopkins, and given that obvious motive, Tommy Sanders has to be the prime suspect.'

That was why he'd been so keen to discount the idea that the front door had been locked, Paniatowski thought – because an *unlocked* door would explain away the problem of how Tommy Sanders could have known Len would be in the lavatory, and make it easier for Beresford to paint a picture of him as the guilty man.

If she'd been dealing with any other inspector but Colin Beresford, she'd have cut him off long before that point, she thought. But it *was* Colin – her friend and loyal lieutenant – and she didn't want to do that to him, especially in front of the rest of the team.

'This isn't America, Colin,' she argued. 'I can't think of a single recorded case in this country of anyone being murdered for their political views.'

'Can't you?' Beresford fired back. 'Try telling that to all the people who've been killed in the Troubles in Northern Ireland!'

'That's a different matter altogether,' Paniatowski said. 'The IRA and the Protestant paramilitary groups see themselves as at war.'

'And how do you think the miners see themselves? Passions are running very deep about this strike – and they're running in both directions.'

Paniatowski sighed. 'You may be right,' she said, 'but when I was at Len's house – which, incidentally, you've still to see for yourself – my gut was telling me, very strongly, that this particular murder was personal. I'm almost certain that the killer was feeling a real rage against his victim *as Len Hopkins*, rather than just as somebody on the other side of the argument.'

'Imagine you were a miner,' Beresford suggested. 'You see this strike as vital for ensuring the future of your family. And this one feller – Len Hopkins – is threatening that future. As far as you're concerned, he's a traitor to his class. Wouldn't you feel a real rage towards *him*?'

'Yes, if he *was* the one feller,' Paniatowski said. 'But he wasn't, was he? There are plenty of other people who oppose the strike.'

'And Martin Luther King wasn't the only black man in the Civil Rights Movement,' Beresford said. 'But King was the symbol of that movement – he inspired others to follow him.'

'I think you're stretching the analogy a bit, Colin,' Paniatowski said.

'And *I* think . . .' Beresford said hotly; then checking himself he continued, in a much calmer voice, 'I think that whoever chose the pickaxe as a murder weapon didn't choose it because it was a weapon of opportunity, or because he was in a rage and wanted to make a real mess of Hopkins. I think he chose it because it was symbolic of the struggle.'

Enough was enough! Paniatowski decided.

'Since you feel so very strongly that this line of investigation is worth pursuing, we *will* – despite any misgivings that I might have – pursue it, Inspector Beresford,' she said.

'Thank you, boss,' said Beresford, finally accepting that he'd gone too far.

'What time is this meeting in the Miners' Institute?' Paniatowski asked.

'Half past seven.'

'I don't think the killer is likely to stand up and confess to his crime in the middle of the meeting – though it would certainly be very nice for us if he did,' Paniatowski said. 'But if he *is* a miner, as DI Beresford is convinced he is, he'll almost definitely be there, and he may just say something – or do something – which will give him away. And in case that happens, I'd like you to be there to see it, Inspector.'

Beresford nodded. 'Right, boss.'

'But at the same time as we're following that line of investigation – the DI Beresford line – I'd like to find out more about Len Hopkins as a man, and the people who he interacted with,' Paniatowski continued. She looked Beresford straight in the eye. 'Is that all right with you, Inspector?'

There was only one permissible answer, and Beresford gave it by nodding his head again.

'Now we know that Len Hopkins was a religious man from some of the books that he had in his house,' Paniatowski continued. 'What was it that the vicar said about him, Jack?'

'That he belongs to some kind of wild Methodist sect in the next valley,' Crane replied.

'Which is not exactly a very Christian attitude, and probably tells us much more about the vicar of Bellingsworth than it does about the Methodists,' Paniatowski said drily. 'I'd like you to go and talk to this pastor of Len's first thing in the morning, Jack.'

'Got it,' Crane said.

'I'd like you, Kate, to find out if the fight in the Miners' Institute was the only example of violence yesterday, and, if there were others, whether or not Len Hopkins was involved – because if he spent his whole day getting into punch-ups, I need to know about it.'

'Hopkins wasn't *in* Bellingsworth for most of yesterday,' Meadows pointed out.

'I know that,' Paniatowski agreed. 'He wasn't here, and neither was anyone he might have come into conflict with. That's why I want you in Accrington tomorrow, talking to the people who organized the brass band competition – and in particular to any of them who were involved in the security arrangements.'

'Right, boss.'

'And there's one more thing that comes to mind,' Paniatowski said. 'Last week – on Thursday, to be precise – a young man, supposedly from the Department of Education and Science, paid Len Hopkins a visit. We don't know what he said to him, but we do know that whatever it was, it made Hopkins absolutely furious. So when you can spare the time, Inspector Beresford, I'd like you to check up on who he was, and what he said.'

'So you think *he* might be the killer, do you?' asked Beresford, with a little aggression creeping back into his voice.

I saw enough of him to know he'd have thought it far too messy to smash in Len's head with a short-handled pickaxe, Susan Danvers had said, sitting in the sad monument to the past that was her front parlour.

'No, I don't believe he killed Len Hopkins,' Paniatowski told Beresford, 'but he's a loose end in this investigation, and I don't like loose ends.'

'I'll deal with it,' Beresford said – though the tone in his voice suggested he wouldn't exactly be making it a priority.

There was the sound of a large van pulling up outside the pub.

Meadows stood up, and looked out of the window.

'I don't want to bother you, boss, but we've got trouble,' she said.

'Trouble?' Paniatowski repeated.

And then she looked out of the window herself, and saw exactly what Meadows meant.

ELEVEN

The trouble that Meadows had spotted through the window of the Green Dragon took the form of Lynda Jenkins, until recently a reporter for Radio Whitebridge and now elevated to regional television.

Lynda had her fans, but her producer, Roger Hardcastle, was definitely not one of them. In his opinion, her soaring career owed less to her innate abilities as a journalist than to her willingness to make the people who mattered at Northern TV aware of her large – and Hardcastle had reluctantly to admit, rather shapely – breasts.

In her own assessment, she had the true reporter's instinct for a good story, which, roughly translated, meant that she considered the accuracy of what she was reporting on to be of lesser importance than the splash it would cause. And as she stepped down from the outside broadcast van in front of the Green Dragon, she was sensing a very big splash indeed.

Terry, her cameraman, followed her on to the pavement, and looked in the direction of the pub.

'Are you going inside, Lynda?' he asked.

'No need,' Jenkins told him. 'Now that we're here, they'll come out.'

'Are you sure of that?'

'Absolutely sure – if they didn't, it would look as if they were hiding from me.'

'Do you want me to have the camera running when they come out?' Terry asked.

It was a tempting idea, Jenkins thought. The image of two bobbies leaving a pub would be good television, especially with the scathing comment she would add during editing. But filming them at that moment might make them less willing to cooperate, and it would be much better – in splash terms – if they agreed to be interviewed live on air.

The door of the Green Dragon opened, and Paniatowski and her inspector stepped out on to the street.

'Told you, didn't I, Terry?' Jenkins said complacently. She switched her attention to the two police officers. 'Good afternoon to you both, Chief Inspector Paniatowski and Inspector Beresford. I'm Lynda Jenkins, and I'm here on behalf of Northern Television News.'

'I know who you are,' Paniatowski said, flatly.

'I've got a time-spot booked for my report on the next news bulletin, and I wondered whether you'd care to appear in it,' Jenkins said.

Paniatowski hesitated. On the one hand, appealing for information could be very helpful at this point in the investigation. On the other, the last time Jenkins had covered a serious crime – the murder of a prostitute whose body had been found in a moorland pub called the Top o' the Moors – the reporter had revealed far too much information on air.

'I'm prepared to be interviewed, but I want something in return,' she said finally.

'And what might that be?' Lynda Jenkins wondered.

'For reasons I'm not at liberty to go into, I want to keep the investigation very low-key at the moment,' Paniatowski said, 'which means that what I really don't need are any outrageous statements from you.'

'Fair enough,' Jenkins agreed, then added hopefully, 'We'll broadcast from here, in front of the pub, shall we?'

'No,' Paniatowski said firmly. 'We'll do it in front of the church hall.'

'The thing is, the church hall isn't very visually exciting,' Lynda Jenkins said. She turned to her cameraman for support. 'I'm right, aren't I, Terry?'

'Quite right,' Terry agreed loyally.

'This isn't some kind of entertainment show, it's a murder inquiry,' Paniatowski said coldly. 'A man has died. So I don't really care

how unphotogenic the church hall is – that's where we've set up
our incident centre, and if we don't do the interview there, we won't
be doing it anywhere.'

'Fair enough,' Lynda Jenkins repeated, but with much less enthu-
siasm this time.

Was she making a mistake in agreeing to the interview at all?
Paniatowski wondered.

It was possible that she was. But the interview just might produce
some helpful results – and given how bloody impossible her right-
hand man was being at that moment, she needed all the help she
could get.

'Well, that last half-hour has certainly been a master class in
harmonious team work, hasn't it?' Meadows asked, as she looked
through the pub window at Paniatowski and Beresford walking
away, with Lynda Jenkins and her cameraman in their wake.

'I have to admit, there've been times when I've felt *more* comfortable with my situation,' Crane replied.

Meadows took a sip of her tomato juice. 'And which of our
esteemed leaders do you believe is thinking along the right lines?'
she asked.

'I'm not sure, Sarge,' Crane said. 'I haven't been with the team
long, but I've come to recognize that when the boss has a gut
instinct, she's usually not far from the mark.'

Meadows smiled. 'A good answer, young Jack,' she said. 'It really
is a perfect combination of gallantry and *realpolitik*.'

Crane grinned back at her. 'Gallantry because the boss is a woman,
and *realpolitik* because she *is* the boss?'

'Exactly! Now stop being so bloody diplomatic, and tell me what
you really think.'

'I'm inclined to go with the inspector's view of the case,' Crane
said.

'And why's that?'

'Because I don't like coincidences, and it seems to me to be far
too much of a coincidence that anybody who hated Hopkins for
personal reasons should have waited until there was this *political*
disturbance before killing him.'

'What a sweet boy you are,' Meadows said, affectionately.

'You don't agree?'

'If I was planning to kill someone for personal reasons, I'd wait for just this sort of opportunity – a time when there might be a completely different reason to kill him – precisely so that a bobby like Inspector Beresford would come along and muddy the waters.'

'So you agree with the boss, do you?' Crane asked.

'I didn't say that,' she replied, enigmatically. 'And whichever of them turns out to be right, there's no doubt that our inspector is being a real pain in the arse, is there?'

'No doubt at all,' Beresford agreed. 'And we both know *why* he's being a pain in the arse.'

'We do indeed,' Meadows said.

Roger Hardcastle looked at Lynda Jenkins' face on the monitor.

'If it had been left up to me, I'd never have let the bloody woman anywhere near a story like this again – not after the cock-up she made on that prostitute murder,' he said. 'But it *wasn't* left up to me.'

'So what happened?' asked Phil, his assistant. 'Has she been waggling her tits in front of the management again?'

'No, funnily enough, I don't think that's it at all,' Hardcastle replied. 'When God came in to work this morning – an hour late, as usual, but that's management for you – he told me that I *had to* use her. But he didn't look too happy about it himself, and when I tried to argue with him about it, he said there was no point, because the order had come from higher up.'

'Who's higher up than God?' Phil asked.

Hardcastle shrugged.

'Beats me,' he admitted.

'You never know, she might just make another prize cock-up soon,' the assistant said.

'That's exactly what I'm banking on, lad,' Hardcastle said. 'And the moment she does, I'll have her back covering cute pets and exotically shaped vegetables.' He switched on his microphone. 'Going live in five seconds, Lynda, love. Five . . . four . . . three . . . two . . . one . . .'

'The murder of Len Hopkins has shocked and horrified the quiet mining community of Bellingsworth,' Jenkins said, having used the five-second countdown to acquire a look of intelligent concern. 'I'm here in the village now to talk to Chief Inspector Monika Paniatowski, who is leading the investigation.'

The camera swung round to focus on Paniatowski and Beresford.

'Do you have any idea what the motive for this terrible murder might have been, Chief Inspector?' asked Jenkins' voice, off screen.

'The investigation is in its earlier stages, and we're still considering all possibilities,' Paniatowski replied. 'What I would like to do now, Lynda, is take the opportunity to appeal to the general public for their help.'

'Go ahead,' Lynda Jenkins said.

Paniatowski shifted her position slightly, and looked directly and earnestly into the camera.

'If you knew Len Hopkins, even slightly, then you may be in possession of information which could help us to find his killer,' she said. 'Whatever you know, and however inconsequential it might seem to you, I urge you to ring Whitebridge Police Headquarters as soon as possible.'

'She's a little cracker, that Monika Paniatowski, isn't she?' Hardcastle asked his assistant. 'The camera loves her, and she could warm her feet on my back any night of the week.'

'She's a bit old for me,' said Phil, who considered any woman over twenty-five beyond the pale. 'Lynda's more my speed.'

'Lynda,' Hardcastle repeated in disgust. 'Comparing her to Monika Paniatowski is like comparing a race horse to a cow. Monika would chew you up and spit you out without even stopping for breath – and I guarantee, you'd love every minute of it.'

'You do know you're talking like a dirty old man, don't you, boss?' the assistant asked.

'Thank you for that, Phil,' Hardcastle said. 'There are not many men who are lucky enough to work with a pimply youth who's brave enough to tell them when they've achieved their ultimate ambition.'

'Thank you, Chief Inspector Paniatowski, and I'm sure our viewers will do all they can to help you,' Lynda Jenkins said. 'If I may, I'd now like to turn to Inspector Beresford. Tell me, Inspector, do you have any theories of your own about the murder?'

'She's doing it again,' Hardcastle groaned. 'She's bloody doing it again.'

'You don't ask questions like that!' he bawled into the microphone. 'Back off.'

'I thought you *wanted* her to make a mess of things,' his assistant said.

'I do, but not over anything as important as this murder,' Hardcastle said. 'I still have some personal integrity, you know.'

'Do you?' Phil asked.

'Yes, I do, you cheeky young bugger. If you haven't noticed it before, that's probably because I usually leave it at home – but today, the wife packed it in with my sandwiches.'

Beresford stared into the camera, the muscles in his face twitching as if he really wanted to say something, but was fighting the urge.

'*Do* you have a theory, Inspector Beresford?' Lynda Jenkins repeated.

'I have nothing to add to what DCI Paniatowski has said,' Beresford replied, almost forcing the words out of his mouth.

The camera swung back to Lynda Jenkins.

'Wrap it up – and keep it uncontroversial,' Hardcastle's voice said to her in her earpiece.

'Whatever DCI Paniatowski might say on the matter, this reporter has discovered that the general feeling here in the village is that Len Hopkins was murdered to stop him campaigning against the proposed strike ballot,' Lynda Jenkins said. 'Furthermore . . .'

'Cut her off!' Hardcastle shouted. 'Take the mad bitch off right now!'

Lynda Jenkins disappeared from the monitor, and was replaced by an image of the anchor man.

'I want you to say that the opinions expressed by Lynda Jenkins are purely personal ones,' he said into the microphone. 'Have you got that! They're purely personal.'

The anchor man gave a barely perceptible nod, and Hardcastle reached for a tissue to mop his brow with.

'That wasn't just the stupid cow losing control in the heat of moment, you know,' he said to Phil. 'I could tell from the look in her eyes that she was always intending to say it. It's almost as if she'd been briefed.'

*   *   *

Beresford took three quick steps forward, and placed his hand firmly over the camera lens.

'It's all right,' Terry assured him, 'there's no need for that, because we're off air.'

'Do you know what you've just done?' Paniatowski asked Jenkins, in a low, rasping voice which should have worried the reporter much more than an outright scream of rage. 'Have you any idea how much you may just have harmed my investigation?'

Jenkins smiled complacently. 'It's called freedom of the press, Chief Inspector. It's something we value quite highly in this little democracy of ours, so you'd better get used to it.'

'Get her out of here!' Paniatowski told the cameraman. 'Get her out while I'm still in control of myself.'

'You can't threaten *me*, you know,' Lynda Jenkins said.

But when Paniatowski took a step towards her, the reporter took an involuntary step backwards, then turned and began to walk quickly towards the Northern Television mobile unit.

'The bitch!' Paniatowski said.

'I did warn you, Monika,' Beresford said.

'Warned me of what?' Paniatowski demanded.

'I warned you that feelings were probably running high, and that there was an obvious suspect in this murder. You *could have* pulled Tommy Sanders in for questioning by now, and if you'd done that – if you'd been able to announce, on camera, that a man was helping us with our enquiries – Lynda Jenkins wouldn't have been able to say what she did say.'

'Let's get one thing straight,' Paniatowski said angrily. 'We've mapped out a strategy for this investigation, and we'll proceed along the lines we've laid down. If that isn't working out – and sometimes it doesn't – then we'll try something else. Have you got that, Inspector? *We'll* try something else? But what I am not prepared to do – under any circumstances – is to let people like Lynda Jenkins dictate what my next move will be. Is that clearly understood?'

Beresford shrugged. 'You're the boss,' he said.

'Yes, I am,' Paniatowski agreed. 'And you'd better not forget it!'

TWELVE

When the school bus pulled up at the approved stop, Becky Sanders was the first one off, and by the time the last of her fellow pupils had disembarked, she was already halfway up the street.

She arrived at her back door panting for breath and almost burst into the kitchen, where her father sat in his armchair reading the evening paper, and her mother was standing up and doing the ironing.

'Mum, Dad, I came second in the history test,' she said. 'Second! And I was the *only* one in the whole class who knew why Henry Tudor had a claim to the English throne!'

Her father lowered the paper just a little. 'Well, I'm sure that'll be a lot of use to you when you're working behind the counter in Woolworth's – I don't think,' he said.

'I came *second*, Dad,' Becky repeated.

'I'm not deaf – I heard you,' her father told her. 'You came second – which means somebody else must have come first, doesn't it?'

Becky felt her lower lip start to tremble.

'Yes, Dad, Johnny Lewis *did* beat me, but his dad's one of the history teachers, and—'

'Well, there you are,' her father interrupted. 'It's not *what* you know in this life – it's *who* you know. Anyway, now you're home, you might as well make yourself useful and put the kettle on. I'm spitting feathers here.'

Her mother looked up from the ironing. 'Your brother was always good at things like that when he was at school,' she said.

'Our Tom was always good at *everything* he did,' her father said. 'And he didn't even have to try – it just seemed to come naturally to him.'

'Now he's in the youth squad at Whitebridge Rovers,' Becky's mother said, with something like awe in her voice.

'And that's only the first step,' her father added. 'You mark my words, Mother, we'll be in the stands watching him play for Manchester United before he's twenty-one.'

Becky's mother suddenly looked slightly guilty.

'I'm very pleased you did well in your test, love,' she said. 'Really I am. What did you say the test was in? Was it science?'

'That's right,' Becky said. 'It was about that world-famous scientist, Henry Tudor.'

'Well, there you are, then,' her mother said. 'And I'm sure your dad's very pleased as well, aren't you, Kevin?'

'I'm over the moon about it,' Kevin Sanders said. 'Now where's that cup of tea I was promised?'

Becky, like the dutiful daughter she always tried her best to be, made the tea and then crept upstairs to her room. Once she'd closed the door carefully behind her – her dad didn't like doors banging, although her brother Tom could crash around as much as he liked – she threw herself on the bed, and burst into tears.

It was ten minutes before her sobbing subsided enough for her to think of looking at the note she'd been handed as she entered school that morning. She didn't really need to read it again – she already knew it by heart – but it was from Gary, and so she *wanted* to.

She read it once more, then forced herself to tear the note carefully into small pieces, and ate them.

She should have done that hours ago, she told herself as she swallowed, and it really had been wrong of her to have waited so long.

I'm a good girl, really I am, she thought, but somehow I can never quite be good *enough*.

As darkness approached, the temperature in the village began to plummet. It was going to be a very cold night, and there would undoubtedly be a heavy frost on the ground in the morning.

Paniatowski, standing in front of the church hall, looked at the heavy grey clouds in the sky.

First there'd been the power cuts, then the three-day week, and now it looked as if it was about to snow, she thought.

And what could Lancashire expect to have heaped on it next, she wondered. Volcanic ash? A plague of frogs?

Snow was the last thing this investigation – already being run under pressure – needed. Snow would make a difficult situation even worse.

She looked first up the street and then down it, and found herself wondering where the murderer was at that moment.

Perhaps he was down the mine, finishing off his shift. Or perhaps his shift was over, and he was sitting at home, waiting for his wife to serve him with his tea.

And what was he *feeling*?

Perhaps it was remorse. Perhaps it was satisfaction. Or maybe, after finally eliminating the object of the hatred which had been eating him up inside, he felt nothing but a kind of numbness.

It was as she was musing that she saw the Rover 2000 approaching.

'Now what the bloody hell is *he* doing here in Bellingsworth?' she asked herself.

The Rover pulled up on the opposite side of the road, and the chief constable's large frame emerged from it.

She watched him as he took his pipe out of his pocket, lit it, and was soon surrounded by a cloud of light grey smoke.

There were still times when she thought of George Baxter as the rather sad, big ginger teddy bear who had undoubtedly deserved the love which he'd so desperately wanted from her, but which she had felt unable to give him. Yet as their affair receded further and further into the past, so she was finding it increasingly easy to see him the way other officers probably did – as a man who carried himself with an air of authority and competence, and who, in an imperfect world, was probably the best chief constable Mid Lancs could ever hope for.

Baxter crossed the road.

'We don't usually see you at a crime scene, sir,' Paniatowski said.

'No, you don't,' Baxter agreed. 'I normally like to leave my people to get on with the job. But I've got a bit of news I know you won't like, and I thought I might as well deliver it personally.'

'I'm listening,' Paniatowski said.

'We've received intelligence that there might be trouble at tonight's meeting in the Miners' Institute, and we got this intelligence *before* your interview with Lynda Jenkins, which, to be honest with you, was a disaster, and certainly won't have improved matters.'

'You sound as if you're blaming the interview going wrong on me,' Paniatowski said.

'You're the one in charge of the investigation, Monika. You're the one who agreed to the interview,' Baxter said.

'And bloody Lynda Jenkins was the one who went rogue,' Paniatowski pointed out.

'That's true,' Baxter agreed. 'If we're apportioning blame, I'd have to say that it was much more her fault than yours – but you still should have handled the whole situation better.'

'Should I?' Paniatowski asked hotly. 'What would you have done in my place, sir?'

'I don't know,' Baxter admitted. 'I can't say with any degree of certainty, because I wasn't *in* your place, was I? But maybe I'd have given her a sterner warning about behaving herself before the interview started. Or maybe I'd have found a way to cut her off before she did any damage. But whatever I'd have done, it would have been better than what you actually *did* do.'

He was right, she thought. If she hadn't been distracted by her almost-argument with Colin Beresford – and if Louisa's words that morning about her being a part-time parent hadn't been nagging away at the back of her mind – she probably would have handled it much better.

'It won't happen again,' she promised.

'It certainly won't happen with Lynda Jenkins,' Baxter said. 'Roger Hardcastle has already been informed that if he wants any further cooperation from us, he'll keep her well away from the police beat.'

'If you think there might be trouble at the meeting, send a few uniformed bobbies down here,' Paniatowski suggested.

'I will,' Baxter told her. 'In fact, they're already on the way. But to get back to the intelligence . . .'

'Yes?'

'It came from your old friend, Mr Forsyth.'

'What's that bastard doing here?'

'He *says* that he's in Whitebridge to monitor the strike, but you can never tell with him. It's more than possible he's here on some entirely different matter, and is only using the strike as a cover. But whatever the case, he's asked Special Branch to send a couple of their officers to Bellingsworth.'

'He's asked what!'

'Forsyth has promised me that they will not impede your investigation in any way. He claims their only purpose here is as back-up.'

'And you believe him, do you?' Paniatowski demanded.

'Honestly, Monika, I don't know,' Baxter admitted. 'It makes sense in policing terms, but then everything Forsyth says seems to make sense at the time, and often, as you know yourself, he's lying through his teeth.'

'I don't want the Special Branch here,' Paniatowski said firmly.

'I'm sure you don't – I wouldn't want them myself – but since there's nothing that I can do to stop them, you'll just have to grin and bear it.'

'But just their presence here will distort the whole investigation,' Paniatowski protested. 'They'll see Len Hopkins' death as simply a political assassination. That's the way they're *trained* to think. That's how they justify their very existence as the Special Branch.'

'And you don't think his death *is* political?'

'Not at all! Len Hopkins' death has *nothing* to do with politics.'

'Have you got your whole team behind you in this, Monika?' Baxter asked, deceptively mildly. 'Do they all think you should focus the investigation on searching for a purely personal motive for the murder?'

It would be nice to be able to say yes to that, wouldn't it, Paniatowski thought. But she couldn't, in all honesty, say that *any* of the team was one hundred percent behind her – and when it came to Colin Beresford, the figure was closer to zero percent.

'Well, of course, we're still keeping all our other options open,' she said, back-pedalling furiously. 'It would be foolish not to.'

'But . . .?' Baxter asked.

It would be pointless to lie to Baxter, Paniatowski thought. And anyway, why the hell *should* she?

'But even though we are investigating other possibilities, I *know* he was killed for personal reasons – I can sense it,' she said.

'I've always had the greatest respect for your hunches, Monika,' Baxter said. 'But the trouble with hunches is that if you put all your effort into following them, and they don't work out, you're left with nothing. Make sure you're not left with nothing this time, Chief Inspector.'

As Becky stepped through the door of the grandfather's kitchen, she bent into a mock-curtsey, and said, 'I am come, your majesty.'

'So I see,' said her grandfather, who was sitting at the table. 'And who might you be, fair damsel?'

'I am no one at all – just a lowly peasant girl, who will work hard and honestly in return for a roof over her head and a few dry crusts.'

It was a game they had been playing since the three-year-old Becky had curled up snugly on her grandfather's knees and listened as he read her fairy tales, and though they had both fully expected it to peter out as the girl grew older, it somehow never had.

'If you are seeking work, then you must speak to my son, the handsome prince, for he is in charge of such matters,' Tommy Sanders said.

'And will he like me?' Becky asked tremulously.

'He'd be a right idiot if he didn't, Becky, love,' Tommy said.

The use of her real name signalled the end of the game, and Becky suddenly grew more serious.

'Have the police been to see you yet, Granddad?' she asked.

'The police?' Tommy repeated.

Becky breathed a sigh of relief. 'So they haven't.'

'Why should the police want to come knocking on my door?' Tommy wondered.

Becky sighed again, though this time with exasperation.

'Because Mr Hopkins was murdered last night – and everybody knows that you and him were enemies.'

'We weren't enemies at all,' Tommy protested. 'We might have disagreed about the direction that the industry was going in, but outside that, we got on well enough.'

'But don't you see, there *was* no "outside that".'

'I'm not sure I quite get the point.'

'The strike's become the only thing that matters to you now. It's all you really care about any more.'

'Now that's not true, our Becky,' Tommy said severely. 'I care about you, Becky. I care about you more than I can tell you.'

'I'm sorry, I should never have said that,' Becky replied, bowing her head to hide the tears that were forming in the corners of her eyes. 'I know you care about me – deep down.'

'What do you mean? Deep down?'

'We used to talk to each other about anything and everything, but for the last few months, all *you* want to talk about is the strike.'

'The strike's important . . .' Tommy began. Then he checked himself, and continued. 'You're right, our Becky, I've become a proper old bore. Well, I promise you that from now on—'

'You still don't get what I'm saying, do you?' Becky asked, frustrated. 'You still don't understand why I'm here.'

'I'd assumed that you were here to give a bit of comfort to your poor old grand—' Tommy began.

'Last night, in the Miners' Institute, you had a fight with Mr Hopkins, didn't you?' Becky interrupted him.

'And how do you know about that?' Tommy asked sharply.

She knew about it because it was all in the note that Gary had given her outside school, Becky thought.

But aloud, she said, 'You had a fight with Mr Hopkins, and now he's dead. What are the police going to think?'

'They'd never think—'

'But of course they would!' Becky began to pace the narrow kitchen, clutching her thin arms across her thin bosom. 'What time did you leave the Institute last night, Granddad?'

'Not long after I had my little disagreement with Len. I didn't much feel like staying on after that.'

'And where did you go?'

'Where do you think I went? I came back home.'

'Alone?'

'Who else would have been with me?'

'So you were here alone, all night?' Becky said. 'You were alone – and you never left the house?'

'Isn't that what I just said?'

She knew he was lying – she could hear it in his voice.

'Granddad . . .' she said.

And it was almost a plea – almost a prayer.

'You're really serious, aren't you?' Tommy asked, suddenly serious himself.

'Of course I'm serious!'

'Listen, love, I don't know if you know this, but Len lives up the hill from me. By the time I'd walked to the end of this street, turned the corner and made my way to his front door, I'd be too knack— I'd be too tired to kill him.'

'You wouldn't have had to do it that way,' Becky said. 'If you went through your backyard into the alley, it's only a few steps to *his* back-yard. And he was *in* his backyard – on the lavvy – when he was killed.'

'You surely don't think . . .'

'It doesn't matter what I think,' Becky said. 'It's what the police think that's important.'

'You've been watching too many cop programmes on the television,' Tommy said.

'It's time we were honest with each other, Granddad,' Becky said.

'Honest about what?'

'We always talk about you being there when I get my degree, but it's all pretend, because we both know that's not going to happen, don't we?'

'Yes,' Tommy agreed. 'We do.'

'Then say it!' the girl demanded. 'Say why it is you won't be there!'

'Because I'll be long dead by then,' Tommy told her.

'Yes, you will,' Becky agreed. 'Long dead. And when you die, I want to be right there with you, holding your hand in mine.'

'I couldn't think of a better way to go,' Tommy said, now almost in tears himself.

'But if that's ever going to happen, there's something you have to do first, to make *sure* it happens,' Becky said. 'And if you won't do that thing for yourself, then at least do it for me.'

'What thing are you talking about, lass?' Tommy asked.

And then Becky told him of her plan.

THIRTEEN

When Louisa arrived home from school, she found Lily Perkins in the kitchen, cooking her tea.

Lily had been Louisa's nanny when she was small, and had graduated from that role to housekeeper as she was growing. Lily was not – as she readily admitted herself – any great shakes in the brain department, but she was warm and good-hearted, and Louisa had come to regard her as a sort of stand-in granny.

'Your mum's out on a job,' Lily said cheerfully.

Louisa grinned. Lily always said it just like that – 'Your mum's out on a job' – as if she imagined Monika was selling brushes door-to-door or fixing somebody's boiler, instead of investigating a grisly murder.

'I know all about that,' Louisa said. 'I was here this morning, when she got the call.'

'So that means I'll be staying over tonight,' Lily told her.

Louisa was not sure whether that was good news or bad news.

It was certainly good news for somebody who wanted to go to a party, because it wouldn't be too hard to con Lily into believing that she had permission.

On the other hand, though she really *did* want to accept Ellie's invitation, she had a nagging feeling that it would be wrong to go, and she'd been half-hoping that her mother would be there, to take the decision out of her hands.

'We'll have a really cosy evening together,' Lily said enthusiastically. 'I bought a special ginger cake on my way over, and we can tuck into it like a couple of little piggies while we're watching television.'

Would now be a good time to tell Lily she would be going out later, Louisa wondered.

No! In fact, it would be a very dangerous time to tell her, because if Mum phoned, and Lily asked her about the party . . .

Better to say nothing now, Louisa decided. Better to leave it and see how things turned out.

For a full twenty seconds after he knocked, Beresford could hear the old man coughing and wheezing, as he slowly made his way from the kitchen to the front door.

But how much of that noisy effort was real, and how much of it was put on? Beresford asked himself.

Was he really struggling, or was it all no more than an act designed to show that Tommy Sanders could not have been *physically* capable of killing Len Hopkins?

The front door was finally opened, and Beresford got his first look at the man he had already decided was the murderer.

Most miners in the village were as short as Tommy was, but whereas their rock-hard muscles visibly strained against the confines of their clothing, his clothes hung loose, as if they had once belonged to a much beefier man.

Tommy Sanders looked up at Beresford with a mixture of mistrust and dislike on his face.

'You're a bobby, aren't you?' Tommy asked.

'I am,' Beresford confirmed.

'Well, you might have gone around the back and saved me a bit of effort,' the old man said.

'I'll remember that the next time,' Beresford promised. 'Can I come inside, please, Mr Sanders?'

'Not unless you've got a warrant in your pocket,' Sanders replied. 'And, incidentally, there won't *be* a next time – because if you come calling again, I'll bloody ignore you.'

'Have you got something against all policemen, or just the ones trying to find Len Hopkins' murderer?' Beresford asked.

'All policemen,' Sanders told him. 'You've sold your souls to the bosses, lad, and in return for a colour television and few bob in the bank, you're more than willing to come and beat us shitless whenever those bosses decide that we're getting out of order.'

'Are you being deliberately provoking?' Beresford wondered.

'Well, of course I am,' Sanders answered. 'And if I say so myself, I'm making a pretty good job of it.' He paused to suck in some air. 'How did you expect me to behave anyway – like a suspect on *Columbo*?'

'I'm not sure I know quite what you mean,' Beresford said.

'Then you must be a bit thick, lad. In every episode of *Columbo*, there's always one character who goes out of his way to help the police, and who's always willing to explain away any questions or doubts that the lieutenant has. And that's how Columbo knows he's the murderer!'

'So by turning the whole thing around by a hundred and eighty degrees, you're hoping to convince me you're *not* the murderer?'

Tommy Sanders chuckled. 'If that *was* the way my mind was working, I'd be a bloody idiot to tell you about it, wouldn't I?'

'*Did* you kill Len Hopkins?' Beresford asked.

'Do *you* think I killed him?' Tommy Sanders countered.

'Well, you certainly had the means, motive and opportunity,' Beresford pointed out.

'Yes, I did, that's certainly true,' Sanders agreed. 'But, you see, I also have an alibi.'

It was plain that PC Mellors was already not a happy man as he stood uncertainly in the doorway of the church hall, and when Paniatowski gestured for him to join her at a desk in the corner of the room, his degree of unhappiness notably increased.

'You sent for me, ma'am?' he asked, standing in front of the desk like an errant schoolboy.

'When I was talking to Susan Danvers, she told me that Len Hopkins had been killed with a pickaxe,' Paniatowski said.

'Well, he was,' Mellors replied.

'I know that, and you know that – because we were there,' Paniatowski said. 'But how did *she* know that?'

Mellors looked down at the floor. 'I might have told her,' he mumbled. 'It might just have slipped out.'

'Might?' Paniatowski repeated.

'It *did* slip out,' Mellors confessed.

'Susan also had the distinct impression that the rest of the village knew as well,' Paniatowski continued. 'Was she right about that?'

'I . . . I didn't know it was such a big secret, ma'am,' Mellors said.

Of course he didn't, Paniatowski thought. He was a country bobby who'd probably never been involved in anything bigger than bicycle theft. He had no idea how murder investigations were run, and when he'd suddenly gained new status in Bellingsworth – as a result of the fact that he alone, of all the villagers, had been to the crime scene – he had not been able to resist revealing a few of the juicier details. In a way, she felt sorry for him, but what he had done had damaged the integrity of the investigation, and it simply couldn't be overlooked.

'I'm going to have to file a report on you,' she said.

'Do you have to, ma'am?' Mellors asked.

'I have to,' Paniatowski said firmly, then, as she noticed that Mellors' lower lip was quivering, she softened. 'You're the one with the local knowledge, and if you learn to keep your mouth shut, you might still be useful to the inquiry. If you can put in a good performance from now, I'll try not to make my report too scathing.'

'Thank you, ma'am,' Mellors said.

'You're dismissed,' Paniatowski told him, 'but keep yourself available, because Inspector Beresford wants you with him at the miners' meeting.'

'I'll do that, ma'am,' Mellors promised. 'And thank you again.'

'Don't thank me until you know you have a reason to, PC Mellors,' Paniatowski cautioned.

It was five minutes after Paniatowski had talked to Mellors that Colin Beresford arrived back at the church hall, and the moment he walked into the room, it was obvious to everyone who saw him that he was in a very black mood.

'He's taking the piss out of me,' he complained, the moment he reached his boss's desk.

'Who is?' Paniatowski asked.

'The feller who's my prime suspect – and notice I said *my* prime suspect, because I know you don't see things that way.'

'Ah, it's Tommy Sanders that you're talking about!' Paniatowski said.

'That's right – Tommy-bloody-Sanders. He thinks he can say what he likes to me, because he's got an alibi. But he's wrong about that – because I'll break that bloody alibi if it's the last thing I do.'

'Who's he offering as his alibi?'

'His granddaughter, Becky.'

'If she's his granddaughter, she can't be much more than a kid,' Paniatowski said thoughtfully.

'He says she's fourteen.'

Fourteen! Paniatowski thought. Louisa's age!

'He claims that she was with him all night, does he?' she asked Beresford.

'Yes, he does.'

'And have her parents confirmed it?'

'That's where our Tommy thinks he's being so bloody clever. He says her parents don't know she was there.'

'How could they not have known?' Paniatowski asked. 'Surely they must have been at home themselves.'

And then she thought, But *I'm* not at home, am I?

'The parents *were* at home,' Beresford said.

'Well, then?'

'According to Tommy's story, Becky was upset about breaking up with her boyfriend, and needed a shoulder to cry on. So she went up to bed as usual, then climbed down the drainpipe into the backyard, and legged it over to her granddad's house. Now I don't believe that for a second, and it won't take me more than a few minutes to get the truth out of the kid.'

'It's probably not a good idea for you to talk to Becky while you're so angry with her grandfather,' Paniatowski said. 'In fact, it's probably not a good idea for you to talk to her at all.'

'And why might that be?'

'Because she's just a kid, Colin, and it might be better if she was questioned by a woman.'

Beresford nodded, reluctantly acknowledging the point, then said, 'So you'll send Meadows to see her, will you?'

She *could* send Meadows, Paniatowski thought, but Meadows didn't have a kid of her own – a kid who was the same age as Louisa.

'I'll go myself,' she said. 'I'll do it while you're attending the meeting in the Miners' Institute.'

'Make sure she tells the truth,' Beresford urged her. 'Break Tommy Sanders' alibi, because he did it, boss – I *know* he did it.'

'Are you sure you don't mean that you'd *like* him to have done it?' Paniatowski asked.

'He did it,' Beresford repeated, 'and he thinks he'll get away with it. But even if he doesn't, he's not particularly bothered, because by the time the case is due to go to trial, he'll be dead anyway.'

'I'm not sure that's quite as strong an argument as you seem to think it is,' Paniatowski said. 'Granted, he may not live long enough to stand trial, but he'll be on remand, and no man wants to die in—'

'He's a man with nothing to lose, so he might as well do what he wants,' Beresford said, almost shouting now. 'And what he wanted to do on Sunday night was to kill Len Hopkins!'

'I hope we're not interrupting a tiff between two sweethearts,' said a voice, and turning round, they saw that a couple of strangers were standing a few feet away from them.

Both the men were tall and lean. One of them was hatchet-faced, the other had a face which looked as if a hatchet had been used on it. They were dressed in dark sober suits, and neither of them was smiling.

'Who the hell are you?' Paniatowski demanded.

'We're Special Branch, darlin',' the hatchet-faced one said.

'Have you got any identification?' Paniatowski asked.

'We have,' Hatchet-face told her, 'but unless you've got some way to prove to us that you've got the right security clearance, we're certainly not going to show it to you.'

'Think yourself lucky that we've even taken the trouble to tell you that we're here,' the second man said.

'I don't *want* you here,' Paniatowski said.

'Course you don't, darlin',' the second man said, 'but you see, it's not really up to you, is it? You may be the law around here, but we're Special Branch – and we're the law around *everywhere.*'

'We'll be at the meeting in the Miners' Institute, but if there's no trouble, you won't even notice us,' Hatchet-face said.

'And if there *is* trouble, we'll neutralize it and be gone before you know it's even happened,' his partner added.

Just listening to their words, you could almost imagine they were a comic double act, Paniatowski thought, but look into their eyes and you soon realized that if they had to break bones, they would do so without a second's hesitation.

Louisa rushed through her homework – it had be done, whatever else happened, because there *was* school the next day – but once she'd finished it, she felt at such a loss that she began to wish she'd taken more time over it.

She still hadn't decided if the evening would end with the fabulous excitement of Ellie's party or the reassuring cosiness of Lily's ginger cake. Her mum had always said that she should learn to make her own decisions, but somehow this seemed just *too* big a decision to make without help.

When the phone rang in the hallway, she dashed to answer it.

'Are you nearly ready?' Ellie Sutton asked chirpily.

'I'm not sure I can come,' Louisa replied.

'You're not going to let me down, are you?' Ellie said, her voice suddenly much colder. 'Robert's already set out to pick you up. Are you saying he'll be making a wasted journey?'

'No,' Louisa said, and then – much more firmly, 'of course not.'

'He'll be there in about ten minutes,' Ellie said, with some of the warmth returning to her tone. 'When he gets there, he'll hoot his horn. And he can be very grumpy if he's kept waiting – so make sure he isn't.'

'I won't – I mean I will,' Louisa promised. She gave a small flustered laugh. 'I don't know what I mean.'

'Just make sure you're ready,' Ellie said, and hung up.

Louisa ran upstairs, and threw open her wardrobe. Now that she'd made her decision – although actually, it felt as if the decision had been made *for* her – she was feeling exhilarated.

She agonized over her clothes for a couple of minutes, then selected a polka-dot dress with a slightly flared skirt.

Once she was dressed and wearing a little of the lipstick her mother allowed her to use, she sat on the bed and waited.

Exactly ten minutes after Ellie had rung off, she heard the horn sound in the street.

She ran down the stairs, then called from the hallway, 'I'll be off now, Lily.'

'Off?' Lily repeated.

'The party!'

Lily appeared in the living room doorway.

'What party?'

'Didn't I mention it? I've been invited to a party. Mum said it would be all right.'

'On a school night? You don't go out on a school night. That's one of the rules.'

'Mum said we could break the rule, just this once.'

Lily looked dubious. 'I think that maybe I'd better give your mum a quick call.'

The horn sounded in the street again, more impatiently this time.

'Ellie's dad's getting cross – and it could take you *hours* to find Mum,' Louisa said. 'Can I go, Lily? Please!'

'Well, if you're sure your mum said it would be all right . . .'

'She did.'

'Then be sure to take your heavy coat with you. I don't want you catching cold.'

'Thank you, Lily,' Louisa said, reaching up to the rack.

'Put it on before you leave the house,' Lily said sternly.

Louisa struggled to put on the coat, which seemed to have developed ten arm holes.

'What time will you be back?' Lily asked. 'Nine o'clock?'

'It might be closer to ten,' Louisa replied.

'I'm not sure about that,' Lily said.

'Mum said that ten o'clock would be fine,' Louisa promised. 'And when I get back, we'll have some of that cake.'

She opened the door and stepped outside. She could, she supposed, have simply sneaked out of the house, but that would have been very bad, and – somehow – telling a few little lies didn't seem quite so bad at all.

FOURTEEN

The Miners' Institute concert room had been the setting for numerous brass band concerts and talent competitions. It had even, on occasion, hosted shows in which professional comedians and singers – some of them with even a few minor television credits to their name – had deigned to perform. But tonight, there was none of the buzz that comes from people expecting to be entertained – tonight, the mood was one of deadly seriousness.

Beresford – standing with his back against the wall, and with PC Mellors at his side – looked around the room. The tables had all been removed to make space for more chairs, and when all the available chairs had been taken, the steward had supplemented them with upended beer crates. And still there was not enough space for everyone who wished to attend, and latecomers had had to settle for standing in the corridor outside.

There was one notable face missing, however. Tommy Sanders was not there. So maybe, after the bravado performance he had put on earlier, the old miner had decided that discretion was the better part of valour.

'I'm in a bit of trouble with your boss, sir,' Mellors said.

There'd been a time – just after his promotion – when Beresford had found it uncomfortable to be called 'sir' by men who were older than him, but now he was starting to take it for granted.

'Trouble?' he said.

'I told people about the murder weapon.'

'Ah!'

'And she says she's going to write up a report on me.'

'She's pretty much obliged to do that.'

'The thing is, you've got a lot of influence with her. In some ways, I think she almost looks up to you.'

'I wouldn't go that far,' Beresford said, though he had not been displeased by the comment, 'but it's true that sometimes, when she thinks she's doing what *she* wants, she's actually doing what *I* want.'

Sometimes, you can be a complete arsehole, Colin Beresford, said a voice in his head.

Yes, he thought, agreeing with the voice, sometimes I can – and I just don't know what to do about it!

'I'll have a word with her, and see if I can get her to tone the report down,' he told Mellors. 'But I'm not promising anything, because she's very much her own woman.'

Is that some sort of long-distance apology to Monika? his inner voice asked. If it is, it's not a very good one. Why don't you tell Mellors that when you hinted you were sometimes in charge, you were talking bollocks?

Yes, that was what he should do, he decided – but he just couldn't force himself to say the words.

He looked around the room again.

'Do you know which of these men are in favour of the strike, and which ones are against it?' he asked.

'More or less,' Mellors replied.

'And could you make a guess at the percentages?'

'Well, the ones in favour of it are sitting to the left of the room, and the ones against it are sitting to the right, so I'd say it's about half-and-half.'

'So the left-wingers are on the left, and right-wingers are on the right,' Beresford mused. 'How very kind of them to make it all so easy for me.'

'I don't think they've done it for you, sir,' Mellors said, completely missing the point.

'Who's going to be chairing the meeting?' Beresford asked.

'The president of the Miners' Institute.'

'He's a miner himself, I take it.'

'He used to be, but he's retired now. The president of the Institute is always a retired miner.'

'And which side is this particular president on?'

'It's hard to say, because he's a bit like the Queen.'

'A bit like the Queen?'

'That's right. When she opens parliament and gives a speech about what the government's going to do in the next year, you never know whether she thinks its bloody brilliant or a load of old cock, do you?'

'True.'

'That's because she's supposed to be above politics.'

'True again.'

'And it's exactly the same with the president of the Miners' Institute.'

*　　*　　*

When Paniatowski knocked on the front door of the terraced house, it was opened by a thin pale girl with mousy brown hair, who seemed to be all elbows and knees.

'Are you Becky Sanders?' she asked.

The girl nodded.

'I'm Detective Chief Inspector Paniatowski, but you can call me Monika,' Paniatowski said. 'I'd like to ask you a few questions.'

'Who is it?' called a woman's voice from inside.

'It's a policewoman, Mum,' Becky replied. 'She says that she wants to talk to me.'

'She'd better come in then,' the woman said.

Paniatowski stepped into the parlour, and saw the thin woman – who could only have been Becky's mother – sitting in an armchair in front of a large television, her eyes glued to the screen as if hypnotized by it.

'You want to talk to our Becky, do you?' she asked, and took the risk of missing a vital part of an advertisement for washing powder by glancing briefly at the visitor.

'That's right, I do,' Paniatowski agreed. 'But since she's only fourteen, a parent or a parent's chosen representative is entitled to be present during the conversation.'

'You what?' Mrs Sanders said, her attention now clearly focussed on the screen again.

'If you or your husband wish to be there when I question Becky, that is your right. Alternatively, you may postpone the interview until your solicitor is present – though I don't really think that in this case it will be necessary.'

'The thing is, you see, her dad's at the meeting in the Miners' Institute, and *Coronation Street* is just about to start,' Mrs Sanders explained.

'Do you wish to be present while Becky is interviewed?' Paniatowski said icily. 'I need a definite decision from you.'

'I don't really know what to say,' Mrs Sanders told her, as she thrilled at the sight of a dog fed on Pal – 'Prolongs Active Life' – jumping over a gate with ease. 'You don't really want me there, do you, Becky, love? You're a big girl now. You can manage on your own.'

'I would strongly advise you to be present,' Paniatowski said.

'She'll be all right,' Mrs Sanders said. She turned briefly to her daughter. 'Take the police lady into the kitchen, Becky.'

The kitchen was separated from the parlour by a narrow hallway, in which there was a steep set of stairs leading to the upstairs rooms.

It must be a real bugger getting a coffin down them, Paniatowski thought, irrelevantly.

Once they were in the kitchen, Becky walked over to the range and picked up the heavy black kettle.

'Would you like a cup of tea?' she asked. 'I can soon make you one. It'll be no trouble at all.'

'I'm fine,' Paniatowski said, sitting down at the kitchen table. She patted the table top. 'Come and join me.'

'It really won't take a minute,' Becky insisted.

Paniatowski laughed. 'You're just like my daughter – you won't take no for an answer. But I really *don't* want a cup of tea, Becky.'

The girl put the kettle back on the hob, and sat down opposite Paniatowski.

'How old is your daughter?' she asked.

'She's about your age.'

'And what's her name?'

'Louisa.'

Becky smiled. 'That's a nice name.' Then the smile disappeared, and was replaced by a wistful expression. 'Do you do a lot of things together? Do you go on picnics and stuff?'

'When we can,' Paniatowski said, feeling vaguely uncomfortable about the number of times that they couldn't.

'I used to go out a lot with my granddad,' Becky said, 'but now he's so poorly, we just stay in the house.'

It was about the best opening that she was likely to be offered, Paniatowski decided.

'My friend Colin was talking to your granddad earlier . . .' she began.

The change in Becky was instantaneous. Her eyes widened, and she looked like a hunted animal.

'He didn't do it!' she said, in what was almost a sob. 'He didn't kill Mr Hopkins.'

'No, he couldn't have, because you were with him all night, weren't you?' Paniatowski said thoughtfully.

'That's right. I was.'

'Without your parents' knowledge?'

'Yes.'

'Is it true you made your escape by climbing down the drainpipe?'

Becky grinned. 'That sounds funny.'

'What does?'

'You saying I made my escape. It makes it sound like I was in one of them old war films or something.'

'But you *did* climb down it?'

'Yes.'

'That must have been rather difficult.'

'No, it was easy.' Becky stood up. 'I'll show you, if you like.'

'That won't be necessary,' Paniatowski said.

'I'll show you,' Becky insisted. 'It won't take a minute.' She moved towards the door. 'Go and stand in the backyard, and you'll see just how easy it is.'

It was a delaying tactic on Becky's part, Paniatowski thought – a way of putting off the questions which she must know she would eventually have to answer. But as she heard the girl's feet clattering up the stairs, she accepted that she had no choice but to go along with it.

She stood up, stepped into the backyard – which was just like Len Hopkins' backyard and every other backyard in the village – and looked up at the back bedroom window. She did not have to wait long before the sash window slid open, and a pair of thin legs appeared.

Grasping on to the inner edge of the window sill with both hands, Becky slowly lowered her trunk. Then, with her feet both pressing against the pipe, she transferred first her right hand from the window sill to the pipe, and then her left. She came down in a shimmying movement, lowering her hands, allowing her body to drop a little, and lowering her hands again. It looked extremely well practised, and it couldn't have taken more than twenty seconds.

'You see,' Becky said, once she had reached the ground, 'I told you it was easy.'

'You must be very good at gymnastics,' Paniatowski said admiringly.

'I'm not bad,' Becky admitted, 'but science is my favourite subject.' She paused, then said hopefully, 'Is that it, then?'

'Not quite,' Paniatowski told her. 'There are just a few more questions I need to ask you.'

*   *   *

The president of the Miners' Institute – who would soon put on another hat and become the chairman of the miners' meeting – entered the concert room and walked over to the table which had been set up for him.

He was in his sixties, with a miner's broad shoulders and compact body, and a mane of grey hair which made him look statesmanlike. He sat down, glanced around him, then slammed his big hand down on the table to call for quiet.

'Point of order, Mr Chairman,' shouted a man from the left, pro-strike half of the room.

The chairman sighed. 'We've not even started yet, Walter,' he said. 'How can you have a point of order already?'

'I want to know why *they're* here,' Walter said, pointing to the four uniformed constables standing by the door.

'This is an open meeting,' the chairman explained. 'Anybody who wants to attend is perfectly entitled to.'

'Even if they're capitalist running dogs?'

'I suppose so, although all *I* can see back there is four bobbies,' the chairman said wearily. 'Now before we get properly started, I want to lay down a few rules. Anybody who wants to speak will be given the chance to speak, and if you don't want to listen to them, then you can just bugger off out. And as for your behaviour in general – I don't *want* to pull down anybody's pants and smack their bare arses for them, but I will if I have to. Is that clear?' He scanned the room for something like assent. 'Good. Then let's get cracking.'

'I thought you were talking rubbish earlier when you said he was a bit like the Queen, but it turns out that you were quite right,' Beresford told Mellors with a grin. 'If I'd closed my eyes just then, I could almost have believed that *was* Her Majesty talking.'

They were back in the kitchen, and Becky was starting to look uncomfortable again.

'What was it that made you feel you had to go and see your granddad last night?' Paniatowski asked.

'I wanted to talk to him about my boyfriend.'

'Do your parents know you have a boyfriend?'

Becky looked down at the table. 'No, it's a secret.' She raised her head again, and there was a look of panic in her eyes. 'It really *is* a secret – and you mustn't tell them.'

'I won't,' Paniatowski promised. 'But I would like it if you told *me* a little about him.'

'His name's Gary,' Becky said. 'He's . . . he's older than me.'

'How *much* older? A year?'

'No, a bit more than that.'

'I see,' Paniatowski said thoughtfully. 'What's he like?'

'He's fabulous. He's very handsome, but he's – you know – nice as well.'

'I bet all your friends are jealous that you've got him, and they haven't.'

'They don't know about him. Like I said, it's a secret.'

'But you must have dropped a few hints to them. I know I would, if I was in your place.'

'I haven't. Gary wouldn't like it.'

'Is he still at school, too?' Paniatowski asked. 'Or has he already started work?'

'He's a student,' Becky said proudly. 'He's going to be a doctor. He'll be brilliant. He's going to travel all around the world, curing sick people wherever he goes, and he's . . . and he's . . .'

'And he's going to take you with him?'

'Yes.'

You poor bloody girl! Paniatowski thought.

She wanted to hold Becky – to comfort her, and to tell her softly that boys were not always what they seemed to be. And then she reminded herself that she was not a social worker but a senior police officer who was investigating a rather nasty murder.

'So what I still don't quite understand is why you felt you had to go and see your granddad last night,' said the senior police officer part of her.

'Pardon?'

'Well, I remember that when I went to talk to my granddad about my boyfriends, it was because there was something wrong between us,' lied Paniatowski, who had never known her granddad, and, by the time she was Becky's age, had been living with an abusive stepfather. 'Do you understand what I'm saying?'

'I'm . . . I'm not sure.'

'I went to him because I had a problem with my boyfriends and needed his advice, but from what you've just told me about you and Gary, everything's going just fine.'

'I . . .' Becky began. 'I . . .'

'Yes,' Paniatowski coaxed.

'I thought something was wrong, and then I found out this morning that it wasn't,' Becky blurted out.

'Well, I'm glad that's cleared up,' Paniatowski said. 'Now there are just a couple of other things I'd like to ask you.'

But Becky had had enough.

'I don't want to say any more,' she announced, folding her skinny arms across her skinny chest.

'I promise you, it won't take long,' Paniatowski said softly.

Becky burst into tears. 'I don't want to say any more,' she sobbed. 'I don't want to say *any more!*'

Paniatowski nodded, and – fighting back the urge to cuddle the child – gave in to the inevitable.

'I'll leave through the back door, so as not to disturb your mum,' she said softly. 'And if I were you, Becky, I wouldn't go and see her myself until I was feeling a bit less upset.'

'She wouldn't notice,' the girl said miserably. 'She doesn't care. Nobody cares – except for Granddad and Gary.'

Paniatowski crossed the backyard, and stepped into the alley.

For a moment, back there, she had thought of breaking her promise to Becky and telling her mother all about the boyfriend who claimed he was training to be a doctor.

But what would be the point of that? Becky's mother would be less involved with the drama in her own family than she was in that being played out in *Coronation Street*. And if Becky's father did anything at all, it would probably be just to give her a good thrashing – which would only make matters worse.

Once this case was over, she might perhaps track down this boyfriend and warn him off, she thought.

You're not a bloody social worker, Monika, a voice in her head reminded her sharply.

No, she wasn't. She was a bobby, and it was her duty – her *only* duty – to analyse the information she'd just collected.

Becky hadn't lied when she'd talked about Gary – she hadn't exactly told the truth, either, but that was only because she didn't realize what a little shit he was – and there was no doubt that he existed, Paniatowski thought. But the girl hadn't been telling the truth when she'd claimed she'd spent the previous night with her grandfather, which was why she had burst into tears when the questions started getting tough.

Paniatowski felt nothing but contempt for Tommy Sanders, and wondered just what *kind* of man would ask his young granddaughter to lie for him?

And if he could do that – if he could so easily betray the trust a child had in him, and so readily abandon the responsibilities that being a grandfather imposed on him – would it be *such* a big step for him to rob another man of his life?

She sighed to herself. Maybe she had been wrong all along, she thought – and if she had been wrong, that probably meant that Colin Beresford had been right.

FIFTEEN

The meeting at the Miners' Institute was well into its second hour, and Beresford, searching for a way to describe the proceedings to himself, had come up with the term 'formal-informality'.

It was formal in the sense that good behaviour was being maintained – and there had been no reason for the chairman to smack any bare arses yet – but informal in that anyone who wished to make a speech did not go to the front of the room, but merely stood up so everyone could see him.

The man standing up at that moment was called Barnes, and was one of the managers from the colliery.

'All you lads know me,' he was saying. 'I'm not some stuffed shirt from Manchester or London. I started down the pit, like the rest of you, and worked my way up.'

'And how do you like the view from the top, Dick?' one of the miners from the left called out.

Dick Barnes grinned. 'I like it just fine,' he said.

At first, Beresford had been surprised at how basically good-natured the meeting had been, but now he was beginning to see that it should have been no surprise at all.

After all, these men lived together, worked together and played together. They had shared triumphs, like the victory of Bellingsworth Colliery brass band. They had shared tragedies – there had been accidents at the pit, and miners had been killed. The relationships they had been building their entire lives were important to them, and while they might disagree – sometimes vehemently – about the proposed strike, they did not want to do or say anything which might imperil those relationships.

Now if they could just get through the evening without anyone mentioning Len Hopkins' murder . . .

'I want to see a decent life for every man jack of you – and for his family,' Dick Barnes was saying, 'and progress is being made. I'd like the men of my age to think about what conditions were like when we first went down the pit. We're much better off now than we were then, and while mining is still a dirty, dangerous job, you have to admit the wages are pretty good as they are.'

'If they're that good, why are six hundred men a week leaving the pits?' one miner called out.

'The National Coal Board is restrained by the Government Pay Policy,' Barnes argued, 'and even if it wasn't, it couldn't pay what some of you are asking, because there simply isn't the money available.'

'Then why doesn't it raise the price of coal?' another miner shouted out. 'Coal does the same work as oil – why shouldn't it cost as much?'

'Because the country can't afford it,' Barnes said.

'And the miners can't afford for the country *not* to afford it,' the other man countered.

Listening, as he was, to the arguments being knocked back and forth, was a bit like watching a tennis match, Beresford thought. And it was a match in which those playing were displaying no obvious signs of weakness, and those that were merely watching were showing no signs of shifting their allegiance to someone who was emerging as an obvious winner.

Victory at the strike ballot, he decided, was still up for grabs.

The Suttons lived in a large detached house, and Ellie's party had taken over the whole of the ground floor. There were flashing lights everywhere, and music boomed out of a dozen speakers. Everyone who'd been invited – and plenty of kids who hadn't, but were there anyway – seemed to be having a real ball.

Or nearly everyone!

It had been a mistake to come to this party, Louisa thought

miserably, as she sat alone on the floor, in one corner of the lounge. Everything about it was wrong, or rather – if she was honest with herself – everything about *her* was wrong!

When she'd examined herself in the mirror at home, her party dress had seemed fabulous, but here, surrounded as she was by people wearing jeans, it just looked silly and very little-girlish.

And she *was* a little girl compared to all the other guests. The girls were all wearing a lot of make-up, the boys were smoking and drinking beer straight from the can. And whenever she made the effort to talk to any of them – when she asked them, for example, what their favourite subject at school was – they simply laughed and walked away.

Well, what did you expect? she asked herself angrily. Ellie's older than you, so why wouldn't her other friends be older, as well?

She was starting to think that she simply didn't understand her new friend at all.

Why had Ellie even invited her to this party, where she must have known she would stick out like a sore thumb?

And she hadn't *just* invited her, had she?

She had insisted that Louisa come – had gone so far as to make it a test of their so recently established friendship.

Yet now that she was here – now she had burned her bridges, and would have to face the consequences later on – Ellie was virtually ignoring her. In fact, it was worse than that – she was acting as if she didn't want to know her!

None of it made any sense at all!

'Is this party boring you as much as it's boring me?' asked a voice.

She turned. The person who'd spoken was a boy – well, almost a man really – who had just squatted down beside her. He had a nice smile, and hair which was the same colour as her mother's – and almost as long.

'*Is* it boring you?' he asked.

'I don't know,' she replied, confused.

'Well, you certainly don't *look* as if you're enjoying yourself very much,' the boy said.

What was the point of pretending?

'I'm having a horrid time,' she admitted.

'What's your name?' the boy asked.

'Louisa.'

'And mine's Colin,' the boy said, and his eyes flickered – but so briefly that Louisa did not even notice it.

'I've got an uncle called Colin,' Louisa said, pleased that this boy had the same name – though not quite sure why.

'Is that right?' the boy asked.

'He's not really my uncle,' Louisa admitted. 'He just works with my mum – but I've known him for ever.'

'What I've been trying to work out is why, if this party makes you so miserable, you're still here,' the boy said.

'I've no choice in the matter,' Louisa said glumly. 'Ellie's dad is going to drive me home, and he's gone out for the evening, and I'll have to wait until he gets back.'

'I could take you,' the boy suggested. 'I was just about to leave this terrible party, anyway.'

'I'm not sure I should,' Louisa said, uncertainly.

'And on the way to your house, we could stop off for a burger – if you're hungry, that is.'

Louisa realized that she *was* hungry. With all the excitement and nervousness, she had hardly been able to eat anything at home – and now she was ravenous.

'I'd better let Ellie know I'm going,' she said.

'Don't do that,' the boy told her.

'But I have to!'

'No, you don't. I've been watching both of you all night, and she's been completely ignoring you. It'd just serve her right if you decided to leave without saying goodbye.'

Yes, it would, Louisa agreed. It really would.

'Where's your coat?' the boy asked. 'Hanging up in the hall?'

'Yes.'

'Let's go and get it, then.'

Louisa stood up and walked to the door, with the boy following just behind her. She didn't go over to say goodbye to Ellie, but she got the eerie impression that Ellie's eyes were following her every step of the way.

The chairman had just called on a new speaker. This man didn't simply stand up and have his say. Instead, he negotiated his way between the chairs until he had reached the chairman's table.

He didn't look much like the rest of the miners in the room, Beresford thought. For a start, he was much bigger – nearly six feet tall. And though his jacket and trousers were clearly bought off the peg, he seemed to wear them with much more confidence and style than most of the people there could have mustered.

'Who's he?' Beresford asked Mellors.

'I don't know,' the constable replied. 'I don't think that I've ever seen him before.'

Most of the previous speakers had said what they had to say in a slightly hurried tone, as if they did not want to take up too much of their fellow miners' precious time, but when this man reached the table, he turned around and took a few moments to survey his audience.

'My name's Ed Thomas, and though this might come as a surprise to you, I'm not from round here,' he said.

There was some laughter – as he'd obviously intended there would be – because no one could ever have mistaken his accent for a Lancashire one.

'No, comrades, I'm not local, I'm from Kent,' he continued, 'and I'm here to convey the fraternal greetings of the Kent branch of the NUM.'

The announcement brought applause from both the left and right sides of the room.

'Thank you, comrades,' Thomas said. 'It's great to see that even in these troubling times – even when we might have our disagreements – there can still be real solidarity among miners.'

He was a good speaker, Beresford thought, not just in the words he used, but in the way he used them, and he already had the men on both sides of the room exactly where he wanted them.

'Now, to be honest with you, I've said all I was sent here to say, and I was going to leave it at that, but after what I've seen and heard while I've been up here in Lancashire, I don't think I can,' Thomas told the miners. He paused. 'Did you catch the television news today? Did you hear what that woman reporter – who certainly seems to know which side *her* bread's buttered on – had to say about Len Hopkins' death?'

Heads were nodding, and Thomas waited until they'd stopped before he carried on.

'The capitalists – and their lackeys who work in Northern Television – are claiming that Len was killed because he opposed the strike. They don't have any proof to back that up – none at all – but they're still using it as an opportunity to paint us miners as black-hearted villains.'

'Bastards!' someone called out from the right side of the room.

'Typical bosses' tricks,' shouted a voice from the left.

'But what if, for once, they've got it right?' Thomas asked. 'What if Len Hopkins *was* killed because he opposed the strike?'

'Nobody in this village would have killed Len Hopkins,' said a voice from the left.

'All right,' Thomas agreed. 'You know the place better than I do, so I'll take your word for that. But what if he was killed by some other miner, from Yorkshire say – or even from Kent?'

An uneasy quiet had settled over the room.

'I say this,' Thomas continued. 'If he was killed by a miner, *then good for that miner* – because he wasn't just killing for himself, he was killing for all of you.'

Several miners – from both the left and the right sides of the room – had risen to their feet and were shouting at Thomas to shut up. Some were even waving their fists.

'Oh, you don't like to hear the truth, do you?' Thomas taunted, all signs of camaraderie now quite absent from his voice. 'You don't mind taking the benefits, but you don't want to dirty your own hands in winning them.'

At least half the miners were on their feet now, and some looked ready to silence Thomas by any means necessary.

The four constables moved rapidly to the table, and formed a protective phalanx round the man from Kent.

'Len Hopkins lived as a traitor and he died as a traitor,' Thomas bawled, to make himself heard above the noise. 'And if another traitor has to die – if another *hundred* traitors have to die – we should give our support to the men who killed them, because this is a war, and they are our front-line troops.'

The two men from Special Branch suddenly appeared next to Thomas, forced his hands behind his back, cuffed him, and frog-marched him towards the exit. The speed of the whole operation took all the miners by surprise, and they were still wondering quite what had happened when the officers and their prisoner reached the door and disappeared.

Beresford rushed after them, but even so, by the time he was outside the club the two officers were already bundling Thomas into the back of their car.

The hatchet-faced man heard his approach, and turned to face him.

'Keep back, sir,' he said. 'This man is being arrested for a breach of the peace, and it has nothing to do with you.'

'Police!' Beresford said, reaching into his pocket and producing his warrant card. 'We met earlier.'

'Oh, that's right, we did,' Hatchet-face agreed. 'You were with that cute little blonde – who you're probably slipping a length to on the quiet – but it's *still* nothing to do with you.'

'I'm investigating a murder, and this man may be germane to my enquiries,' Beresford insisted.

'Ed had nothing to do with your murder, son,' Hatchet-face said. 'He's been stirring up trouble in the Kent coalfield for years, which means we've been keeping an eye on him for years – and we know exactly where he was at the time Len Hopkins was killed.'

'And where exactly was he?'

Hatchet-face smiled. It wasn't pleasant.

'I'm not allowed to tell you that – but he was at least a hundred and fifty miles away from this shithole,' he said.

Beresford looked down at the prisoner, who was still handcuffed, and was now sitting in the back of the car.

Thomas didn't look particularly shaken by what he had just gone through, but then, Beresford supposed, an agitator like him must regard being arrested as no more than an occupational hazard.

'Why don't you get back to your nice little murder, and leave the important work – protecting this country – to us?' Hatchet-face suggested.

And then he climbed into the car, and his partner, who was already behind the wheel, pulled away.

'When I went back into the concert room, it was like attending a completely different meeting,' Beresford told the rest of the team, at their 'specially reserved' table in the Green Dragon. 'You could have bottled the hostility in the air – and it wasn't just hostility towards Ed Thomas, it was hostility towards *each other*.'

'Are you saying that he managed to convince some of the miners that Len Hopkins *was* killed because he was against the strike?' Paniatowski asked.

Beresford shook his head. 'It was more subtle than that. It was as if . . . I don't know quite how to describe it.' He took a sip of his pint. 'It was as if they were already thinking, deep down, that he'd been killed because of the strike, but they were trying to keep the thought buried. Then Thomas made that speech of his, and it all came to the surface.' He had another slug of beer. 'Anyway, nobody seemed to want to say much after that – or maybe they *did* want to say something, but thought they shouldn't – and the meeting more or less broke up.'

'So, in your opinion, Colin, there are now quite a number of men in this village who are willing to accept that Len Hopkins was killed by a pro-strike miner?' Paniatowski said.

'That's right,' Beresford agreed. 'And it's also my opinion that a lot of them might be starting to think not just that it was any pro-strike miner, but that that miner is Tommy Sanders.'

Paniatowski nodded. 'And they may well be right,' she said.

Beresford almost choked on his beer. 'So you've come round to my way of thinking, have you?'

'I have,' Paniatowski admitted. 'I can't think of any reason why Tommy Sanders would have put his own granddaughter through what he has put her through if he wasn't the murderer.'

Beresford seemed to swell in size.

'So Tommy Sanders is our prime suspect – like I always said that he should be?' he asked.

'So Tommy Sanders is our prime suspect,' Paniatowski agreed.

'Right,' Beresford said firmly, 'then the first thing we need to do is break his alibi.'

An image of Becky Sanders – all thin arms and big frightened eyes – came into Paniatowski's mind.

'If that's absolutely necessary, then that's what we'll do,' she said. 'But I'd rather get at him some other way, if that's at all possible.'

'Oh, come on, boss, be sensible!' Beresford protested. 'Breaking the alibi is the obvious way to—'

Paniatowski raised a hand to silence him. 'It's not up for negoti-ation,' she said, and there was a firmness in her voice which even Colin Beresford – in his moment of triumph – could not ignore. 'Anyway, breaking the alibi will only prove that Becky's lying – and that's not enough to arrest Tommy on.'

'It would prove that Sanders was lying, as well,' said Beresford, who had not yet *quite* given up.

'We'll go about it another way,' Paniatowski said briskly. 'I want Len Hopkins' house thoroughly examined again, in case we've missed anything the first time that might suggest Sanders was there last night. And I want another door-to-door, looking for possible witnesses, and this time I want special attention paid to people whose bedrooms overlook the back alley which could have been the route from Tommy's house to Len's.'

'Got it,' Beresford said, with as much good grace as he could muster.

'Everything else I've already laid out will go ahead as planned, but with a slightly different focus,' Paniatowski continued. 'I still want you, Jack, to talk to Len's minister, but now I'd be particularly interested to learn if Len had told him anything about Tommy Sanders.'

'Are you saying you think there might be a personal motive behind the murder, *as well as* a political one?' Beresford asked, as if he suspected Paniatowski of trying to steal his thunder.

'I'm saying that if you've convinced yourself you have to kill somebody for the good of the mining community as a whole, it certainly wouldn't be a drawback if you already hated his guts,' Paniatowski replied.

'Good thinking, boss,' Crane said, and tried to ignore the black look that Beresford shot at him.

The phone rang behind the bar. The landlord answered it, then called out, 'Phone call for *Detective Chief Inspector* Paniatowski!' in a voice loud enough for all the customers to hear.

'Must be something wrong with my beeper,' Paniatowski said.

Crane grinned. 'Maybe the landlord's found some way to sabotage it. You're a real feather in his cap, you know.'

'You're not wrong,' Paniatowski agreed. 'If I had a heart attack and died while I was in this pub, I swear he'd want me stuffed and mounted.'

She stood up, and walked across to the bar.

'You should take what you've just witnessed as an object lesson, young Jack,' Beresford said.

'How do you mean, sir?'

'When you're investigating a murder, you shouldn't overlook the obvious suspect just because he *is* obvious – nine times out of ten, he'll be the man you're looking for.'

I used to like you, Colin, Crane thought. I *really* used to like you. But I don't think I like you much any more.

'If you're right about that, sir – and I'm sure you are, given that you seem to be right about most things – then we're a bit of an irrelevance, aren't we?' he said aloud.

'What do you mean by that?' Beresford asked.

'Well, if solving murders is as simple as you seem to think it is, we might as well leave it in the hands of country constables like PC Mellors.'

'Are you trying to be funny?' Beresford demanded

'No, sir, he's not trying to be funny – he's trying to make a point,' Meadows said.

'And what point might that be?'

'That you've suddenly become a complete bloody prick.'

Beresford reddened. 'I think you've forgotten who you're talking to, Detective Sergeant Meadows,' he said.

'And when you're talking to the boss, *you* seem to have forgotten who *you're* talking to, Detective Inspector Beresford,' Meadows countered.

'I don't have to tolerate this insolence from you,' Beresford said angrily.

'Oh, I see, you can dish it out, but you can't take it,' Meadows taunted. 'Well, if you don't like it, why don't you file a complaint?'

'Shut up, the pair of you,' Crane hissed. 'The boss is coming back, and she looks a bit upset.'

Paniatowski looked more than a *bit* upset. Her face was as pale as death, and her whole body was shaking.

'What's happened, Monika?' Beresford asked, turning pale himself.

'That . . . that was Lily Perkins on the phone,' Paniatowski said. 'Something's . . . something's happened to Louisa, and I have to go home straight away. But I . . . but I don't know what I've done with my car keys.'

Beresford sprang to his feet and hugged her to him. 'Don't worry about it,' he said softly. 'I'll find your car keys for you. But you can't drive yourself home in this state.'

'But I have to . . . I have to . . .'

'I'll leave my car here, and drive you home in yours,' Beresford said. 'Now that would be better, wouldn't it?'

'Yes,' Paniatowski replied, in a tiny, tiny voice.

SIXTEEN

There had been no snow, despite the threatening grey clouds the day before, but a heavy frost had formed during the night, and the hills which surrounded Bellingsworth glimmered and twinkled in the weak early sunlight.

In the village itself, the air was clear and sharp that Tuesday morning, and as DC Jack Crane stood on the steps of the church hall, watching the patrol car driven by Inspector Beresford pull up opposite, he clutched his cup of steaming coffee tightly in an effort to keep his hands warm.

Beresford climbed out of the car, walked across to his own vehicle, which had been parked in the village overnight, and ran a finger through the thick frost on the bonnet.

'If I can get this started again without help, it'll be a bloody miracle,' he said grumpily.

'How's Louisa?' Crane asked.

'I don't know any more than I did when I rang you at home last night,' Beresford told him.

'So you haven't called the boss this morning?' Crane asked, surprised.

'No,' Beresford replied. 'And before you accuse me of being completely insensitive to anyone's problems but my own, I should perhaps inform you that I went one better than just calling her on the phone, I drove round to the house!'

'But you didn't talk to the boss?'

'No, I didn't. It was Lily Perkins who answered the door, and she was in such a state herself that she hardly made any sense at all. The one thing I did manage to gather from her was that Monika was upstairs with Louisa, and didn't want to be disturbed.'

'So I take it the boss won't be coming to the village today,' Crane said.

'The boss won't be coming to the village *at all*,' Beresford replied. 'She's asked the chief constable to grant her some compassionate leave.'

'Then who'll be taking over from her?' Crane asked, running

through his mind the list of available DCIs, and quickly deciding that none of them was immediately appealing.

'*I'll* be taking over from her,' Beresford said.

'You!' Crane exclaimed, before he could stop himself.

'Me,' Beresford replied. 'The chief constable seemed to think I was perfectly capable of leading the investigation, but, of course, if *you* have any doubts about me, Detective Constable Crane, I'm sure he'll be more than willing to reconsider his decision.'

'Sorry, sir, I didn't mean it to sound like that, but it just took me by surprise, coming out of the blue,' Crane said.

But he was thinking to himself, Well, shit! That's the last thing this investigation needs.

It only took him a moment to realize that if he was stuck with working for Colin Beresford, then he'd better make the best of it – and part of making the best of it involved clearing the air.

'I'm sorry about last night, sir,' he said.

'Last night?' Beresford repeated vaguely, as if he had no idea what the detective constable was talking about.

He wants his pound of flesh, Crane thought, and to *get* his pound of flesh, he's going to make me spell it out.

'I was a bit sarcastic to you in the Green Dragon, sir,' he said.

'It was rather more than *a bit*, don't you think?' Beresford asked.

No, it bloody wasn't! Crane thought. Given what you were like last night, it was a model of restraint.

'I went too far,' he said.

'Forget it, Jack,' Beresford said, patting him on the shoulder. 'As your new boss, I'm sure that I can overlook one minor indiscretion.' He made great show of checking his watch. 'Aren't you supposed to be over in Brigden this morning, having a little talk with Len Hopkins' vicar?'

'Yes, sir.'

'Well, half the morning's gone already, so you'd better get moving, hadn't you, lad?'

'I'm on my way,' Crane said.

The new boss was trying to act like a patrician, he thought, as he walked over to his car, but he couldn't carry it off, and instead he was coming across as just bloody *patronizing*!

*   *   *

The phone was ringing when Beresford entered the church hall.

'Taylor the Cutter here,' said the unreasonably cheerful voice of the caller. 'Have scalpel, will slash.'

'Do you have some information for us on the cadaver, Dr Taylor?' Beresford asked.

'I do indeed, young man. Your stiff died sometime between ten o'clock at night and two o'clock in the morning, as near as I can tell. Death was, as you've no doubt already concluded yourselves, the result of being smote on the noggin with the sharp end of a pickaxe. There wasn't *that* much force behind the blow, and a younger and fitter man might well have survived it. Your chap wasn't so lucky. He died instantly.'

'Thank you, Doctor,' Beresford said.

'There's something else,' Taylor told him. 'I don't know if you wondered what would drive a man to visit an outside shithouse on a cold winter's night, but I certainly did.'

'Yes, we were puzzled by that,' Beresford said, 'especially as we know he had a chamber pot under his bed.'

'Unless it was as big as a bath tub, the chamber pot simply wouldn't have been up to the job,' Taylor said. 'He'd have filled it in two minutes.'

'What do you mean by that?'

'The man had enough laxative inside him to have given a bull elephant Montezuma's Revenge. Now I'm not in a position yet to say exactly what laxative it was, you understand . . .'

'Could it have been self-administered?'

'It could, I suppose, but the man would have had to be a complete idiot to have exceeded the instructions on the bottle by the amount that's banging around in his system now.'

'Thanks a lot, Doc,' Beresford said.

'I'll get back to you when I have more,' the doctor promised.

When Beresford hung up the phone, there was a puzzled expression on his face.

If Len Hopkins hadn't administered the laxative himself – and according to the doctor, he'd have to have been insane to take such a large dose voluntarily – then somebody else had been responsible.

And that somebody else had done it to make sure that Len would visit his outside lavatory in the middle of the night – which turned everything they'd thought about the crime so far completely on its head!

The assumption had been that the killer had planned to murder Len in the house, but finding him on the toilet, had realized that made him an easier target. But that assumption had been wrong. It must always have been his intention to do it while his victim was sitting on the bog, weakened by an attack of diarrhoea.

In other words, he hadn't *taken* the opportunity at all – he had *created* the opportunity.

And just *how* could their prime suspect have managed that?

How could a man who had come to blows with his victim just a few hours earlier ever get close enough to him to administer the laxative?

The nameplate on his desk announced that the managing director of Brough's Premium Brewery (Accrington) was called William Radcliffe, and the letters which followed the name – OBE – provided the additional information that he had been awarded the Order of the British Empire in recognition of some unspecified service he had done for the nation.

Radcliffe was a bald man, with a broad walrus moustache which seemed to belong to another era, and when his secretary showed Kate Meadows into his office, he greeted the visitor with a broad walrus smile.

'Ah, Lady Katherine,' he said, gesturing that she should take a seat, 'what an absolute delight to see you again.'

Meadows groaned inwardly, as she always did when her past managed to catch up with her.

'As far as I'm concerned, Lady Katherine's dead and buried,' she said. 'My name's just Kate Meadows now, or, when I'm working, *Detective Sergeant* Kate Meadows.'

'Ah, yes, of course,' Radcliffe said awkwardly. 'I *did* hear that after you . . . I mean, I should have *realized* that you wouldn't want to be—'

'I appear to be at something of a disadvantage here, since you seem to know who I used to be, but I have no idea who you are,' Meadows interrupted him. A half-amused, half-embarrassed smile came to her face. 'God, that's awful, isn't it? "I appear to be at something of a disadvantage here." I must sound to you like a real toffee-nosed bitch.'

'No, no, not at all,' Radcliffe protested.

'Let's start again, shall we?' Meadows suggested. 'From your reaction to me, we've clearly met before, but being the flighty, scatterbrained sort of person I am, I'm rather ashamed to admit that I can't remember it. So would you be so kind as to enlighten me?'

'It was at one of your husband's famous weekend house parties,' Radcliffe said. 'He was thinking of expanding his business interests at the time, and I was invited down there in order to—'

'Of course, that was it! I remember you perfectly now, Mr Radcliffe,' Meadows lied. 'So now that we've established that we're old friends, do you think it would be possible to get down to the business which has brought me here?'

'Certainly, Lady Kath . . . Sergeant,' Radcliffe said.

'I'm investigating the murder of Len Hopkins,' Meadows said. 'No doubt you'll have read about it in the papers.'

'The name sounds vaguely familiar, but I can't say I've exactly got the details at my fingertips,' Radcliffe admitted.

'Hopkins attended the brass band competition which you sponsored last Sunday. In fact, it was his local band which won.'

'Yes, the . . . err . . . Bellingsworth Colliery Band,' Radcliffe said, with a sudden hint of caution in his voice which took Meadows by surprise.

'We're interested in any incidents which occurred during the competition,' Meadows told him.

'And . . . err . . . what exactly do you mean when you say "incidents"?' Radcliffe asked.

'Did any serious fights break out? Were there disturbances of some other kind? You know the sort of thing.'

'Ah, if that's what you need information on, then you'll have to speak to our security people,' Radcliffe told her, picking up the phone. 'Ask John Tweed to pop upstairs, will you, Marjorie,' he said. He replaced the phone on its cradle. 'John's our head of security. Very sound chap. He should be here in five minutes.'

'You're being most helpful,' Meadows said sweetly.

'Always pleased to assist the forces of law and order,' Radcliffe said. 'Now about the other matter – there's no need for the police to get involved in it, is there? I mean, strictly speaking, no crime has actually been committed.'

'What other matter are you referring to?' Meadows asked, puzzled.

'Ah, you haven't heard!' Radcliffe said. 'I thought you must have done. To be perfectly honest with you, my first thought, when I heard you'd asked for an appointment, was that that was what you wanted to know about.'

'You talk in riddles, o wise one, and I, a humble disciple at your feet, have no idea about that of which you speak,' Meadows said.

'I beg your pardon?'

'I still haven't got a clue what you're talking about.'

'Oh, I see,' Radcliffe said. 'Well, Sergeant, this company has invested a great deal of money in the brass band competition. We advertise it extensively on television and in the newspapers, and on the actual day of the competition, we hire four large marquees and a number of smaller tents in which to stage it. But what's more important than the cost is that the company's also investing its prestige—'

'Forgive me, but I don't quite see where you're going with all this,' Meadows interrupted.

'No, I don't suppose you do,' Radcliffe agreed. 'Let me put it this way, then – since we are so closely associated with the brass band competition, its integrity and the integrity of our beer have become almost synonymous. So it is very important to us that the competition is seen as the embodiment of British fair play, just as Brough's Premium is the embodiment of British beer.'

'I'm a big fan of Watney's, myself,' lied Meadows, who was teetotal.

Radcliffe looked shocked. 'Have you never tried Brough's Premium?' he asked.

'I can't say that I have.'

'Would you like a crate to take away with you, Sergeant? Or perhaps even two crates?'

'Two crates would be lovely,' Meadows said sweetly.

Crane would enjoy it, and if Beresford stopped being such a dickhead, she might even give some of it to him.

'Two crates it will be, then,' Radcliffe said. 'Now where was I?'

'British fair play, Brough's Premium beer,' Meadows prompted.

'Ah, yes. Given the importance of the competition to the brewery's image, we were not at all happy with Sunday's result. I'm no expert in brass band music myself, but according to the people who do know about these things, Bellingsworth Colliery Band, whilst more than competent, is scarcely championship material. And yet it romped to victory.'

'Maybe it just had a good day, while some of the other bands had a bad one,' Meadows suggested. 'That can happen.'

'Indeed it can,' Radcliffe agreed, 'but there are very few people who think it *did* happen at last Sunday's competition. Bellingsworth, of course, had no doubts that it should have won – the winning team never does. But I think it would be fair to say that when the results were announced, a wave of disbelief swept over a large part of the audience.'

'So the judges were nobbled?' Meadows said.

'I am reluctant to reach such a conclusion, but we are certainly investigating the possibility.'

'What's the prize for winning the competition?'

'The winners are awarded the Brough Premium Cup.'

'Is it valuable?

'Yes, it is. It's solid sterling silver. But it's only *awarded* to them, not *given* to them.'

'What's the difference?'

'They have their name engraved on the base, and they're allowed to keep it for a year, in the special security case that we provide them with. But come next year, when there's a new winner, they have to hand it back.'

'What else do they get out of it?'

'The brewery throws a party for them in whichever of our pubs is closest to their home base, and they are allowed to replace either three or four of their instruments – depending on the cost – at our expense.'

'In other words, it's peanuts,' Meadows said.

'I suppose that's one way of looking at it,' Radcliffe agreed, just slightly miffed.

'Yet someone was prepared to bribe the judges to get the result he wanted,' Meadows said.

'And that's what makes the whole idea so apparently inconceivable,' Radcliffe told her. 'The judges are all respectable men – pillars of their communities. Some of them are even quite wealthy. They simply do not strike me as the kind of chaps who would be interested in taking bribes. And even if they were prepared to sacrifice their hard-won integrity for financial gain, who would be willing to pay them?'

'Who indeed,' Meadows agreed.

'And yet if they weren't bribed, how did Bellingsworth manage to win?' Radcliffe asked helplessly.

*   *   *

Louisa lay in her bed, looking pale and exhausted.

'I'm sorry, Mum,' she said, for perhaps the hundredth time.

'It doesn't matter, baby,' Paniatowski cooed softly, as she looked down at the child with tired, prickling eyes. 'It doesn't matter at all.'

But it *did* matter, she thought. It mattered that someone had invited her child to a place where she would be in danger. It mattered that someone – perhaps the same someone – had dropped her off at her home in such an unsteady state that she couldn't even find her front-door key, and had only just managed to ring the doorbell before collapsing on the garden path.

'Do you feel strong enough to tell me what happened, baby?' Paniatowski asked.

'I think so.'

'Then take your time. There's no need at all to rush.'

'I was at Ellie's party – I shouldn't have gone, Mum, I shouldn't . . .'

'Don't worry about that now. Just tell me what happened.'

'I didn't like the party, and there was this boy called Colin – he seemed nice – who said he'd drive me home.'

'Go on.'

'He took me for a burger, and I think it was soon after that I started to feel funny.'

'*She's been drugged,*' Dr Green, the family doctor, had said, when Paniatowski had called him the previous night.

'*And is she . . . is she . . .?*'

'*There's no need to panic. It was a very mild dose – I doubt she even completely lost consciousness – and it's already starting to work its way through her system. She's over the worst of it, and by morning she should be fine.*'

'What happened after you started feeling funny, sweetheart?' Paniatowski asked.

'I don't know, Mum, I just don't know. The next thing I remember, I was at the front door.'

Paniatowski patted her daughter's hand. 'When you're feeling a little bit stronger, we'll get you dressed and go and see the doctor,' she said.

'Which doctor? The one I saw last night?'

'No. It will be the doctor I work with.'

'Why do I have to see a different doctor?' Louisa fretted.

Because, if it ever came to court, evidence from the police doctor would carry more weight from that of an ordinary general practitioner, Paniatowski thought.

'I'm taking you to him because I know you'll like him,' she told her daughter. 'He's a nice man, and he tells funny jokes.'

Louisa bit her bottom lip. 'Why do I have to go and see him?' she asked tremulously. 'Is it to find out if I've been interfered with?'

'Of course not,' Paniatowski said, a little too quickly.

Louisa gave her a sad smile. 'I'm a big girl now, Mum. I know I don't always act like it – but I am. You can tell me the truth.'

She wasn't a big girl at all, Paniatowski thought, she was still such a baby – but she wasn't a *stupid* baby.

'All right, if you want the truth, here it is,' she said. 'There was no evidence at all that your clothes had been disturbed, so it's almost certain that nothing happened to you.'

What she'd just said was perfectly true, she thought. The police officer in her *knew* it was true.

But the mother in her – already wracked with guilt – was preparing for the worst.

SEVENTEEN

The vicar of Bellingsworth had not merely been snobbish when he'd described Len Hopkins as belonging to some sort of wild Methodist sect in the next valley – he'd been completely wrong. Hopkins, it turned out, had not been a Methodist at all, but an evangelical.

And this was where he worshipped, Crane thought, looking at the Brigden Evangelical Church.

The church stood on a hill overlooking the village itself, and Crane wondered whether the decision on locating it there had been made by the evangelicals (to maintain their purity), or by the parish council (on purely aesthetic grounds).

Whichever the reason, the tin-clad building was certainly ugly, and had it not been for the small spire – little more than a pimple – which was precariously balanced at one end, it could easily have been mistaken for a large shed or a middle-sized industrial chicken coop.

The pastor, who was standing in front of the church at that moment, went by the name of the Reverend Eli Mottershead, and was probably a couple of years short of his thirtieth birthday. He had a slight – almost puny – build, yet walked with the swagger of a much larger man, and Crane, who could recognize an out-and-out fanatic when he saw one, knew that he was looking at one now.

'How long have you been working in this village?' the detective constable asked.

'Ministering,' Mottershead said. 'I do not *work*, I *minister*.'

So it was going to be like that, was it?

'How long have you been *ministering* in this village?' Crane asked.

'I was called by the Lord God to minister here only six months ago,' Mottershead replied.

Now that was a pity, Crane thought, because he'd been hoping that Len Hopkins' pastor would have known the man for much longer than that, and could tell him something interesting about Tommy Sanders.

'Is your predecessor still in the area?' he asked hopefully.

'No,' Mottershead said. 'He is not.'

'Then do you know where I can find him?'

'We can only pray that he has ascended to Heaven, there to bask in God's infinite mercy,' Mottershead intoned.

'In other words, he's dead?'

'That is correct.'

'And we can *only pray* he's ascended into Heaven?' Jack Crane repeated, slightly puzzled. 'Why would you phrase it in quite that way? Is there any real doubt about it?'

'My predecessor was, by all accounts, a kind and gentle man,' Mottershead said, 'but he lacked the faith – the conviction – to go about God's work as it should be gone about, and as infinitely forgiving as the Lord is . . .'

'He has to draw the line somewhere?' Crane suggested.

'Indeed he does,' Mottershead said, completely missing the irony. 'I arrived here to find not a sheep dip from which my flock could emerge purified, but a cesspit in which they were allowed to wallow in their own sin.'

He wasn't just a fanatic, Crane thought – he was a genuine, prize-winning religious nutter.

'I expect it wasn't long before you started cleansing the cesspit,' he suggested.

'It was not,' Mottershead agreed. 'It has been a hard path I have chosen for myself and my flock, and some – the weaker brethren – have fallen by the wayside as we followed it, and so condemned themselves to eternal damnation. But those who have persevered – and continue to persevere – will undoubtedly find their reward in Heaven.'

'Did Len Hopkins fall by the wayside?' Crane asked.

'He did not,' Mottershead said. 'He struggled constantly with his demons, and he was slowly triumphing over them.'

'Do you have any specific demons in mind?' Crane wondered.

'When he was a younger man, he had carnal knowledge of a woman who was not his wife,' Mottershead said, 'and the demon which had led him to that abomination remained with him.'

A woman who was not his wife! That would be poor Susan Danvers he was talking about, Crane thought.

'But surely, Mr Hopkins had stopped committing that particular sin a long time ago,' he said aloud.

'And so he had.'

'Then I don't see—'

'He had not yet divested himself of the source of that sin.'

'The source?'

'There was not only his own particular demon to consider – there was also the one which dwelt in her.'

'You told him he had to get rid of his housekeeper,' Crane gasped.

'It was the only way.'

'And how did he take it?'

'There were tears, as the demon sought to hold on to his soul, but in the end, armed with the strength of the Lord, I prevailed.'

And that was why Len hadn't taken Susan to the brass band competition, Crane thought, because this so-called 'pastor' – this vindictive scarecrow powered by bile – had told him he had to dump her.

'I'd better have a look at this church of yours while I'm here,' Crane told the pastor.

Mottershead smiled. It was a smile of grisly, complacent triumph, the sort of smile which would have been completely at home on the face of the Spanish Inquisitor General.

'My words have touched you,' he said.

'You're not wrong,' Crane agreed.

'You have begun to see your path, and now you wish to enter my church and throw yourself on God's mercy. Isn't that true?'

'I wouldn't put it quite that way,' Crane admitted.

'Then how *would* you put it?'

'I wish to enter your church and see if you're complying with the fire regulations.'

The idea seemed to rock Mottershead.

'But this is a church – a sacred place,' he protested. 'It is above the merely temporal concerns and—'

'Render unto Caesar what is Caesar's,' Crane interrupted him. 'And Caesar, in this case, is the local borough council.'

He strode across to the church, with Mottershead, like an agitated puppy, at his heel. Once inside, he walked up and down, making loud clicking noises with his tongue.

'This place is a death trap,' he pronounced. 'Section 14/36/B of the Fire Code clearly states that you must have Paniatowski sliders attached to all windows, and a Meadows' rotating hinge on the door. And don't even get me started about the lack of Beresford bolts.'

'But . . . but . . .' Mottershead whimpered.

'Don't get your cassock in a twist,' Crane said cheerfully. 'It's true that, as it stands, we'd have to close the place down, but I estimate that the whole lot can be put right for around six thousand pounds.'

'Six . . . thousand . . . pounds,' Mottershead gasped.

'Well, I suppose I'd better say seven, just to be on the safe side,' Crane told him.

'But . . . but this is a poor church. Where could I possibly be expected to lay my hands on that kind of money?'

Crane walked over to the door, and out into the clear, crisp air.

'Where can you lay your hands on that amount of money?' he said, over his shoulder. 'I expect the Lord will provide it.'

As he walked down to his car, he tried to convince himself that in causing Mottershead no more than temporary discomfort – and changing nothing at all in the long term – he had been childish and petty, and had not lived up to either the standards that the police had set for him, nor the ones he had set for himself. He *tried* to convince himself, and he failed – because the simple fact was that he felt good about what he'd done.

*   *   *

Detective Constables Smalley and Higgs had been searching the kitchen of Len Hopkins' terraced house for over an hour, and so far they had found nothing to even mildly excite them.

'It might help if we knew what we were looking for,' Higgs complained, as he carefully emptied the kitchen cupboard of its tins of baked beans, rice pudding and stewed fruit.

'We're looking for clues,' said Smalley, withdrawing his head from the fireplace, after shining a torch up the chimney.

'But what *kind* of clues?' Higgs asked.

'We don't know, do we – that's why we're looking,' Smalley replied, running his finger across his forehead, and discovering, just as he'd suspected, that there was soot on it.

'Still, it's the best job going at the moment,' Higgs said philosophically. 'It's certainly better than freezing our balls off walking the streets, like most of the lads.' He paused, as a new thought came to him. 'Why *did* we get the plum job? Does Inspector Beresford fancy you, do you think?'

'If he did fancy one of us, it'd be more likely to be you, you pretty little thing,' Smalley countered. 'But you've got him all wrong – there's nothing queer about old Beresford.'

'I heard there was.'

'There were rumours at one time, largely based on the fact that he never seemed to have a girlfriend,' Smalley admitted, 'but according to a mate of mine who works in Whitebridge HQ, he's become a real ram in the last month or so.'

He had only just finished speaking when he became aware of the stony-faced Inspector Beresford standing in the doorway.

'Oh, hello, sir,' Smalley said weakly. 'We were just . . . we were just . . .'

He trailed off, painfully aware that it was perfectly obvious what they'd just been doing.

'If you were going to poison somebody, what – from the things you've found in this kitchen – would you put the poison in?' Beresford asked.

'A cup?' Higgs suggested.

Beresford sighed theatrically. 'I sometimes wonder where we're getting our detective constables from these days.'

'Oh, do you mean, what would we mix it with to disguise the taste, sir?' Smalley suggested.

'Go to the top of the class,' Beresford said dourly.

'Something strong,' Smalley said thoughtfully. 'How about this, sir?' he added, holding up a tin of baked beans for Beresford's inspection.

'Brilliant!' Beresford said. 'And how, exactly, would you get the poison in there?'

'I'd have to open it, I suppose,' Smalley said.

'You'd have to open it,' Beresford repeated. 'So you'd open the tin and put the poison in. Is that correct?'

'Yes, sir, I suppose so.'

'And then along comes your victim, Len Hopkins. "I don't remember opening that tin of baked beans," he says to himself. "In fact, I'm bloody certain I didn't, so somebody else must have broken into my house and done it while I was out. Never mind, I think I'll eat them anyway."'

'No, that wouldn't work,' Smalley admitted.

'So what *would* work?' Beresford demanded.

Smalley looked around, and picked up a jar of cocoa.

'This might do the job, sir,' he suggested.

Yes, it very well might, Beresford agreed.

And now he thought about it, there was something in Monika's notes about Hopkins making himself a cup of cocoa on the night he died, and Susan Danvers washing it up before she found the body.

'What I want you to do now, DC Smalley, is to take the cocoa tin – and anything else that poison could be mixed in with – straight to the police lab,' he said. 'Tell them I want it all analysed as soon as possible, and that I'd like them to begin with the cocoa.'

'What about me, sir?' Higgs asked.

'You stay here, and keep searching for clues,' Beresford replied.

That's just typical, Higgs thought. Smalley gets to take a trip to Whitebridge, and I'm left rooting around in this old man's kitchen.

Beresford turned around, and walked down the backyard.

It still bothered him that it would have been very difficult for Tommy Sanders to have slipped the laxative into the cocoa – or into anything else in the kitchen, for that matter – unless Len Hopkins had left his front door unlocked.

And *would* Len have left the door unlocked while he was away at the brass band competition in Accrington?

Besides, Tommy had been in Accrington himself.

He squeezed his eyes tightly shut, and tried to come up with another scenario which he might be able to squeeze the facts into.

After the fight in the Miners' Institute, Len comes home, and five minutes later, Tommy knocks on his door. Len is obviously surprised to see him, but Tommy says he's come to apologize for the unpleasantness earlier, which he now sees was entirely his fault, and Len accepts his apology. Then, while Len is distracted in some way – making a cup of tea, or paying a quick visit to the lavvy – Tommy slips the laxative into the cocoa.

That was *just* possible, but it was not really very likely at all, he accepted miserably.

On the brighter side, he thought, as he stepped out into the alley, he had enjoyed overhearing the conversation between the two detective constables in Len Hopkins' kitchen.

One of them had said that he was gaining a reputation as a real ram, he recalled, as a broad smile came to his face.

A real ram!

He rather liked that.

Monika Paniatowski and Lily Perkins were sitting in the waiting room in Dr Taylor's private practice. Both of them had old, well-worn magazines open on their knees, but neither was making any pretence of reading.

The consulting room door opened, and Dr Taylor stepped out.

'I asked Louisa to stay inside for the moment, while I had a word with you,' he said.

'Is it . . . has she . . .' Paniatowski began.

'You can relax, Chief Inspector,' Taylor told her with a smile. 'There is some recent bruising on Louisa's right arm, right leg and thigh, all of which are consistent with a fall . . .'

'She fell over on the garden path last night, when she was trying to open the front door,' Lily said.

'. . . but other than that, there is absolutely no indication she has been assaulted – either sexually or in any other way.'

'Thank you, Doctor,' Paniatowski gasped. 'Thank you *so* much!'

'Would you like to see Louisa now?' the doctor asked.

'More than anything,' Paniatowski told him.

Taylor opened the door again, and Louisa came rushing out. Paniatowski bobbed down, then mother and daughter threw their arms around each other and burst into tears.

Dr Taylor glanced at his watch. 'Giving Louisa the once-over has meant I've rather fallen behind on my slashing and gouging this morning,' he told Lily Perkins. 'Could I leave these two in your charge?'

'Yes, I'll look after them,' promised Lily, who was almost crying herself.

As Taylor retreated back into his consulting room, Paniatowski pulled away from her daughter, and looked into her tear-stained eyes.

'I want you to go back home with Lily now,' she said. 'Would that be all right?

'What about you?' Louisa asked. 'Won't you be coming with us, Mum?'

'No, I . . .' Paniatowski began.

'Of course,' Louisa said, disappointedly, 'you've got your murder to investigate.'

Oh my God, how can she possibly think that, even for a moment? Paniatowski wondered.

And then she realized that she could think it because her mother had never given her cause to think anything else.

'I don't care about the murder, my darling,' she told Louisa, feeling fresh tears forming in her eyes.

'Really?' Louisa asked.

'Really,' Paniatowski confirmed. 'I only care about you – and I want to find out what happened to you.'

John Tweed, the head security man at Brough's Premium Brewery, was in his late thirties and had eyes which suggested both curiosity and intelligence.

'I was a military policeman – a redcap – and when I came out, going into security seemed the logical next step,' he said.

'Didn't you consider joining the police?' Meadows asked.

Tweed smiled. 'Not really,' he said. 'No offence, Sergeant Meadows, but given the choice of living on my salary or yours, I'd much rather live on mine.'

'No offence taken,' Meadows assured him. 'Tell me about the brass band competition.'

'It went like a dream – very little trouble at all,' Tweed said. 'Of course, you wouldn't expect trouble, would you? Brass bands are a strange combination of the macho and the gentle, but it's the gentle which usually prevails. Besides, I took precautions beforehand.'

'What kind of precautions?'

'I talked the brewery into producing a beer especially for the competition. I called it Championship Ale. It proved to be very popular.'

Meadows grinned. 'Let me guess – it wasn't as strong as the regular beer?' she suggested.

'It wasn't as strong as the regular beer,' Tweed agreed, 'so anyone who knocked back six pints on Sunday was nowhere near as intoxicated as if they'd knocked back six pints in their local.'

'You said there was very *little* trouble,' Meadows reminded him. 'That means there must have been *some.*'

'Nothing to write home about,' Tweed told her. 'A couple of heated arguments, one or two minor scuffles, but my lads were ready for it, and they soon sorted them out.'

'It's precisely that kind of minor incident that I'm particularly interested in,' Meadows said. 'I'd like to know if you recognize any of the people in these photographs.'

She reached into her briefcase, and laid all the photographs she'd managed to collect on the desk. It was a pathetic collection, she acknowledged to herself – a few group photographs that she'd scrounged from the Miners' Institute, plus some she'd taken from Len Hopkins' house – but, for the moment, it was the best she could do.

'Anyone here who looks familiar?' she asked, showing Tweed a photograph of the Miners' Institute Bowls Club, which had Tommy Sanders sitting squarely in the centre of it.

Tweed studied the photograph carefully.

'I don't really think so,' he said finally.

'Then do you recognize him?' Meadows said, laying several pictures from Len Hopkins' album in front of him.

'Can't say he rings a bell, either,' Tweed said, after examining the first couple of photos in the pile.

Well, it had always been a long shot, Meadows thought. Even if Hopkins and Sanders had clashed at the competition, the chances of anybody from outside Bellingsworth noticing it were minimal.

Tweed picked up another photograph.

'Now, her, I *do* recognize,' he said. 'Not that it will probably be much help to you.'

'Let me see that,' Meadows said, with a hint of expectancy creeping into her voice.

The picture had been taken on the seafront at Blackpool – the

Tower was clearly visible in the background – and there were two people framed in it, a man and a woman.

The man was Len Hopkins. He was staring into the camera, and it was almost impossible to tell what he was thinking. There was no such problem with the woman. She was looking up at Hopkins, and the expression on her face was one of near-adoration.

Tweed must be mistaken, Meadows thought. Susan Danvers had specifically told DCI Paniatowski that Hopkins hadn't taken her to the competition.

'Are you sure she was there?' she asked Tweed.

'Have you got any more pictures of her?' the head of security asked.

Meadows flicked through the pile, and found two more. In one of them, Hopkins was smiling, in the other he wore an expression similar to the one in the Blackpool photograph. In both, Susan had the same look of love on her face.

'Yes, that's her,' Tweed confirmed. 'But she didn't look quite like that when I saw her.'

'Go on,' Meadows encouraged.

'I noticed her initially because, unlike everybody else, she wasn't part of a group,' Tweed said. 'It's a very sociable thing, a brass band contest, but she was there all on her own. And the reason she's stuck in my mind,' he continued, 'is because I don't think I've ever seen anybody look quite as miserable as she did last Sunday.'

EIGHTEEN

The admiring comments on his virility had kept Beresford buoyed up until he had reached the High Street. Then his doubts about the case – and his own ability to solve it – had returned with a vengeance, and by the time he reached the church hall, he was feeling very down.

If it hadn't been for the laced cocoa – or whatever else it was that had been mixed with the laxative – he would have had a rock solid case against Tommy Sanders, he told himself. But then, he supposed, if it hadn't been for the laced cocoa, the murder wouldn't have been exactly *this* murder at all.

Then, in the middle of the dark night of his failure, two lights suddenly appeared. The first was a call from Crane, who was still in Brigden, the second, a call from Meadows in Accrington. And when he put the phone down after talking to Meadows, he had a whole new perspective on the murder.

The revelation that the cocoa had been spiked was not an impediment to making his case, he now realized – it was a sturdy cornerstone on which he could build it.

He needed just one more piece of information – a piece of information that Monika Paniatowski had wrongly called a loose end – before he was ready to make his move.

The university was one of the new crop which had sprung up in the ambitious years of the early sixties. It was sited on its own campus, midway between Whitebridge and Bolton, and had been designed by an architect who had obviously believed that if you used enough concrete and plate glass, you could easily dispense with both imagination and creativity.

Paniatowski, walking across the spacious piazza which was supposed to create a feeling of the Mediterranean in damp Lancashire, noticed neither the curly roof of the building to her right, nor the fountain which was bubbling lethargically to her left. All her attention was focussed on the history department which lay ahead of her, and the man who – she'd been told in the registry – occupied an office on the second floor of it.

She entered the building, and walked up the stairs. She kept urging herself to calm down, because the best way to accomplish what she wanted to accomplish was to approach this investigation as if it were any other.

'But it's *not* any other investigation,' she said aloud, to the empty stairwell. 'It's *nothing like* any other investigation!'

Dr Robert Sutton's office was located halfway down the second floor corridor.

There was a handwritten sign on the door which said, 'I'm in. Please knock and enter.'

Paniatowski grasped the handle, flung the door open, and stepped inside.

Sutton was sitting at his desk. He was in his mid-forties, had sandy hair and was wearing a corduroy jacket with leather patches on the elbows.

On the wall behind him were expensively framed posters of Karl Marx and Che Guevara, and in between them a third, more recent one, had been tacked up, which said simply, 'Support the Miners' Right to Strike!'

The police officer part of Paniatowski's mind noted this, and quickly decided that Sutton was trying just a little *too* hard to establish his left-wing credentials. But it was the civilian part of her mind which was in control – and that part was fighting the urge to rip the man's head off.

Sutton looked up at Paniatowski, over the top of his half-moon glasses.

'I'm a great advocate of informality in all situations,' he said mildly, 'but even allowing for that, I don't think it's being *too* authoritarian of me to expect you to knock before you come in. Who are you, anyway?'

'I'm Louisa Paniatowski's mother,' Monika told him.

'Oh?' Sutton said, quizzically. 'Is that a fact? And you've come to see me because . . .?'

'Because I want to know what the hell happened to my little daughter last night.'

'Since I don't know your daughter from Adam – or perhaps, more correctly, I should say, from Eve – I'm afraid I have absolutely no idea what happened to her,' Sutton said. He paused. 'Wait a moment. I think I *do* know who you're talking about. Isn't Louisa the name of Ellie's little friend?'

'She went to your daughter's party. You were the one who picked her up from home.'

'That's right, I was.'

'You took my *fourteen*-year-old daughter to your *seventeen*-year-old daughter's party!'

'It's not for me to question my daughter's choice of friends, however strange I may think that choice is. Ellie said she wanted Louisa to be there, and I assumed Louisa had her mother's permission.'

'You assumed!' Paniatowski bellowed.

'Wouldn't you assume it, in my place?' Sutton asked. 'I drive up to the house and hoot my horn – not once, but twice. When the girl comes out, she is wearing her party dress, so I *naturally* take it that she has her mother's permission. If you didn't want her to go the party – as you now seem to be claiming – why didn't you simply, at that point, stop her from leaving the house?'

Paniatowski felt a sinking feeling in her stomach.

'I wasn't there,' she said, before she could stop herself.

'Ah, you weren't there!' Sutton said, seizing on the admission. 'So who's *actually* responsible for her going to the party? Is it her friend's father? Or is it her own mother?'

No mother can be there all the time, Paniatowski told herself. No mother, however caring, can possibly be there *all* the time. And yet she couldn't entirely dismiss the idea that Sutton might have a point.

'All right, perhaps you did think that Louisa had my permission,' she agreed. 'But when you picked her up, you – as an adult – made yourself responsible for her, and that meant you were also responsible for seeing she was safely returned home again. And you didn't do that!'

'No, I didn't,' Sutton conceded. 'I went out for the evening, so as not to be a damper on the party, and by the time I returned, someone else had already taken her home.'

'I want the name and address of this boy who drove Louisa home,' Paniatowski said.

'I suppose that's reasonable,' Sutton agreed. 'But I have no idea who he was – I have no idea who half the people at the party were – so you'll have to ask Ellie. If you'd like to call around at my house tonight, at about, say—'

'I'm going to talk to her *now*,' Paniatowski told him. 'And you're coming with me.'

'No, I'm bloody not!' Sutton said, with a sudden blaze of anger. 'If you seriously think that just because you're a police officer, I'll drop everything and follow you like some kind of faithful hound, then you don't know me.'

It had all been an act, Paniatowski suddenly realized. The initial reasonableness and the sudden anger were both part of the same act!

'Police officer?' she asked.

'What?'

'You just said I was a police officer. Yet when I arrived, you pretended you had no idea who I was.'

'And I didn't know who you were then,' Sutton said, defensively.

'It was only during the course of our conversation that I remembered seeing your photograph in the *Evening Telegraph* on a couple of occasions, and finally put the name and the image together.'

'You're lying,' Paniatowski said.

'You shouldn't even be here,' Sutton said, going onto the attack. 'It's totally inappropriate for a police officer to be investigating an incident which involves her own daughter.'

'So it's an incident now, is it?' Paniatowski demanded.

Sutton folded his arms. 'I assume there *must* have been an incident of *some* kind, since you're here, frothing at the mouth like a mad dog. But I know nothing about it, and I certainly have no intention of answering any more questions until they are put to me by someone acting in an *official* capacity. And even then, I shall insist that my lawyer is present.'

'You're making a big mistake in crossing me,' Paniatowski said.

Sutton laughed. 'Why? Because you're a chief inspector in some tinpot little police force? That doesn't frighten me. I have powerful friends, Ms Paniatowski, as you'll find out if you push this matter any further.'

'It's a big mistake to cross *any* mother,' Paniatowski said, ignoring the comment, 'especially one who's feeling as guilty as I am!'

The detective constable who Beresford sent to collect Hopkins' correspondence returned with a mountain of paper.

'The man never seems to have thrown anything out, sir,' he said.

And that was good, Beresford thought, because when he didn't find what he was looking for – and he was almost sure that he wouldn't – he could assume that the reason it wasn't there was not because it had been thrown out, *but because it had never existed.*

Hopkins had kept bills stamped 'paid' which went back ten years, Beresford discovered as he worked his way through the pile.

And he had been a prolific letter writer, too, though all the letters seemed to be on high-minded religious or political subjects, and – on first glance, at least – contained nothing of a personal nature.

There were programmes from concerts in the pile, as well as

birthday cards and embossed invitations to weddings and christenings. Hopkins had kept the death certificates which had been issued for his wife and sons twenty years earlier, and a copy of the coroner's inquest report which stated that the three deaths had been no more than a tragic accident.

There was all that, but there was no trace of the letter from the Department of Education and Science, offering him a grant to study his family's history – the letter which Susan Danvers said she had seen with her own eyes.

Beresford picked up the phone, and rang the DES.

The chief constable listened without interruption to Paniatowski's account of her interview with Dr Sutton, and when she'd finished, he ran his hands through his shock of ginger hair and said, 'Difficult.'

'Difficult?' Paniatowski repeated, incredulously. 'What's so bloody difficult about it?'

'You have to try and look at the whole situation through the eyes of a police officer, rather than through the eyes of a parent,' Baxter said. 'I know it's hard, but you have to try.'

'All right,' Paniatowski agreed.

'We could probably charge Dr Sutton with child endangerment, but I'm not sure we could make it stick. His brief will argue that he had reasonable grounds for assuming that Louisa had your permission, and may even slip in the suggestion that if anyone's guilty of child endangerment, it's the mother. And I've heard Dr Sutton give a lecture. He's a convincing speaker. Put him in the witness box, and he'll feed the jury a line about how he now real-izes it was a mistake to leave the party, and he's very sorry it happened. And then, in his summing up, his barrister will point out that no real harm came to the girl, so what's all the fuss about anyway?'

'No real harm was done!' Paniatowski exploded.

'That's not what I think,' Baxter said firmly, 'but that's certainly how it will appear in court.'

'But Sutton's not just a well-meaning man who made one mistake – he set the whole thing up!'

'You can't prove that,' Baxter said.

'His seventeen-year-old daughter – who my fourteen-year-old daughter has never even really spoken to – rings up at eight o'clock in the morning, and invites her to a party. Why should she do that, unless her father had told her to?'

'I don't know.'

'And when I meet him, he pretends that he doesn't know who I am, even though – and I'm sure of this – he's already game-planned the way that meeting might develop, so he'll be ready to deal with anything I throw at him.'

'My problem, Monika, is that I can't see *why* he would have done it,' Baxter said. 'He's a middle-aged man, with a very good job and solid standing in the community. Why would he risk all that by arranging the abduction of a chief inspector's daughter? And what could he possibly stand to gain from it?'

'I can't answer that.'

'Nothing, Monika! He stood to gain nothing!'

'I don't know why he did it, sir, I only know that he did do it,' Paniatowski said.

Baxter sighed. 'I'll put a couple of men on the case, but I wouldn't want to raise your hopes by promising they'll get anywhere.'

'I don't want a couple of men – I want DS Meadows.'

'Why Meadows?'

Because Meadows was a Rottweiler, Paniatowski thought, and once she'd got her teeth into something, she wouldn't let go until she'd drawn blood.

'I just think that Meadows, being a woman, is the best person for the job,' she said aloud.

'Sergeant Meadows is currently involved in the murder investigation in Bellingsworth,' Baxter reminded her.

'I'm prepared to wait until DI Beresford thinks he can spare her,' Paniatowski countered.

'That could be days – or even weeks.'

'I don't care. Sutton isn't going anywhere.'

'All right, Monika, I'll assign DS Meadows to the case as soon as it's practicable,' Baxter promised. 'But I want it clearly understood that Meadows will be working for the Mid Lancs Constabulary, and not Louisa's mother.'

'That *is* clearly understood, sir,' Paniatowski said – though neither of them thought, for even a moment, that she meant it.

The woman at the DES who took his initial enquiry had promised Beresford that they would get back to him within the hour, and it was, in fact, just thirty-five minutes before someone – a man this time – was on the line.

'I'm John Ryan, Inspector Beresford,' he announced. 'And you're Colin, right?'

'Right,' Beresford agreed.

'Well, Colin, I must admit that your enquiry came as quite a surprise to us, because we simply don't award grants for that kind of personal research.'

'And you told Mr Hopkins this in your answer to him, did you?' Beresford asked, crossing his fingers.

'Well, no.'

'No?'

'We never wrote him a letter. And though correspondence does occasionally go missing, I'm almost one hundred percent certain that we never received one from him, either.'

Of course you didn't, Beresford thought.

'Then if you didn't receive a letter from Mr Hopkins, why did one of your staff pay him a visit?' he asked – just to make certain that he had got things absolutely right.

'He may have been visited, but it certainly wasn't by any of our chaps,' Ryan said.

'You're sure of that?'

'Listen, Colin, even if we did give out grants for research of that nature – which we don't, and never have – we certainly wouldn't send one of our chaps to . . . where did you say it was?'

'Bellingsworth. It's in Lancashire.'

'To Bellingsworth in Lancashire. We simply don't have the manpower for that kind of indulgence.'

'Thank you,' Beresford said. 'You've been very helpful.'

'It's all part of the service, Colin, old chap,' Ryan replied, and rang off.

When Beresford put down the phone, there was a broad smile on his face.

He had cracked it!

He was convinced he had cracked it!

And within the next two hours, he would be arresting his murderer.

NINETEEN

The detective constables were all out conducting house-to-house enquiries, Sergeant Orchard was on his break, and there were only four people left in the church hall. Two of these people – Susan Danvers and the police sketch artist – were sitting at a desk close to the stage. The other two – Beresford and Crane – were watching them from a distance.

'I don't understand why you're going through all this rigmarole, sir,' Crane said.

Beresford smiled complacently. 'Don't you?' he asked.

'You don't seem to think the sketch will be of any use . . .'

'It won't.'

'. . . yet you've brought the police sketch artist all the way from Whitebridge to draw it.'

'The sketch will be of no value in itself, but the act of producing the sketch is serving a very valuable purpose indeed,' Beresford said.

'You've lost me,' Crane admitted.

'Then I suppose I'd better spell it out,' Beresford said, a little wearily. 'An interrogation is a bit like a conjuring trick. You don't want your suspect to see which direction it's taking until it's far too late. Are you following me?'

'Yes, sir.'

'Because we have the sketch artist here, Susan Danvers thinks she knows which way the questioning is going to go. She thinks we'll want to question her about the man who she says visited Len Hopkins last Thursday, and all her energy and effort is being spent on working out what questions we're likely to ask her about him, and what answers will best serve her own interest. And what that means, Detective Constable Crane, is that she's not thinking about either the brass band competition or the evangelical church, so that when I hit her with *those* questions, she'll be completely at sea.'

'Clever,' Crane said, with reluctant admiration.

'Yes, isn't it?' Beresford agreed.

The police artist ripped the page he'd been working on from his pad, laid it carefully on the desk, and stood up.

'Job done!' he said.

Susan Danvers stood up, too.

'Could you sit down again, please, Miss Danvers,' Beresford said, walking quickly towards her.

'Why?' Susan Danvers asked. 'You said you wanted me to describe the man, and I've done that.'

'There are a few more questions we still need to ask you,' Beresford told her, sliding into the seat the sketch artist had been using.

'But I've already told your chief inspector everything I know,' Susan said uneasily.

'She's not here, and we need to go over some of the details,' Beresford told her. 'Do, please, sit down, Miss Danvers – you're making me tired just looking at you standing there.'

Slowly and reluctantly, Susan Danvers sank back into her chair.

Beresford picked up the sketch. 'Now this is what I call a fine piece of work,' he said. He turned slightly. 'Come and look at this, Jack.'

Crane walked over to them, carrying a chair in his hands. He put the chair down next to Beresford's and sat.

'I see what you mean,' he said, 'it is a very fine piece of work. Of course, the artist's pretty good – we already knew that – but it's all the detail you've given him that really makes it.'

'I'll always been good with faces,' Susan said.

'Are you sure the nose is quite right?' Beresford wondered. 'Might it not have been a little larger than it is in the sketch?'

'His nose was *just* like that,' Susan Danvers said firmly.

'Well, you're the one who saw him, so I suppose you should know,' Beresford said. He glanced down at the sketch again. 'It really is a remarkably vivid portrait, considering that you only saw the man who visited Len Hopkins for a few seconds, as he passed you on the street.'

'You're forgetting that I also saw him through the front window, when Len was arguing with him,' Susan pointed out.

'You're quite right, I did forget that,' Beresford agreed. 'Well, I don't think we have any more questions on the artist's impression, do we, Jack?'

'No, sir, I don't think we do,' Crane replied obediently.

Susan looked relieved, and well she might, Beresford thought.

Since she first sat down with the artist, she'd been steeling herself to defend the details of the picture that would be produced, and now it looked as if she wouldn't have to.

She thought she was in the clear – and she couldn't have been wronger!

'There are still a few more questions we'd like to ask you before we're finally done, aren't there, Jack?' Beresford asked.

'Just a few,' Crane agreed. He reached into his pocket and produced a tape recorder. 'And, if you don't mind, Miss Danvers, we'd like to record the conversation. It'll save taking notes, you see – and I'm *dreadful* at taking notes.'

'He's not exaggerating,' Beresford said. 'His notes really are indescribably dreadful.'

'You are happy about us recording this, aren't you, Miss Danvers?' Crane asked.

'Well, I wouldn't say I was exactly *happy* about it . . .' Susan Danvers began.

'That's fine then,' Crane said, pressing the 'record' switch.

'We'll be showing this picture of yours to everyone in the village,' Beresford told Susan Danvers, 'but we're not very hopeful of getting any results, because, as far as we can tell from the questions we've asked already, nobody else seems to have seen him at all.'

'Len saw him,' Susan said.

'Ah, yes, but you see, Len is dead,' Beresford pointed out.

'Do you think I need reminding of that?' Susan asked, with a hint of anger in her voice.

'You said he'd been sent by the Department of Education and Science, didn't you?'

'Yes.'

'And that Len showed you the letter they'd written to him?'

'Yes.'

'We couldn't find that letter anywhere in his house.'

'Then maybe he'd thrown it out.'

'You knew him better than most people, Miss Danvers,' Beresford said. 'Did he normally throw his letters out?'

'Not normally, no,' Susan Danvers admitted. 'Maybe he threw this one out because the young man had upset him so much.'

'Yes, that could be it,' Beresford agreed. 'But I'll tell you what's strange – the DES says it never sent Len a letter. In fact, it says it never *received* one from him, either.'

'It must have done. I posted it myself.'

'And you're sure it was addressed to the DES, and not to some other government department?'

'I'm sure.'

'And they say that not only did they neither receive a letter nor send one, but they're certain they never sent a man to visit Mr Hopkins. Now how would you explain that?'

'They must be mistaken.'

'Are you sure you're not the one who's making a mistake?' Beresford asked. 'Are you quite sure you're not making this man up?'

'I saw him.'

'Fine. Well, since that's settled, let's move on to something else, shall we?' Beresford suggested. 'Now what shall we talk about? I know – how about last Sunday's brass band competition? You weren't with Len in Accrington, were you, Miss Danvers?'

'No.'

'So he didn't take you to the competition, and yet he'd taken you to so many other places – to Blackpool, for instance.'

'He didn't take me to those places – we went together.'

'So why didn't you *go together* to Accrington?'

'I . . . I wasn't feeling well,' Susan said. 'I decided to stay here.'

It was the first lie they could be sure they'd caught her out in – but it was a beauty.

'So you never went to Accrington that day?' Beresford asked.

'No.'

'We have witnesses – quite a number of them – who saw you there. But perhaps they were mistaken – just like the people at the DES were mistaken.'

'I . . . I did go to the competition in the end.'

'But you've just said you *never* went to Accrington.'

'What I meant was, I didn't go when everybody else did. But then, when I started feeling better, I changed my mind.'

'Everyone else got there in specially chartered coaches, but you'd have been too late to catch one of them. So how *did* you get to Accrington?

'I . . . I took the ordinary bus.'

'That would have involved changing buses once you got to Whitebridge, wouldn't it?'

'Yes.'

Beresford produced a bus timetable from his pocket, and studied it for a few moments.

'And if I've read this properly, once you'd got to Whitebridge, you'd have had to wait half an hour at Whitebridge bus station for the Accrington bus,' he said.

'There was a wait,' Susan admitted.

'Indeed there was – a half an hour wait, in the middle of winter, when, being Sunday, the station café wasn't even open.'

'It wasn't so bad,' Susan said weakly. 'I walked up and down, and that kept me warm.'

'It still seems like a long and arduous journey for a woman who, just a few hours earlier, hadn't felt well enough to even travel in a luxury coach,' Beresford reflected. 'Still, I expect you thought it was worth it, because once you were there, you could be with Len.' He paused. 'You did join Len, once you'd got to the competition, didn't you?'

'No.'

Beresford raised his eyebrows in surprise. 'You didn't? Why not?'

'He . . . he was with some other people by the time I arrived. I didn't want to disturb him.'

'You didn't go to Accrington with Len because he didn't want to take you,' Beresford said harshly. 'He was getting rid of you, wasn't he?'

'No, he—'

'We've spoken to the minister at the evangelical church. We *know* he was going to dump you.'

Tears began to trickle down Susan Danvers' cheeks. 'It wasn't Len's fault,' she said.

'Then whose fault was it?'

'It was the new minister's fault. The old minister said that what was past was past, and as long as we didn't touch each other in *that* way, there was no harm in me looking after Len now. But this new one has no love or compassion in him at all – he's an evil man.'

'So how did you feel when, after twenty years of caring for him – of giving up your life for him – Len was about to dump you?'

'How do you think I felt?' Susan sobbed. 'I was heartbroken!'

'But there wasn't just the heartbreak, was there? You were also very angry,' Beresford said.

'No, I wasn't. I . . .'

'For a while, you kept hoping he'd come back to you.'

Susan nodded. 'Yes, I did.'

'And on Sunday, when he ignored you at the brass band competition, something finally snapped. You arrived back in the village before him, went up to his house, and got in using the key he'd given you.'

'No!'

'I don't know why you decided to kill him while he was on the lavatory. Maybe it was because you wanted to rob him of his dignity, just as he'd robbed you of yours. Maybe it was just that he'd be easier to kill when he was sitting down with his pants around his ankles. But whatever the reason, you made sure he'd need to go to the lavatory in the night by spiking his cocoa powder – which you knew he always drank before going to bed – with laxative.'

Susan said nothing, but from the look on her face, it was plain that at least one of the inspector's comments had really hit home.

'And then we come back to this,' Beresford continued relentlessly, holding up the sketch that the police artist had drawn. 'You wanted to make sure that suspicion didn't fall on you, so you invented this mysterious stranger who had an argument with Len, and who just possibly might have killed him.'

'You're right, he did rob me of my dignity,' Susan said. 'He didn't mean to, but he did. Even so, I could never have robbed him of his, because I loved him too much.'

'Did you hear what I said about inventing the mysterious stranger?' Beresford asked.

But it was plain that she hadn't – or that if she had, she didn't care.

'*Because I loved him too much*,' she repeated. 'Even when he was dead, I tried to rescue his dignity by pulling his trousers up again, but it was too awkward, and I was too weak and upset. I . . . I got them as far as his knees, and then I just had to stop.'

'So you tried to pull up his trousers again after you'd killed him?' Beresford said.

'I tried to do it after I found him in the morning,' Susan replied.

'Listen, Susan, we've got more than enough evidence to convict you, so why don't you make it easier on yourself and just admit you did it?' Crane said persuasively. 'If you tell the truth now – to the two of us – your barrister will be able to argue in court that your mind was unbalanced by the horrible way you'd been treated.

He'll say that you just lost control, and that you're very sorry for what you've done.'

'Then he'd be telling lies,' Susan said.

'You'd have both the judge and the jury on your side. You could be released after no more than a couple of years.' He paused to let his words sink in. 'But if you say nothing, you'll start to look like a cold-blooded killer, and they'll lock you up for life.'

'Do you really think I might only get two years?' Susan asked.

'Well, I'm not giving you any guarantees, but with a bit of luck, it could well be only two years,' Crane said awkwardly.

'And what would I do when they released me?' Susan asked.

The question seemed to knock Crane off balance.

'Well, I suppose you could come back here,' he said finally.

'To *what*?' Susan demanded. 'What is there here for me, now that Len's dead?'

'You'd still have time to build a new life,' Crane said weakly.

'You're a fool,' Susan told him. She turned to Beresford. 'I might as well go to prison for life, because my life is over,' she said. 'But I still have a little pride left – and I won't confess to a murder I didn't do. I just won't!'

TWENTY

Paniatowski parked her red MGA in front of the church hall. It had been less than thirty-six hours since she had first arrived in this village, she thought, but so much had happened in that time.

Thirty-six hours ago, she had thought herself as happy as any woman who had lost the love of her life could be.

Thirty-six hours ago, she had believed she was making a reason-able job of being a mother.

And now?

And now, the only thing she was sure of was that she needed to know what had happened to her daughter, and *why* it had happened.

She knew there'd been a breakthrough in the case the moment she entered the church hall.

She could feel it in the air. She could see it in the expression on the faces of the four or five detective constables who were sitting around the horseshoe – expressions which said that the investigation was all but over, and now all that was necessary was to tie up the loose ends.

Beresford, who had been talking to the sergeant, noticed her arrival, and walked over to her with a broad grin on his face. Then, perhaps remembering that the whole world was not made up exclusively of his personal triumphs, he grew more sombre.

'How's Louisa?' he asked.

'The doctor found no evidence of assault . . .'

'Thank God for that!'

'. . . but she's still pretty shaken up. As a matter of fact, I'm still pretty shaken up myself.'

'It'll be rough at first, but it will get better,' Beresford promised her. 'And if there's anything I can do, Monika – and I do mean *anything* – then you only need to ask.'

He was a good friend, she thought. He was her *best* friend.

She smiled. 'Thank you for your concern, Colin – and now you can tell me your news.'

The grin was back on Beresford's face.

'We got her, boss,' he said.

'Her?' Paniatowski repeated.

'Susan Danvers.'

Paniatowski's stomach turned an instant somersault.

Susan Danvers!

That just didn't feel right.

'They say that Hell hath no fury like a woman scorned – and in this case they're spot on,' Beresford continued.

'Has she confessed?'

'Not yet. But I've sent her back to Whitebridge, and after a couple of hours in the holding cells, she should be more than willing to come clean. Anyway, it's time for a celebratory piss-up in the Green Dragon, don't you think?'

'That sounds like a good idea,' Paniatowski said, hoping she sounded more enthusiastic than she felt.

Crane joined them in the Green Dragon, but not Meadows.

'Where's Kate?' Paniatowski asked.

'She's still not got back from Accrington,' Beresford said, 'and, as a matter of fact, I'm rather glad she's not here.'

'Why's that?'

'She was really rather rude to me in here last night, wasn't she Jack?' Beresford said.

Crane looked embarrassed. 'I think we were all a little tense last night,' he said.

'Anyway, she's done a splendid job in Accrington – I'd never have been able to put the case together without her contribution – and as soon as she's apologized for her behaviour, I'll be more than willing to welcome her back into the fold,' Beresford said.

Wrong attitude! Paniatowski thought sadly. It was completely the wrong attitude.

'Why don't you tell me about the case that you've built up against Susan Danvers?' she suggested.

'I'd be delighted to,' Beresford told her.

He outlined the whole thing – Len Hopkins' rejection of Susan, her trip to Accrington, the spiking of the cocoa – which had now been confirmed by the lab – with laxative, and the fact that Susan had a key to Len's house.

'We should have thought of her from the start,' he said, as he drew to a close. 'After all, she found Len's body, didn't she, and how often has it happened that the person who "found" the body turns out to be the killer?'

'That is quite common,' Paniatowski admitted, cautiously.

'There's a few "i"s to dot and "t"s to cross, so we'll probably be here in the village for a couple more days, but essentially, it's in the bag,' Beresford said confidently.

He was so pleased with himself that it was pity to burst his bubble, Paniatowski thought – but it had to be done.

'You are aware that all the evidence is circumstantial, aren't you, Colin?' she asked.

'Yes, as it happens, I am,' Beresford said, bristling slightly. 'But you have to admit, it's a classic case of means, motive and opportunity.'

'Yes, it certainly is,' Paniatowski agreed.

But she was still thinking, It doesn't feel quite right, it just doesn't feel quite right.

'So is there a problem?' Beresford asked.

'Probably not,' Paniatowski said. 'But it does seem to me that the prosecution might be a little bit happier if he had something more concrete to take into court with him.'

'And by the time we finish up here, we'll probably be able to *give* him something more concrete,' Beresford said confidently. 'But even if we haven't, we'll have Susan's confession – and that's all we really need.'

'And you're sure she'll confess?'

'No doubt about it.'

Paniatowski turned to Crane. 'What do you think, Jack?'

Jack Crane looked distinctly uncomfortable again. 'Inspector Beresford's got a lot more experience in these matters than I have,' he said, 'and he certainly thinks she'll confess.'

Which, on one level, wasn't answering the question at all, Paniatowski noted – although, on another, it most certainly was.

'She didn't even want to admit that she'd been to the brass band competition at first,' Beresford said, 'but I soon got that out of her. Of course, I started the interview rather cleverly, I think, by tricking her into a false sense of security.' He reached into his briefcase, took out a sheet of thick paper, and laid it on the table. 'And this is what I used.'

'What is it?' Paniatowski asked.

'It's the man who never was – Len Hopkins' mysterious visitor. I got the police artist to draw it from Susan Danvers' description, and she was so intent on creating her fake that she had no idea what was coming next. That's right, isn't it, Jack?'

'It certainly is, sir,' Crane agreed, and this time there were no reservations in his tone at all.

Paniatowski took a glance at the sketch of the young man, and felt an unexpected shiver run through her entire body. There was something familiar about him, she thought – something *unpleasantly* familiar – but she couldn't quite pin down what it was.

'It's a very detailed sketch for somebody who Susan simply made up,' she said.

'Oh, she probably didn't make him up entirely,' Beresford said airily. 'Chances are, it looks very like someone she knows.'

But it didn't look remotely like anybody she'd seen in the village, Paniatowski thought – and *they* were the only people who Susan really knew.

'And you're sure he's nothing more than a figment of Susan's imagination?' she asked.

'I'm absolutely convinced of it. She needed to blame someone else for the murder, you see, and who better than a man we'd never find because he never actually existed?'

Paniatowski cast her mind back to the conversation *she'd* had with Susan about the man.

'*What did Mr Hopkins tell you about him?*'

'*Not a thing. He refused to discuss it. But while I was making his tea, he kept muttering the same thing over and over to himself.*'

'*And what was it?*'

'*He kept saying, "It's all true. You read about it, and you think it's an exaggeration – but it's all true."*'

'*And you have no idea what he meant by that?*'

'*Not a clue.*'

Why would she have complicated her story – if a story was what it was – by adding to it something she couldn't explain herself?

Wouldn't it have been far simpler to invent something that would strengthen her case, rather than distract from it?

She could have said something like, '*He told me the man wanted him to do something – he wouldn't tell me what it was, only that he'd refused – and then the man had said that if he didn't do it, he'd kill him.*'

But she hadn't said anything like that. In fact, she'd gone out of her way to suggest that the man wasn't the murderer.

'*Do you think the young man might have been responsible for Len's death?*'

'*Good heavens, no.*'

'*Why not?*'

'*Because if he'd killed Len – and I'm not saying he ever would have, but if he had – he'd have shot him, or maybe strangled him. I didn't see much of him, but I saw enough to know that he'd have thought it far too messy to smash his head in with a short-handled pickaxe.*'

Of course, if the man did really exist – and Paniatowski was *convinced* that he did – it was still perfectly possible that he had had nothing at all to do with the murder, and that Susan was, in fact, the killer.

So perhaps Colin had got everything right. Perhaps, when they got back to Whitebridge, Susan Danvers would be ready to confess that she had killed Len Hopkins in a jealous rage.

Paniatowski's gut told her that wasn't going to happen, but it was Colin's investigation now, and she had no right to interfere.

Besides, she had another concern at that moment – the concern that had brought her to the village in the first place.

'The chief constable's willing to launch an investigation into what happened to Louisa, but, naturally enough, he doesn't want me involved personally,' she told Beresford.

'That's sensible.'

'He suggested that when you could spare her, the job could be given to DS Meadows.'

'I can spare her now,' Beresford said airily.

'Are you sure about that?' Paniatowski asked – hating herself for saying it, but feeling obliged to anyway. 'Susan Danvers hasn't been charged yet, so the investigation's still—'

'I can spare her,' Beresford interrupted, 'and, to tell you the truth, I'd rather not have her around until she's prepared to apologize.'

If you're waiting for Kate Meadows to apologize, you'll be waiting a long time, Paniatowski thought.

TWENTY-ONE

Kate Meadows thought she knew something about the penchants of middle-aged academics, so even though it was a cold night, she was wearing a short skirt under her coat – and as she walked up the path to the front door of Dr Sutton's detached house, she began unbuttoning the coat to reveal the treasures beneath.

It was Dr Sutton himself who answered the bell.

'Well, well, what have we here?' he asked, running his eyes appreciatively up and down her body. 'A door-to-door salesperson, perhaps? Or a young lady with a survey which she'd like me to complete?'

'I'm afraid I'm neither of those, Dr Sutton,' Meadows said, producing her warrant card.

Sutton groaned.

'I thought I'd made it quite plain to your DCI Paniatowski that if she wanted my daughter to talk to the police, it would have to be by appointment, and only in my solicitor's presence,' he said.

'You might have made it plain to her, but she certainly didn't make it plain to me,' Meadows said. 'So I've wasted a journey, have I?'

'It would appear so.'

Meadows stamped her foot angrily on the path. 'She doesn't listen, does she?' she demanded, of no one in particular. 'The bloody woman never listens to anybody. So not only am I sent out to investigate something that should never have been investigated in the first place, but I'm going to have to do the whole thing again tomorrow.'

'You don't think that it should be investigated?' Sutton asked interestedly.

'Of course not. The bloody kid runs off – and if I was Paniatowski's kid, I'd run off, too – and when she's caught, she spouts out the first crappy little excuse which comes into her head, and her stupid mother swallows it wholesale.'

'Yes, that is probably what happened,' Dr Sutton agreed.

'And as a result of that, I end up on a cold street in the middle of winter, when I could be snugly tucked up at home with a nice glass of wine,' Meadows ranted. She stopped suddenly, as if she'd realized she'd said too much. 'I'm sorry, Dr Sutton, I should never have let my feelings show like that. But when you're working for *Ma'am*, it can sometimes be a bloody hard life.'

'I'm sure it can,' Sutton agreed, sympathetically.

Meadows sighed. 'Well, I suppose we'll just have to play it by the book,' she said. 'I'll contact your solicitor in the morning, make an appointment, and we'll wrap things up then.'

She turned, and began to walk down the path.

'Just a minute,' Sutton called after her.

'Yes?'

'Am I right in assuming that if I agreed to you talking to Ellie now, we could get the whole thing over with tonight?'

'I don't see why not.'

'Then you'd better come inside.'

The Suttons' living room was what Meadows immediately christened 'socialist cool', which was another way of saying that it was furnished in the style in which an average worker's living room might be furnished, only much more expensively.

'Please take a seat,' Sutton said, indicating an armchair modelled on mass-production lines – but covered in soft, luxurious leather – which was positioned opposite the sofa on which his daughter was already sitting.

Meadows sat, and took out her notebook. 'What a lovely home you have,' she said enthusiastically.

'I'm glad you approve,' Sutton said. 'Could I perhaps get you a glass of wine?'

Meadows shook her head, with a show of reluctance.

'Better not,' she said. 'I don't want to wake up in the middle of the night and find Paniatowski standing over me with a breathalyser.'

Sutton laughed, then crossed the room and sat down on the sofa next to his daughter – from where he would have an excellent view of the detective sergeant's legs.

The daughter was even easier to classify than the room, Meadows thought. She was one of those quite pretty girls – though nowhere near as pretty as she thought she was – who seem to have been issued with discontented mouths and greedy eyes at birth.

'I suppose I'd better start by asking you why you made friends with Louisa Paniatowski in the first place, Ellie,' Meadows said.

Ellie shrugged. 'I felt sorry for her. Who wouldn't feel sorry for her, with a mother like that?'

Meadows laughed. 'You're telling me,' she agreed. 'So when you decided to have a party on Monday, you thought you might as well ask her.'

'That's right.'

'Hang on a minute,' Meadows said. 'The party wasn't going to be on Monday, was it? It was planned for Friday. Or have I got that wrong?'

'Does it really matter?' Dr Sutton asked.

'Not to me,' Meadows replied. 'But if Paniatowski asks about it, I'd better have an answer ready.'

'The party was originally planned for Friday,' Sutton conceded.

'So why was the date changed at the last minute?'

'Some of Ellie's closest friends simply couldn't make it on the day we'd planned.'

'Good,' Meadows said. 'Now, when Paniatowski tries to twist the fact that you changed the date into some kind of evil conspiracy, I can nip it in the bud. The next thing I'd like to ask you—' She stopped, suddenly. 'Oh my God! Is that ring you're wearing from the Queens of the Nile range, Ellie?'

'It certainly is,' the girl said complacently, holding out her hand so that Meadows could get a better look at it. 'It's the Nefertiti.'

'It's beautiful,' Meadows said. 'I'd love to have one myself, but they're rather expensive.'

Sutton laughed uneasily. 'They're *very* expensive,' he said, 'but if you can't spoil your own beautiful daughter, then who can you spoil?'

'So, to get back to the party,' Meadows said. 'I assume you gave Louisa strict instructions not to take a lift with anyone else, but to wait until you could drive her home, Dr Sutton.'

'Naturally.'

'But by the time you returned home, of course, the wilful child had already gone.'

'That's right.'

'When did she leave, Ellie?' Meadows asked.

'I don't know,' the girl said carelessly. 'I didn't even realize she had gone until Robert started looking for her.'

'So one of your friends must have taken her home,' Meadows said.

'No, it was definitely not one of Ellie's friends,' Sutton said firmly.

'How can you be so sure of that?'

'Because after DCI Paniatowski burst into my office and had her rant, I rang up all Ellie's friends and asked them.'

Meadows consulted a blank page of her notebook.

'I know it's here somewhere,' she muttered to herself. 'Ah, yes. I thought you told *Ma'am* that you didn't even know the names of half the people at the party, Dr Sutton.'

'I asked Ellie.'

'There you are, another simple explanation to what, on the surface, was an apparent contradiction,' Meadows said. 'But there is one thing I still don't understand – if one of your friends didn't drive the brat home, then who did?'

'It must have been one of the gatecrashers,' Ellie said.

'Were there many of them?'

'Quite a few. I give really cool parties.'

'And you didn't try to get rid of these gatecrashers of yours?'

'Now that would have been distinctly *un*cool.'

Sutton laughed again. 'Young people!' he said.

'Young people,' Meadows agreed. She turned her attention to Ellie again. 'Louisa described the boy as being tall, and having blond wavy hair. Was he a gatecrasher?'

'He must have been.'

'You do remember him being there, don't you?'

'I'm not sure.'

Meadows closed her notebook. 'Well, that's about it – apart, of course, for the names and addresses of the guests who you changed the date of the party to accommodate.'

'What!' Sutton said.

'You heard,' Meadows told him.

'But you said we could wrap the whole thing up tonight.'

'I lied – but then, you've been lying to me ever since I walked through the door.'

'I resent being called a liar in my own home,' Sutton said, 'and if you wish me to hand over any information at all – however trivial it might be – you'll need a warrant.'

'Oh, I don't see much of a problem there,' Meadows said. 'Would you like to know my thoughts on what I've heard so far?'

Both father and daughter remained silent.

'Not very curious, are you?' Meadows said chirpily. 'But I think I'll tell you anyway. Firstly, my thoughts on Ellie's friendship with Louisa. Now, Louisa's a lovely girl, as I know from personal experience.'

'You *know* her?' Sutton asked.

'Yes. Didn't I make that clear from the start?'

'No, you bloody well didn't!'

'That was rather careless of me. Anyway, I can almost believe, at a push, that a girl three years older than Louisa would want to make friends with her – even though, as we all know, a three-year gap is such a huge one at that age. But if she did make an older friend, it wouldn't be a girl like you, Ellie. The other girl would be a sensitive, intelligent, caring soul – not a self-absorbed sulky brat.'

Sutton sprang to his feet. 'How dare you talk to my daughter in that manner? If you don't leave this house immediately,' he continued, taking a step or two towards her, 'I'll throw you out myself.'

Meadows raised a single finger in the air. It was hard to say exactly what made it seem so threatening, but it stopped Sutton in his tracks.

'I'm not big, but I'm highly trained, and if you lay one hand on me, I'll break you in half,' Meadows said calmly. 'Now sit down again, Dr Sutton.'

'I . . . I refuse to answer any more of your impertinent questions,' Sutton blustered.

'But I'm not asking questions – I'm telling you how things were,' Meadows said. 'So sit down and listen!'

Sutton stepped backwards, and sank heavily into his seat.

'Ellie made friends with Louisa specifically so she could invite her to the party, and the party was planned specifically so that Louisa could come. There's a rather nice symmetry in that, don't you think?'

Sutton and Ellie said nothing.

'The expensive ring Ellie is wearing is her reward for the part she played in all this,' Meadows continued. 'Now I admit that statement is no more than a guess at the moment, but if turns that it was bought this morning – and that's how it *will* turn out – then the guess will become a certainty. So Ellie got the ring as a reward. What did you get out of this whole shabby business, Dr Sutton?'

'No comment,' Sutton growled.

'I see you're already getting prepared for the grilling you'll be given tomorrow,' Meadows said. 'Good idea. Now where was I? Oh yes. Whoever wanted Louisa to come to the party changed his mind about the date it would be held on – I don't know why that should be, but then that's hardly surprising, since I don't even know yet why he wanted her there. But I'll find out in time. Anyway, at the party, it all goes according to plan. The boy – let's call him Boy X – offers Louisa a lift home and drives her to a deserted spot, where he first rapes her, and then sodomizes her—'

'He . . . he promised me that no harm would come to her!' Sutton gasped.

And the moment the words were out of his mouth, he looked as if he could cheerfully have eaten his own tongue.

'That was a trick!' he said accusingly. 'If the girl had been raped and sodomized, DCI Paniatowski would have said so this morning.'

'If she had been raped and sodomized, I don't imagine DCI Paniatowski would have been in a fit state to say *anything*,' Meadows countered. 'Still, you have rather let the cat out of the bag now, haven't you?'

'No comment.'

'It really is time to come clean, Dr Sutton.'

'No comment.'

'Suit yourself,' Meadows said, standing up. 'I'll show myself out.

See you tomorrow then – when we'll be looking at each other across the table in Interview Room A.'

It was standard police procedure for the victims of attacks to describe their attacker to the police sketch artist, but Paniatowski had not wanted to take her daughter down to Whitebridge Police Headquarters, and had asked the police artist – as a favour – to come to her home instead. And he was there now, working with Louisa in the living room, while a chain-smoking Monika paced the length of her study and wished they would hurry up.

The phone rang, and Paniatowski grabbed at it.

'The whole thing was a complete set-up, boss,' Meadows said from the other end of the line. 'It wasn't a case of Louisa being in the wrong place at the wrong time – she was targeted. She was the whole point of the party.'

'You're sure?' Paniatowski gasped.

'I'm sure,' Meadows confirmed. 'For a bright man, Sutton's awfully stupid, and he let it slip out that he was working for someone else.'

'Someone else? Who else?' Paniatowski asked. 'In God's name, Kate, *who?*'

'I don't know yet,' Meadows admitted, 'but I'm putting the investigation on an official basis, and I'm going to call our Dr Sutton in for questioning first thing in morning.'

'I appreciate this, Kate, I really do,' Paniatowski said.

'It's all part of the service,' Meadows said. 'Try to get a good night's sleep, boss.'

And then she hung up.

Paniatowski began pacing the floor again, with Meadows' words echoing round her brain.

Louisa was targeted! Louisa was targeted!

But why had she been targeted? What reason could there possibly have been for targeting her?

If there had been a phone call demanding a ransom, that would at least have explained matters.

If she'd been raped – or worse, never seen again because she'd been sold into sex-slavery – there would have been some evil, twisted logic about it.

But apart from her being slipped some mild sort of drug, she hadn't been touched.

An elaborate plan had been constructed – involving a university lecturer, his daughter and God knew how many other people – with the sole purpose of snatching Louisa. And yet once she'd been caught – once he'd got what he wanted – her captor had simply let her go!

There was a gentle tap on the study door, and she looked up to see Louisa standing there.

'We've finished, Mum,' the girl said.

Paniatowski gave her a hug.

'You've been a very brave girl, and I'm so proud of you,' she told her daughter.

'Hugo would like a word with you before he goes,' Louisa said.

'Would he, now?' said Paniatowski in a light singalong voice – a voice which she hoped would completely disguise from Louisa the anguish that she was feeling. 'Well, I'll tell you what, you stay here, and when he's gone, I'll make us both something special to eat.'

'Something wicked?' Louisa asked, with a grin.

'Something really wicked,' Monika promised.

She walked slowly from her study to the hallway, and the hallway to the living room. She hadn't wanted to walk – she'd wanted to run – but it was important that Louisa think she was calm, so the girl could be calm herself.

The police artist was standing in the centre of the living room, under the ceiling light, and studying the sketch.

'This is really weird, ma'am,' he said. 'It's the second time today that I've drawn—'

'Give me the picture, Hugo,' Paniatowski said. 'For Christ's sake, give me the bloody picture!'

The sketch artist held his pad out, and Paniatowski grasped it with trembling hands.

'Oh no!' she moaned softly.

She had been bracing herself for her first sight of the man who had threatened her daughter, but she had never – even in her wildest imaginings – thought it would be anything like this, and it required an effort of will from her not to go straight into a dead faint.

Taking a deep breath, she forced herself to take another look. She felt the same unease as she had when looking at the picture which had been drawn from Susan Danvers' description – the same sense that she had seen the man before, and that it had been a horrible experience.

And that was not surprising, because though the hairstyle in this picture was slightly different, it was undoubtedly the same man.

TWENTY-TWO

I f there'd been a competition to find the dreariest room in the whole of the Whitebridge Police HQ, then Interview Room A would only have won second prize, having been beaten – but only by a nose – by Interview Room B. The room was painted in chocolate brown to waist height, and sickly cream above that, and as Beresford and Crane entered it at eight twenty-five on Wednesday morning, Crane found himself wondering whether it had been skilfully designed by a team of expert psychologists whose aim was to break the human spirit.

'Susan Danvers will crack,' Beresford said, as they sat down at the table. 'By ten o'clock – at the latest – she'll have told us all we need to know.'

Crane looked up at the small window, set high in the wall, and noted that the outside of the glass was frosted over.

No, this room hadn't been *designed* at all, he decided. It was like the least favoured child in a large family, and was simply uncared for.

Beresford looked impatiently at his watch.

'How long have we been here, Jack?' he asked.

'Can't be more than a minute or two, sir,' Crane replied.

Beresford checked his watch again. 'What the hell's keeping them?' he demanded.

At eight thirty-one, Susan Danvers arrived with her WPC escort.

She looked tired, Beresford thought – and that was all to the good, because although he'd spent a fitful night himself, he felt wide awake.

Susan Danvers' escort guided her to the chair facing them, and when she'd sat down, Beresford said, 'I hope they gave you a good breakfast, Susan.'

'Do you?' Susan replied, sounding slightly puzzled. 'And why would you hope that?'

'Because I've got your best interests at heart,' Beresford told her. 'You may not believe that at the moment, but it's true. I want to make this whole process as painless as possible for you.'

'Then let me go,' Susan suggested.

'You know I can't do that,' Beresford said.

'I know you don't *want* to do that, because you need to convict somebody of killing my Len, and you think you've got a good chance of convicting me,' Susan countered.

Maybe this was going to be a little harder than he'd first thought, Beresford decided.

'I'd like you to account for your movements from Sunday afternoon onwards,' he said.

Susan sighed. 'I went to the brass band competition because I wanted to talk to Len.'

'If you wanted to talk to him, why didn't you wait until he got back to the village?'

'I thought it would be easier at the competition. I thought if I did it there, he'd *have to* listen.'

'And did you talk to him?'

'No.'

'You didn't? Not after you'd travelled all the way to Accrington for just that purpose?'

'I've told you once I didn't. I'll not tell you again.'

'*Why* didn't you talk to him?'

'Because it turned out that I was wrong when I thought it would be easier there.'

'I'm not sure I know quite what you mean,' Beresford told her.

'Don't make me say it,' Susan pleaded.

'I have to know what happened,' Beresford said firmly.

'All right, then,' Susan said angrily. 'I didn't talk to him because when he saw me walking towards him, he turned his back on me.'

'So what did you do then?'

'I caught the next bus back to Bellingsworth, and went straight home.'

A lie! Beresford was sure it was a lie, and glancing at Crane, he could see that Jack thought so, too.

She hadn't gone straight home at all. Of course she hadn't. Because *before* she could go home, she'd needed to spike Len's cocoa with laxative.

'What time did you get home?' he asked.

'At about half past five.'

'And when did you leave your house again?'

'When I set out the next morning to make Len's breakfast for him.'

'You didn't go out again that night, say between ten o'clock and two o'clock in the morning?'

'No.'

'Why did you go to make Len's breakfast?'

'I was his housekeeper.'

'But he'd sacked you.'

'I was going to work out my notice.'

'You were going to work out your notice,' Beresford repeated sceptically. 'And you were going to do it even though he didn't want you to – even though you knew that what *he* wanted was a clean break?'

It was as Susan folded her arms across her chest that he realized he'd made a mistake by pushing too hard – and Susan's next words were only a confirmation of what he already knew.

'I'm not going to say any more,' she said. 'You can question me as much as you like – you can go on for days and weeks, if you want to – but you'll get nothing more from me.'

She meant it, Beresford thought, as he felt his stomach knot up into a tight ball.

There was no bravado to her words, just a rock-solid certainty. She would *never* confess.

By ten o'clock, Beresford was standing at the apex of the horseshoe in the church hall, looking down at all the detective constables who had thought their job was almost done, and were now being told that it wasn't.

'We need something concrete,' Beresford was saying, bitterly aware that he was echoing the words that Monika Paniatowski had used – the words he had airily dismissed – only the day before. 'It would help, for example, if we had a witness who saw Susan Danvers go into Len Hopkins' house shortly after she got off the bus from Accrington.'

One of the constables raised a tentative hand.

'Yes,' Beresford said.

'The problem with that, sir, is that nearly everybody from the village was still in Accrington when she arrived back. It was a big thing to them, that brass band competition.'

'Do you think you're telling me something I don't already know?' Beresford snapped. 'Yes, it was a big thing for them, and yes, most of the village will have been there, but there must have been some people who didn't go.'

There must have been some people who didn't go, he repeated in his head.

He had meant the words to sound like a supposition, but they had emerged from his mouth more like a prayer.

'We also need witnesses who saw Susan later that night, either on her way to kill Len or returning home after the deed was done,' he continued. 'I know they won't be easy to find, given that all the power had been cut off by then, but I've been watching the way you lads have been working over the last couple of days, and I know,' he forced himself to smile, 'that you just love a good challenge.'

The detective constables should, by rights, have smiled back at him – or perhaps nodded their heads in agreement – but instead of that, they merely looked embarrassed.

They know just how desperate I am, he thought miserably. They can almost *smell* it.

OK, lads,' he said aloud, 'get out there and bring me back what I need.'

The detective constables had been gone for less than five minutes when Paniatowski arrived at the church hall, carrying a large folder.

'Have you still got the sketch of the man who visited Len Hopkins last week?' she asked.

'The imaginary visitor?' Beresford replied. 'Yes. I saw no reason to keep it myself, but I thought there was just a chance that either the prosecution or the defence might want a look at it.'

'Could I see it?' Paniatowski said.

Beresford pulled it out of his briefcase, and laid it on the desk.

'Now look at this,' Paniatowski said, laying her sketch next to it. 'This is the boy who abducted Louisa.'

Beresford felt the knot in his stomach tighten even more.

'They're similar,' he admitted.

'Apart from a few minor details, they're exactly the same!' Paniatowski exclaimed.

'Except that Louisa's was drawn from memory, and Susan's was made up,' Beresford said.

Paniatowski shook her head, almost pityingly.

'Didn't Charlie Woodend always tell us that when the facts didn't fit the theory, it was time to jettison the theory?' she asked.

'And what's that supposed to mean?' Beresford demanded.

'It means that while it might be convenient for you to believe that Susan made up Len's caller, it's now perfectly clear that she didn't.'

'So let's assume for a moment that the man Susan described does actually exist,' Beresford said, with an edge entering his voice. 'Is the next step to assume that he killed Len Hopkins?'

'It's a possibility. Not the only one, by any means, but it's certainly a possibility.'

'Is it, now?' Beresford asked. 'Then let's follow that line of thought through to its natural conclusion, shall we? He kills Len on Sunday – we don't know why yet, but we'll say, for the sake of argument, that he did it because Len was against the strike. Are you still with me?'

'I'm still with you.'

'He's achieved his objective, hasn't he? So what does he do next? The logical thing would be for him to put as many miles between himself and Bellingsworth as he possibly can. But he doesn't do that at all, does he? Instead, he hangs around until Monday night – nearly twenty-four hours after the murder – and then abducts your daughter. Now why would he do that?'

'I don't know,' Paniatowski admitted.

'You don't know,' Beresford repeated scornfully. 'Does kidnapping Louisa do anything to make the strike – which we've agreed is his main interest – any more likely to happen?'

'No.'

'No! It doesn't have any effect at all. So does the man abduct her because he thinks that will lengthen the odds of him getting caught?'

'This is pointless, Colin,' Paniatowski said weakly.

'No, it doesn't lengthen the odds,' Beresford ploughed on. 'In fact, he must know that what he's done will have quite the reverse effect! By sticking his head above the parapet again, he's actually *increasing* the chances of getting caught.' He paused. 'Well?'

'I can't explain why he acted as he did,' Paniatowski admitted.

'It seems to me that the one who should be jettisoning the theory because it doesn't fit the facts is you,' Beresford said. 'I'm disappointed in you, Monika. I've supported you all these years, and now that I need your support for once, I simply don't get it.'

'I want to support you, Colin, I really do,' Paniatowski said. 'It's just that the more I think about it, the more I'm convinced that in arresting Susan Danvers, you've arrested the wrong person.'

'And you've reached that conclusion simply because you now think that Susan *didn't* invent the caller?'

'That's certainly part of it,' Paniatowski said. 'If she didn't lie about that, it's equally possible she didn't lie about other things, either. But there's more to it than that.'

'Like what?'

'She's not a calculating woman – you can see that for yourself. She might have possibly killed Len Hopkins in a rage, but she'd never have been capable of planning it in the cold-blooded way that the killer did.'

'And that's it?' Beresford asked.

No, Paniatowski thought, there was also the gut feeling that however little sense it made, Louisa's abduction and Len's murder were connected – and Louisa's abduction was something Susan could have had no control over.

'Susan wouldn't have wanted him to be found in such a humiliating position,' she said. 'Didn't you tell me that when she found him in the morning, she tried to pull his trousers up?'

'I certainly told you that that was what she *said* she'd done.'

'And doesn't that have the ring of truth about it? Doesn't it sound like something she would have been incapable of making up?'

'Not to me,' Beresford said hotly. 'What this all boils down to, Monika, is that I look at her and see a guilty woman, and you look at her and see an innocent one. And you have to be the one who's right, don't you – because you're the great Detective Chief Inspector Monika Paniatowski?'

'If you want my support, you've got it – my *unqualified* support,' Paniatowski said. 'If you believe that Susan Danvers is the murderer, I'll do everything I can to prove that you're right.'

'Don't patronize me,' Beresford said harshly.

'What do you *want* me to say?' Paniatowski pleaded.

'There's nothing you *can* say – not now,' Beresford told her.

And then he saw that though she was fighting hard against it, Paniatowski was almost in tears.

He took a deep breath. 'I'm sorry, Monika, this has all got a bit out of control,' he said, 'and that's probably my fault.'

'We could both have handled it better,' Paniatowski said.

'I don't want to lose your friendship.'

'And, God knows, I don't want to lose yours. There've been times when it was the only thing that kept me sane.'

Beresford smiled. 'We won't lose it. We'll be fine. As soon as I've put this case to bed, we'll be fine.'

'I meant what I said,' Paniatowski told him. 'If you want me to, I'll work like a horse to make the case against Susan.'

Beresford shook his head. 'You go home to Louisa. She needs your strength even more than I do.'

They hugged each other for a few moments, then Paniatowski said, 'I'd better go.'

It was as she was walking to the door that she remembered why she had come to Bellingsworth in the first place, and turned around.

'I'm having the picture of the man who abducted Louisa plastered all over Whitebridge,' she said.

'That's a good idea,' Beresford replied, but there was a note of caution in his voice, as if he suspected she might say more – and it would be a more that he didn't like.

'Don't you think it might be a good idea to do the same in Bellingsworth – on the off chance that Len's visitor wasn't imaginary after all?' Paniatowski asked tentatively.

Beresford glared at her, then the glare slowly turned into a smile.

She was trying to help him, he thought. She was wrong – but at least she was trying. And the least *he* could do, as a friend, would be to accept that help.

'It's worth a try,' he said. 'I'll send one of the lads over to Whitebridge to pick them up.'

Paniatowski grinned sheepishly. 'There's no need to do that,' she said. 'I've got them in the car.'

TWENTY-THREE

When Dr Robert Sutton was shown into Interview Room A of Whitebridge Police HQ at ten fifteen that morning, his solicitor – an unsmiling man called Mr Coppersedge – was by his side.

'My client wishes it to be clearly understood that he is here of his own free will, and that he is willing to cooperate with the police in every way possible,' Coppersedge said, when he and Sutton had sat down, and Meadows had switched the tape recorder on.

Meadows looked across the table at them, an expression of amused contempt on her face.

'Beautifully put, Mr Coppersedge,' she said. 'Why, it was almost poetry. Now, shall we get down to business?'

'Before he answers your questions, my client would like to read out a prepared statement,' Coppersedge said.

Meadows yawned and stretched. 'Must he?' she asked.

'He must,' Coppersedge said firmly.

'Then let's get it over with.'

Sutton took a folded piece of A4 paper from his pocket, and smoothed it out on the table.

'I wish to apologize for the way in which I have behaved throughout this whole unfortunate incident,' he read. 'I accept that it was my responsibility to take care of Louisa Paniatowski, since I knew her to be a minor, and that I should not have delegated that responsibility to my daughter, who is herself still legally a child. I deeply regret the distress my carelessness has caused, and I am more than willing to offer DCI Paniatowski and her daughter compensation, either financially or in any other way that is deemed appropriate.'

'Interview interrupted at ten seventeen,' Meadows said, switching off the tape recorder. 'Off the record,' she told Sutton, 'I think my boss *would* be willing to settle for compensation, if it was the *right* compensation.'

'My client is willing to accede to any reasonable demands,' Coppersedge said. 'What exactly are we talking about?'

'I think she rather fancies the idea of having Robert's balls delivered to her on a platter,' Meadows said.

Coppersedge scowled. 'That is a most inappropriate comment, Detective Sergeant Meadows,' he said.

'Of course it is,' Meadows agreed, 'that's why it's off the record.' She clicked on the recorder again. 'Interview resumed at ten eighteen. Last night, Dr Sutton, you admitted to me that that you had known in advance that the victim, Louisa Paniatowski, would be abducted.'

'My client strongly denies ever having made such a statement,' Coppersedge said.

'You must have known you were building up a lot of trouble for yourself by pulling a stunt like that on the daughter of a chief inspector, yet you went ahead with it anyway,' Meadows mused.

'And that leads me to believe that whoever's jerking your strings must have a *great deal* of dirt on you.'

'To reiterate, my client denies knowing, before the event, that Miss Paniatowski would be abducted,' Coppersedge said.

'Your client is sweating like a pig on a slaughterhouse conveyor belt,' Meadows replied. She turned her attention to Sutton. 'Whoever it is who's got this hold on you, he won't save you, you know. Your only chance, Robert, old chap, is to make a deal with me.'

'We've heard enough,' Coppersedge said. 'Either charge my client or allow him to leave.'

'All right,' Meadows agreed easily. 'If that's the way you want to play it, then I'll charge him.'

Coppersedge and Sutton exchanged anxious glances, but said nothing.

'Well?' Meadows asked. '*Is* that the way you want to play it?'

'What would you be charging my client with?' Mr Coppersedge said cautiously.

'I've been thinking about that, and I've decided that facilitating paedophilia has a nice ring to it,' Meadows told him.

Coppersedge relaxed. 'You'll never make that charge stick,' he scoffed. 'The girl was not sexually assaulted in any way.'

'How do you know that?' Meadows wondered.

'Well, was she?' Coppersedge asked, avoiding the question.

'No, she wasn't.'

'Then there you have it,' the solicitor said complacently.

'Ah, but you see, Dr Sutton didn't *know* that she wouldn't be molested when he set the whole thing up,' Meadows pointed out. 'And you don't get off a charge of bank robbery just because you find out when you open the safe that there's no money in it.'

'It's not the same thing at all,' the solicitor protested.

'Isn't it?' Meadows asked. 'Maybe you're right. I wouldn't know, because I'm not as clever as you. But the one thing I am sure of is that if Robert here doesn't take a deal, his daughter will – because if there's only one seat in the lifeboat, Ellie will make damn sure she's got her pert little bottom on it.'

'Ellie?' Sutton gasped.

'Oh, I'll be arresting her, too. Didn't I mention that?'

'But you can't!'

'Of course I can. She was the one who invited Louisa to the party – she's as guilty as you are, Robert.'

'This is blackmail!' the solicitor said.

'It's a statement of intent,' Meadows countered.

Sutton really was sweating now.

'If . . . if I tell you what I know, will I go to gaol?' he asked.

'I couldn't even begin to guess at that until I know what it is that you know,' Meadows said. 'But whatever punishment you receive, it will be considerably reduced if you cooperate.'

Sutton glanced at his solicitor, and Coppersedge nodded to confirm that was true.

'And what will happen to Ellie?' Sutton asked.

'If I'm happy with what you tell me, I'm willing to give Ellie a free pass,' Meadows said.

Sutton took a deep breath. 'I got a phone call at four o'clock on Monday morning,' he said. 'The man who called told me to organize a party and to make sure that Louisa was there.'

'What's the man's name?'

'I don't know. I didn't ask, and he didn't tell me. It wouldn't have been his real name, anyway.'

'Well, that sounds perfectly reasonable, doesn't it?' Meadows asked Coppersedge. 'A man you don't know asks you to do something thoroughly reprehensible, and you agree immediately.' She turned back to Sutton. 'Did he offer you money?'

'No – he reminded me that I had once known a girl called Brenda. And that was all he *needed* to say.'

'What's that supposed to mean?' Meadows demanded.

'It's a long story.'

'I like stories,' Meadows said, 'and as far as I'm concerned, the longer they are, the better. So let's hear it, Robert.'

The note from Tommy Sanders had arrived a few minutes after Paniatowski had left. In it, Sanders said that he wished to talk to Beresford as soon as possible, on a matter of some urgency, and that Beresford should not go to the back door, because the old man would be waiting for him in his front parlour.

The words 'front parlour' had been underlined.

And now here I am, in the front parlour of a man who, only yesterday, I suspected of being Len Hopkins' murderer, Beresford thought, as he looked around the room.

The parlour was immaculately clean and over-furnished. Neither the armchair in which he was sitting, nor the one in which the old man was hunched, showed much sign of wear, and the walls were covered with photographs of people long dead. A fire burned cheerily in the grate, but the room still had the musty smell of a place which is only used on special occasions.

'You can stuff your gas fires and your electric heaters up your backside,' Tommy Sanders said. 'There's no heat like that that comes from a coal fire. I love the stuff – even if it is bloody killing me.'

'You said you wanted to talk to me urgently,' Beresford pointed out.

'All in good time, lad, all in good time,' the old man said.

He coughed into a white handkerchief, and Beresford could see the flecks of blood.

'Do you know why I'm seeing you here, rather than in the kitchen?' Sanders asked.

'Because the kitchen is where you entertain your friends, and this is serious business,' Beresford said.

The old man laughed. 'Well done, lad. Nicely worked out. There's a chance you might turn out to be a good bobby in time – but you're not there yet, not by a long chalk. At the moment, to be honest, you're a bit of a bloody idiot.'

'I didn't come here to trade insults,' Beresford said.

'It's not an insult,' Sanders said. 'I'm just speaking the truth as I see it. I mean to say, who else but a bloody idiot would have arrested Susan Danvers for Len Hopkins' murder?'

Beresford stood up. 'I think I'll be going,' he said.

'You've arrested the wrong person, lad – and I can prove it,' Tommy Sanders said.

'You can *prove* it?'

'That's what I said. Sit down again, lad.'

Beresford sat.

'But *before* I prove it to you, we need to make a deal,' the old man said.

'What kind of deal?'

'What I'm about to tell you could give you grounds for charging my granddaughter, Becky, with obstructing the course of justice. You have to promise me that won't happen.'

Jesus Christ, he was going to admit that the alibi was a fake! Beresford thought. And then he was going to explain why he had *needed* the alibi. Or to put it another way, he was going to confess to the murder of Len Hopkins.

And if he did that – and if it was a true confession – it meant that despite all the evidence that seemed to be stacked up against Susan Danvers, the officer in charge of the case – Detective Inspector Colin-bloody-smart-arse-Beresford – had got the whole thing wrong.

'Would this obstruction of justice have anything to do with the alibi that Becky gave you?' he asked cautiously.

'It would,' Tommy Sanders confirmed.

So there it was. It was starting to look like he *had* been wrong about Susan – and Monika had been right.

How do you feel now, Inspector Hotshot? he asked himself. Still think you're capable of running an investigation on your own? Still think you know better than your boss?

'Becky won't be prosecuted for lying about being with you on Sunday night,' he said. 'You have my word on that.'

'All right, then, let's start at the beginning,' Tommy Sanders said. 'I . . . I didn't see Len . . . Hopkins at the brass . . . band competition . . .'

He was having another coughing attack, and this one was much more violent than the one he'd had earlier.

'It'll . . . it'll pass, this,' Sanders said between coughs, 'but it'll . . . take time . . . and you're . . . you're going to . . . have to be . . . patient.'

'Take your time, Mr Sanders,' Beresford said soothingly. 'There's no hurry at all.'

Nor was there, he thought, because no man is ever in a hurry to find out just how *big* a bloody idiot he's been.

It is young Robert Sutton's first term in Oxford and he is drinking in the Bulldog pub, across from Christchurch College, when he sees the girl sitting in the corner. She has long brown hair, and is strikingly beautiful, and when she notices him looking at her, she smiles.

'I went over to talk to her,' Sutton told Meadows. 'She said her name was Brenda, and that she hated it because it was so old-fashioned. I said I thought it was a beautiful name.'

'Men will say anything when they want to get into a girl's knickers,' Meadows said.

'Yes,' Sutton agreed, 'they will. We had a few drinks – more than I intended; I wasn't used to alcohol in those days – and then she suggested we went back to her flat.' He paused. 'It wasn't really her flat, of course.'

'Of course it wasn't,' agreed Meadows, who could probably have written the rest of the confession herself.

'She'd appeared to be rather shy in the pub, but the moment we got to the flat, she became a completely different person. It seemed like she couldn't wait to get me into bed. We made love for hours.' Sutton sighed. 'I'd never experienced anything like it before.'

'But when you woke up the next morning, she was gone, was she?' Meadows suggested.

'That's right,' Robert Sutton agreed. 'She was gone – but somebody else was there.'

Sutton wakes up feeling gloriously happy, and instead of opening his eyes, he just lies there, reliving the previous night.

And then he hears the man cough, and what had seemed like a dream rapidly turns into a nightmare.

The man is sitting on an upright chair quite close to the bed. He is in his thirties, and though the rest of his face is virtually expressionless, his eyes are hard and cold.

'Well, well, well, Mr Sutton,' he says, 'you have been a naughty boy, haven't you?'

There is a part of Sutton which wants to jump out of bed – naked as he is – and demand to know what this man is doing in Brenda's flat. But there is another part of him which simply wants to hide under the bedclothes.

'Are you interested in photography, Mr Sutton?' the man asks. 'Because if you are, you might like to see these.'

He slowly and carefully lays a series of photographs on the bed. They are all in sharp focus, and are all of Sutton and Brenda. Even though he is scared – and he is very scared – Sutton feels both proud of himself and aroused.

'So I went to bed with a girl,' he says, attempting to bluster his way out of the situation. 'What's that got to do with you?'

'You might also like to see this,' the man says.

He hands Sutton a birth certificate. The name on it is Brenda King, and from the date of birth, it seems she is fifteen years old.

'It was probably a fake, of course,' Sutton told Meadows. 'I realize that now. But at the time, I was little more than a kid myself, and I believed it was all true.'

'What did he want you to do?'

*'You're quite the little radical, aren't you, Robert?' the man asks.
'You've only been here a couple of months, but you're already
making an impact in the university's Communist Party, and there's
talk of co-opting you on to the committee.'*

*'I will not apologize for my beliefs,' Sutton says pompously. 'The
downfall of capitalism in inevitable, and it is the duty of the intel-
ligentsia to—'*

*'You really don't want to go to gaol for rape, now, do you?' the
man interrupts him.*

Sutton's mouth is suddenly very dry. 'No, I . . . no, I don't,' he croaks.

*'Then we'll have to see what we can do to prevent that terrible
thing happening, won't we?' the man says, and suddenly his voice
has a kindly, almost avuncular tone to it.*

'He told me that if I reported back to him on everything that happened
in Communist Party meetings, I'd have cleared my debt in three
years,' Sutton said. 'That's what he called it – clearing my debt. So
I did it, and I never heard from him – or any of his kind – again,
until the early hours of Monday morning.'

'The incident he was threatening you with happened over twenty
years ago, when you were a naïve student,' Meadows pointed out.
'You know now it was probably all faked, so why didn't you simply
call his bluff?'

'You don't understand,' Robert Sutton said. 'He wasn't threatening me with Brenda.'

'Then what was he threatening you with?'

'He was threatening me with *them* – the people behind him. By
mentioning Brenda, he was just underlining the fact that there's
nothing they won't do to get what they want.'

'You didn't even argue with him, did you?' Meadows asked
contemptuously. 'You didn't even *try* to put up a fight?'

'You're wrong,' Sutton replied. 'I told him that I wasn't going
to do it. I said that even if he continued to assure me that nothing
bad would happen to Louisa Paniatowski, I would never play a
part in the abduction of a child.'

'And what did he say to that?'

'He reminded me that I'd got a daughter of my own – and that's
when I knew I had no choice.'

Meadows was starting to feel sorry for the man, but there was
still a job to do, and she pushed all pity aside.

'What made them switch the day of the party from Friday to Monday?' she asked.

'It wasn't switched,' Robert Sutton said. 'It was always going to be on Monday.'

'But when Ellie called Louisa on Monday morning, she told her that it would be Friday.'

'The man said we had to do it that way, because if Ellie had told Louisa it was being held on Monday, Louisa would have said she couldn't go, because Tuesday was a school day.'

'But by the time you switched the days, Louisa would be so looking forward to it that she'd be prepared to break the rules?' Meadows guessed.

'That's right.'

'And did he tell you what you were supposed to do if her mother wouldn't let her go to a party on a Monday?'

'He told me not to worry about the mother. He said she'd be somewhere out in the sticks, investigating a murder.'

'And he said this to you at four o'clock on Monday morning?'

'Yes.'

At four o'clock on Monday morning, even Monika Paniatowski hadn't known she'd be investigating a murder, Meadows thought. At four o'clock on Monday morning, Len Hopkins' body hadn't even been *found*.

TWENTY-FOUR

The coughing fit had gone on for over half an hour, and the bottom of the enamel bowl which Tommy Sanders held shakily on his lap was spattered with spots of red and black.

He looked up at the waiting Beresford.

'This is how it will all end,' he gasped. 'One day, I'll start coughing and I'll never stop. I'll spew up what's left of my life into this bloody bowl, and then I'll be gone.'

'If you'd like me to come back later . . .' Beresford began.

'Haven't you been listening to what I've been saying, lad?' Tommy asked. 'There might not *be* a later, so let's get it over with now.'

The sick man was right, Beresford thought – he could go at any time.

'Do you mind if I take notes, Mr Sanders?' he asked, wishing he'd brought a tape recorder, so that he could have on record what would be – for him – a necessary humiliation.

'I don't mind what you do, lad, as long as you listen,' Tommy said. 'Now where was I? Oh yes, I was telling you that I didn't see Len Hopkins at the brass band competition.' The old man paused for a moment. 'No, that's not strictly true,' he continued. 'I did see Len, though it was only at a distance. But there was someone else I saw—'

'I couldn't really give a toss about what happened at the competition,' Beresford interrupted. 'It's the events of the night which followed it that I'm interested in.'

The moment the words were out of his mouth, he regretted saying them. He had broken one of the cardinal rules of questioning, he told himself – you *never* hurried a suspect, not even if you were desperate – as he was – to learn if you'd made a mistake.

Tommy was glaring at him through watery eyes. 'I'll tell my story in my own way, and at my own speed, lad,' he said, 'and if you don't want to listen, then you can just piss off.'

'I'm sorry,' Beresford said.

'And so you should be,' Tommy agreed. He was about to say more, then shook his head with frustration. 'Now see what you've done,' he continued, after a few moments, 'with all your interrupting. I've completely lost my train of thought.'

'You were saying that you didn't see Len close up at the competition,' Beresford prompted.

'That's right. I didn't see him close up – but I did see Susan Danvers. She was standing all by herself, behind the refreshment tent, and she was sobbing her eyes out. So I asked her what was wrong, and she said that bastard Len had kicked her out, just because his bloody pastor had told him to.'

And that gave you one more reason – on top of the political one you already had – to drive a pickaxe into Len's skull, Beresford thought.

But how had he managed to lace Len's cocoa with laxative?

Easy! Susan had a key to Len's front door, Tommy had asked her for it, and she had handed it over. So maybe Susan had been part of the murder plot after all – and if that were the case, arresting her would begin to look, in retrospect, like a very smart move by a young inspector in charge of his very first major investigation.

'Are you listening to me, lad, or are you off in a dream world of your own?' Tommy demanded.

'I'm sorry,' Beresford said. 'Go on with your story.'

'I can't describe how sorry I felt for her at that moment. Anyway, it was obvious to me that she was in no state to be left on her own, so I asked her if she'd like to come round here for a while when we got back to the village, and she said she would.'

'Did she come back on the coach with you?'

'No, she couldn't have faced that – not with all those people she knew looking at her – so we both came back on the regular service bus.' He paused again. 'Don't you believe me, lad?'

'I'm not sure,' Beresford admitted. 'I thought everybody in the village was very keen on the brass band competition.'

'We were.'

'And yet you were willing to leave before the end?'

Tommy shrugged. 'The results had already been announced, so it was all over, bar the shouting. Besides, the state Susan was in, I couldn't let her make the journey all by herself. And if you still doubt I'm telling the truth, just ask the other people who took the coach if they saw me on the return trip, and they'll tell you they didn't.'

'I didn't realize before that Susan was such a good friend of yours,' Beresford said.

'She isn't,' Tommy said. 'I knew her, of course – I know most people in this village – so we'd nod to each other if we passed in the street. But that was about as far as it went.'

'Then I don't see . . .'

'You don't see why I'd have gone to all that trouble for a casual acquaintance?'

'Yes.'

Tommy shook his head sadly. 'Let me tell you a story,' he said. 'It might not make sense to you at the start, but it should do by the time I get to the end.'

'I'm listening,' Beresford said, determined not to repeat his earlier mistake of rushing the old man.

'It's a terrible thing when the roof of a coal seam collapses,'

Tommy said. 'You can tell it's going to happen before it actually does – I can't explain how, but you do – and you know there's nothing you can do about it. When it does come down, the whole seam rocks as if it was being shaken by an angry giant, and the air gets so thick that you can't see your hand in front of your face.'

'That happened to you, did it?' Beresford asked.

'It happened to me,' Tommy agreed. 'For a few seconds, I was in shock, and then I realized that I was one of the lucky ones, because I hadn't been buried alive. After a while, the air started to clear a bit, and I could see the caved-in section about a dozen yards away from me. Now what I was *supposed to do* in them circumstances was make my way to the cage and wait for the rescue team to arrive. They've got all the right equipment, you see. They shore up the roof as they go along, to make sure it doesn't collapse on *them*.'

'But you didn't do that,' Beresford guessed.

'I didn't,' Tommy agreed. 'I was going to, but then I heard this voice. It wasn't a voice I recognized – I found out later that the feller had only been taken on a couple of days earlier – but it was calling out, "Help me, please help me." I knew it was madness to go any closer to the cave-in, but I did it anyway, and I pulled him clear.' Tommy paused. 'Do you get the point, lad?'

Beresford nodded. 'When you heard his cry for help, you felt you had no choice but to go and help him.'

'And when I heard Susan's cry for help, I didn't stop to ask myself whether she was a mate or not, I went to help her,' Tommy said.

Beresford nodded for a second time, and realized he was feeling slightly ashamed of himself.

'So you returned to Bellingsworth on the service bus,' he said, doing his best to sound like a crisp and efficient police officer again.

'That's right. I brought her back home, and we had a cup of tea and a bit of a chat. Then, when it got to about half past six, I asked her if she fancied coming to the Miners' Institute to celebrate the victory, and she said she'd rather not, but she didn't mind if I went. So I left her here, and went on my own.'

The key! a voice screamed in Beresford's head. Tell me when she gave you the key to Len Hopkins' front door!

'You know what happened next,' Tommy continued. 'I got into a fight with Len. Now there's a real comic turn for you – two old men battling it out. Anyway, at the time, I thought I'd lost my temper with him over the strike, but looking back on it, I think I hit him because I was so angry about what he'd done to Susan.'

And *that* was when you finally decided that you were going to kill him! Beresford's inner voice yelled.

'I left the Institute soon after Len, and came straight back here,' Tommy said. 'Me and Susan spent some time together . . .'

'Spent some time together? What you really mean is that you had sex,' Beresford said, before he could stop himself.

'Sex!' Tommy repeated in disgust. 'That's all that you young fellers these days call what goes on between a man and a woman, isn't it? There's no tenderness any more. No compassion. You just "ram it home", don't you?' Tommy paused for a moment to cough into the enamel bowl. 'So tell me, Inspector Beresford, how many women have you *had sex with* in the last month or so?'

Too many, said the voice in Beresford's head.

He was shocked to hear his own mind betray him like that.

Too many!

How could it be *too* many?

But it was, he thought. It was too many because it was turning him into a person he didn't like very much – a person who was constantly challenging Monika, who took offence far too easily, who just had to be *right*.

'Well?' Tommy asked.

Beresford took a deep breath. 'We're not here to talk about me,' he said. 'I asked you a question you've still not answered, so I'll ask it again. Did you have sex with Susan Danvers?'

'We didn't go upstairs, get stark bollock naked, and jump all over each other, if that's what you mean.'

'So what *did* you do?'

'We did what a dying man and a broken-hearted woman *could do* to give each other a little comfort,' Tommy said. 'It wasn't very satisfactory – neither of us ever thought it would be – but at least we did it for the right reasons.'

'And then what happened?'

'And then we talked – until about half past four in the morning.

I wanted her to stay for the rest of the night, but she said she had to get home.'

Half past four is too late! Beresford's voice said. Len was already dead by then!

'I told her it was pointless leaving at that time, but she said she needed to get a couple of hours' sleep before she made Len's breakfast for him,' Tommy said. 'I asked why she wanted to go making his breakfast, when he'd already sacked her, and she told me she'd been paid her wages till the end of the week, and she intended to work out her notice.'

That's what she told me, too, Beresford thought.

'That was just an excuse, of course,' Tommy said. 'It was nothing to do with her wages at all. I think she was still hoping to get back with him. And I think that the real reason she went home was because she was already regretting what we'd done, and had convinced herself that if she woke up in her own bed that morning, it'd be like it had never happened.'

He was lying about the whole thing, Beresford thought. He just *had* to be lying.

'Why did you use your granddaughter as your alibi for Sunday night?' he asked.

'I agreed to use her because that was what she wanted. My little Becky was terrified that I might end up going to prison, you see.' Tommy chuckled, though it was a sad, wounded chuckle, and it started him coughing again. 'I think . . . I think that maybe there was a part of her that thought I *had* killed Len. Anyway, she asked, and I couldn't turn her down.'

'But if you already had an alibi – as you claim – you wouldn't have needed one from her.'

Tommy shook his head, almost despairingly. 'You just don't see it, do you, Inspector Beresford? I would never have used Susan as an alibi, not even if I'd been arrested – not even if I'd been tried and found guilty.'

'Why not?'

'Why not? Because they're nice people in this village – as nice as you'll find anywhere – but even nice people can be cruel sometimes.'

'I'm not following you,' Beresford admitted.

'I know you're not,' Tommy Sanders agreed. 'If I'd used Susan as my alibi, it would have made her an even bigger laughing stock than she already was. Poor Susan Danvers, folk would say. She was so desperate for a man – any man – that when the feller she'd faithfully looked after for twenty years jilted her, she fell right into the arms of some poor old bugger with only half a lung. I couldn't have done that to her, and the only reason I'm telling you now is because, like me, *she'd* rather go to gaol than admit where she was – and I can't let that happen.'

It could all still be a lie, Beresford told himself – but he knew, deep down, that it wasn't.

'I want to ask you a favour, Mr Beresford,' Tommy said. 'It wasn't part of our deal, but I want to ask it anyway.'

'Go ahead,' Beresford said.

'I want you to try and stop what I've just told you from becoming public knowledge around the village. I'm not asking that for myself, you understand – I'm too close to death to give a bugger what people think about me – I'm asking it for poor Susan.'

'If what you've told me is true, then I *will* try,' Beresford promised. 'It's the least I can do.'

'Aye,' Tommy Sanders agreed. 'It is.'

TWENTY-FIVE

Monika Paniatowski sat with Kate Meadows at their usual table in the public bar of the Drum and Monkey, her whole body trembling with rage at her enemies – and anger at herself.

'I should have worked it out much sooner,' she told Meadows. 'I knew that Forsyth was in Whitebridge. I should have seen that when something as senseless – as absolutely bloody pointless – as Louisa's abduction happened, he just had to be behind it.'

'You're being too hard on yourself, boss,' Meadows said.

'And if that wasn't enough, there was the fact that the bastard who kidnapped Louisa told her his name was Colin. Why would he have done that?'

'Because he knew that Louisa was very fond of her *Uncle* Colin, so she'd associate the name with nice people, and that would make her more vulnerable to what he suggested next?' Meadows suggested.

'Exactly,' Paniatowski agreed. 'We'd never have come up with that idea, but Forsyth did – because that's the way his twisted tortuous mind functions. And I should have spotted that mind at work. *Why* didn't I spot it?'

'You were so worried about your daughter that you weren't thinking straight,' Meadows said, 'which, of course, is probably what he was banking on.'

'And even now that I know he did it, I've no idea *why* he did it,' Paniatowski agonized. 'Was he punishing me? And if he was punishing me, what was he punishing me *for*?'

'I don't know,' Meadows admitted.

'There's something else I don't understand,' Paniatowski said. 'When Forsyth rang Sutton, at four o'clock on Monday morning, he already knew that Len Hopkins was dead. I'm right about that, aren't I?'

'You are.'

'So if he knew Hopkins was dead long before anyone else knew – anybody, that is, apart from the killer – we have to assume that the murder was carried out on Forsyth's instructions, don't we?'

'I don't see that there's any other conclusion we *could* draw,' Meadows agreed.

'But of all the people he could have chosen to have killed, why did he select Len Hopkins? Forsyth wants to prevent the strike, and Len was one of its biggest opponents within the village. From Forsyth's perspective, the old man must have seemed like a real asset. Having Len murdered would be like shooting himself in the foot and—'

Paniatowski suddenly stopped talking, and turned pale.

'What's the matter?' Meadows asked worriedly.

'Knowing what we know now, who do we think killed Len Hopkins?'

'The chances are, it was the young man who visited him, claiming to be from the DES, and . . . and . . .'

'And that was the same young man who abducted Louisa,' Paniatowski said shakily. 'Forsyth deliberately chose to put my daughter in a car with a murderer!'

She picked up her glass, and knocked back the rest of her vodka.

'I'll make the bastard pay for that. I don't know how I'll do it yet – but I swear I'll make him pay.'

'You can't, boss,' Meadows said softly.

'Can't I? Is that what you really think?'

'Listen, there'll be no way you can get at him legally – he'll have covered his tracks too well for that to happen.'

'Yes, he will,' Paniatowski agreed, already starting to look defeated.

'So what are you going to do instead?' Meadows asked. 'Are you going to kill him?'

'Yes – if that's the only option open to me, then that's what I'll bloody well do.'

'No, you won't. Once you've calmed down, you'll realize that if you do kill him, you'll end up in gaol – or maybe even dead yourself.'

'I don't care. I'll take the risk.'

'And are you prepared to risk Louisa's future, as well?' Meadows asked.

Paniatowski sighed. 'You know I'm not.'

'So you're stuck, aren't you? He's got all the power of the state behind him, and you've got nothing. And however much you might hate that particular idea, you'll have to learn to accept it – because you've really got no other choice.'

'What a bloody mess,' Paniatowski said.

'Yes, that's what it is,' Meadows agreed. 'A bloody mess.'

The poster which Monika Paniatowski had had printed – and which Beresford had instructed two of his detective constables to paste up all over Bellingsworth – was the size of a large envelope, which meant it was small enough to paste to lamp posts, yet too large to be easily overlooked.

Two-thirds of the poster was taken up by the sketch that the police artist had produced from the description which Louisa had given him, and the text underneath it said:

The Whitebridge Police want to question this man.
If you think you might have seen him,
please ring the number below immediately.

The poster had already been up all over Bellingsworth for several hours when Becky Sanders, stepping down from the school bus, saw an example pasted to the bus shelter.

Two other school kids – a boy and a girl – had followed her down the steps, and noticing the effect the poster seemed to be having on her, went to see what all the fuss was about.

'It's just like one of them wanted posters you see in westerns,' said the boy with some relish. 'Wanted – dead or alive!'

'Do you think he was the one what did in poor old Mr Hopkins?' the girl asked.

'Bound to be,' the boy said confidently. 'They wouldn't have bothered putting it up if he wasn't.' He tilted his head to one side. 'He's an ugly-looking bugger, isn't he?'

'He most certainly is not,' the girl disagreed. 'If you want the truth, I think he's rather cute . . .'

'Cute!' the boy scoffed.

'. . . and if I had the choice of waking up beside him or waking up beside you, I know which one I'd choose.'

'If you think he's better looking than me, you must be going soft in the head,' the boy said, stung. 'I'm so good-looking, I could be in films.'

'Yeah – horror films!' the girl said. 'Who do *you* think is cuter, Becky – the feller on the poster or young Frankenstein here?'

They'd been totally absorbed in their own little argument, and it was only now – when they turned their full attention on to Becky, in anticipation of her supporting one or the other of them – that they noticed she was sobbing uncontrollably.

It was said that the first forty-eight hours of any murder investigation were the most crucial ones, Colin Beresford thought, as he stood on the pavement outside the church hall and looked down the street. Well, they'd been running this investigation for more than forty-eight hours, and they were no further on now than when they'd arrived in the village on Monday morning.

'I've made a mess of this whole case, haven't I, Jack?' he asked DC Crane, who was standing by his side.

'No, sir,' Crane replied. 'You've made a series of perfectly logical assumptions which, as chance would have it, happened to be wrong.' He paused for a moment. 'But if I could just make one criticism . . .'

'Yes?'

'Forget it. It's not my place to say.'

'Were you about to say that ever since I started bedding women,

I've been strutting around like I was the king of the jungle?' Beresford wondered.

'I wouldn't have put it quite like that,' Crane said cautiously.

'Yes, you would,' Beresford told him.

'Yes, I would,' Crane agreed.

'And is there any cure?'

'It'll wear off in time,' Crane promised. 'It's a stage that all fellers have to go through.'

Beresford grinned. 'But most of them don't have go through that stage when they're already in their thirties and a detective inspector in the Mid Lancs CID?' he suggested.

Jack Crane returned the grin. 'Look at it this way, sir, if I'd been given the choice of being a complete arsehole for a couple of months, or a virgin for the rest of my life, I'd have plumped for being a short-term arsehole any day of the week. And besides that—'

He broke off abruptly, as he caught sight of a schoolgirl running frantically – almost dementedly – down the street towards them.

'Isn't that Becky Sanders?' asked Beresford, who had noticed her too.

'I think it is,' Crane said.

The girl came to a halt in front of them, and for a few seconds just stood there, gasping for breath as the tears poured down her face.

'What's the matter, Becky?' Beresford asked.

'Why have you put up those pictures of my boyfriend all over the village?' Becky demanded. 'Is it because you think he killed Mr Hopkins?'

'I think you'd better come inside, and wait while we fetch your mother,' Beresford said softly.

'He didn't do it!' Becky screamed. 'You have to believe that! Gary didn't do it!'

The Drum and Monkey had closed its doors to its customers more than an hour earlier, but the normal rules did not apply to what had been once been Charlie Woodend's team and was now Monika Paniatowski's, and the two women were still sitting at the table as the landlord cleared up around them.

'Do you know where Forsyth will be right at this minute?' Paniatowski asked.

'No,' Meadows replied. 'Do you?'

'Oh yes,' Paniatowski said bitterly. 'He'll be in a suite at the Royal Victoria – waiting for me.'

'Waiting for *you!*'

'He likes to see me. He likes to play his little mind games with me. It's almost like sex to him. It may even be *instead of* sex.'

'Will you go?' Meadows asked.

Paniatowski shook her head. 'Not this time. I daren't. Despite what you said, I still don't trust myself enough to get within striking distance of him.'

The phone behind the bar rang, and the landlord picked it up.

'It's for you, Chief Inspector,' he said.

Paniatowski walked over to the bar and took the phone from him.

'Is that you, boss?' asked the troubled voice on the other end of the line.

'It's me,' Paniatowski confirmed. 'Is something wrong, Colin?'

'I need you over here in Bellingsworth,' Beresford said. 'I need you right now.'

TWENTY-SIX

The three of them sat at a table in the church hall, Beresford and Paniatowski on one side, a thin, sobbing Becky Sanders on the other.

'Tell me what you told Inspector Beresford earlier, sweetheart,' Paniatowski said softly.

'I killed him,' Becky sobbed. 'It wasn't Gary, it was me. Gary wasn't anywhere near here when it happened.'

'You're going to have to give us a little more detail than that,' Paniatowski said.

'I hit him with the short-handled pickaxe, while he was sitting on the lavvy,' Becky said.

'How did you know he'd be on the lavvy?'

'I just *knew.*'

'I don't think that's quite true,' Paniatowski said. 'I think the reason you knew he'd be there was because you'd put laxative in his milk.'

'That's right, I did. I'd forgotten that,' Becky said.

'You must have slipped the laxative in while Mr Hopkins was in Accrington, at the brass band concert,' Paniatowski suggested.

'Yes, that's when I did it.'

'So how did you get into the house? Did you have a key?'

'No, the . . . the door wasn't locked.'

'How did you get to the toilet, later that night? Did you go through the house again?'

'No, I was waiting in the back alley. I heard him come down the yard, and open the lavvy door, and then I counted very slowly to twenty.'

'That sounds like something you were *told* to do,' Paniatowski said.

'It wasn't. I just did it.'

'What happened next?

'I had the pickaxe in one hand, and my flashlight in the other, but once I was in the yard, I put the flashlight in my mouth, so I'd have two hands free for the pick. I opened the lavvy door, and I could see him sitting there. His eyes were very big. I think that was because I was shining the light in them.'

'It would have been.'

'He said, "Is that you, Susan?" I wanted to say it wasn't, but I couldn't speak because of the flashlight.' Becky paused. 'I don't know why I wanted to say that I wasn't Susan.'

'It doesn't matter.'

'Did he try to pull his trousers up?' Beresford asked.

'No, he just sat there.'

'But his trousers were round his ankles, were they?'

Becky blushed. 'I don't know.'

'You don't know?'

'I didn't want to look down, in case I accidentally saw his thingy.'

'Carry on,' Paniatowski said.

'I . . . I swung the pickaxe at him. When it hit him, it really shook, and my wrists tingled. That was when I dropped my flashlight. I didn't mean to, it just fell out of my mouth. And when it hit the ground, it went out.'

'We didn't find any flashlight at the scene,' Paniatowski said.

'No, you wouldn't have. I picked it up again. It wasn't easy in the dark, but I knew I had to find it, because I'd been told that I should make sure I didn't leave anything behind.'

'You'd been *told*?'

'I mean, I thought that. *I thought* I shouldn't leave anything behind.'

'Then what did you do?'

'I went into the back alley . . .'

'No, you didn't,' Paniatowski said firmly. 'If you want us to believe you, Becky – if you want to convince us it was you, and not Gary, who killed Mr Hopkins – then you can't lie to us about *anything*.'

'I ran back towards the house,' Becky said miserably. 'I was nearly there when I realized I still had the pickaxe in my hand.'

'So what did you do with it?'

'I threw it against the wash house wall.'

'Why did you decide to leave through the house, instead of going into the alley?'

'I don't know.'

'And how did you manage to lock the front door behind you?'

'I don't remember.'

Paniatowski risked a sideways glance at Beresford. It was clear from the expression on his face that he believed that Becky really had killed Len Hopkins – and so did she.

'What I still don't understand is why you killed him, Becky,' Paniatowski said. 'He was a nice man.'

'He wasn't a nice man at all,' Becky said stubbornly.

'You killed a nice man, who everybody liked,' Paniatowski prodded. 'You robbed him of his life. You *murdered* him!'

It was those last words that connected – that hit the switch in Becky's brain. Her eyes widened, and her face was suddenly transformed into a mask of arrogance and pitilessness.

'It's not murder to kill a man like Len Hopkins,' she said, in a harsh voice, quite unlike her own. 'He's a louse. He's scum. He's against everything your grandfather ever worked for or believed in. And he'll still be alive when your granddad's dead. He'll stand there, looking down at your granddad's grave, and laughing. And don't you think your granddad knows that? Don't you think it's eating away at him worse than the coal dust? If only Len Hopkins was gone, your granddad could die happy. And it wouldn't be any worse than squashing a bug, Becky – it wouldn't be any worse than swatting a fly.'

The mask melted away, revealing the frightened child beneath it.

'That was what Gary told you, wasn't it?' Paniatowski asked gently.

'No,' Becky said, in a dazed voice. 'No, he . . .'

'I'll tell you what I think happened on Sunday night,' Paniatowski said. 'You went up to your bedroom, and then you climbed down the drainpipe. You're very good at that, aren't you? Remember. you showed me how easy it was?'

'I remember.'

'Gary was waiting for you in the alley . . .'

'No!'

'He was waiting for you in the alley,' Paniatowski repeated firmly. 'He told you that Mr Hopkins would have to go to the lavvy at some time in the night . . .'

'No!'

'. . . and the reason he was sure of that was because he'd already spiked Mr Hopkins' cocoa with laxative. Not his *milk*, Becky – his *cocoa*!'

'I meant his cocoa when I said his milk,' Becky whimpered. 'You've been getting me all confused.'

'It was Gary who told you to use the pickaxe, because that was the weapon a miner would have used. And when you'd killed Mr Hopkins – when you'd *murdered* Mr Hopkins, when you'd smashed the poor man's skull in – it was Gary who was waiting for you in the house. Isn't that true?'

'No!'

'It just as we thought,' Paniatowski said to Beresford. 'She's making the whole thing up. She was the one waiting in the house, and Gary was the one who killed Len Hopkins.'

'That's not true,' Becky said. 'It was Gary who was in the house.'

'And what was he doing there?' Paniatowski asked.

'He . . . he . . .'

'You can't go back on it now – you've already admitted he was there.'

'He . . . he was looking for a bit of paper,' Becky mumbled. 'He said it was very important that he took it away with him.'

That would be the letter which was supposed to have come from the Department of Education and Science, but, in fact, had come from a very different department, Paniatowski thought.

'He found what he was looking for, didn't he?' she asked.

'Yes,' Becky admitted. 'And when he found it, he screwed it up, and put it in his pocket, as if it didn't matter at all.'

It didn't matter. All that was important was that the police didn't find it in the house after Hopkins' death, and start asking awkward questions.

'You left through the front door, didn't you?' Paniatowski asked.

'Yes.'

'And Gary locked it behind him, so he must have had a key.'

'Not a proper key. It was like a lot of metal rods.'

'Skeleton keys?'

'I think that's what he called them.'

And he'd locked the door behind him to muddy the issue, Paniatowski thought – he'd done it so they'd waste time wondering who had a key.

'When you persuaded your granddad to lie about you having been together Sunday night, he thought that was because you wanted to give him an alibi. But that wasn't it at all, was it? You wanted *him* to give *you* an alibi. And you didn't think that up yourself, did you? That was another one of Gary's ideas.'

'Gary said he couldn't stand the thought of me going to gaol. He said that if I had an alibi, everything would be all right.'

'Do you ever feel sorry for killing Mr Hopkins?'

'Sometimes. But Gary said I shouldn't. Gary said I'd done a wonderful thing – a *kind* thing.'

'I think that's all we need,' Beresford said to Paniatowski.

'You do believe me now, don't you?' Becky asked pleadingly. 'You do believe that Gary was in the house at the time I killed Mr Hopkins, and that he had nothing at all to do with it.'

'I believe he was in the house,' Paniatowski said.

'I couldn't bear it if anything bad happened to him,' Becky told her. 'I love him, you see. I'm having his baby.'

TWENTY-SEVEN

The cold wind had blown in from the moors – where it had been doing all it could to freeze the sheep to death – and now it was rushing along the streets of Whitebridge in search of human victims. What few pedestrians there were out on those streets walked with their hands in their pockets and their heads bent forward, but even then, the wind's icy fingers clawed at their faces and found a way under their tightly wrapped scarves to their vulnerable necks.

The two women standing in front of the Royal Victoria looked up at the suite on the top floor of the hotel.

'I don't want you going up there to talk to him, boss,' Kate Meadows said. 'I really don't.'

'I don't much like the idea myself, but I've no choice in the matter,' Paniatowski replied. 'A deal has got to be made – and I'm the only one who can make it.'

'Then let me come with you,' Meadows pleaded.

Paniatowski shook her head. 'If you're there, we'll get nothing. He likes it to be just me. He thinks we have a special relationship.'

'You *do* have a special relationship,' Meadows told her.

'Yes, I try to deny it, but deep down inside myself, I know that we do,' Paniatowski admitted. 'And some nights, I wake up in a cold sweat, just thinking about it.' She braced herself, and took a step closer to the hotel's main entrance. 'Wish me luck.'

'Good luck, boss,' Meadows replied, and then, when Paniatowski was almost at the door, she added, 'I'm half-hoping that he'll refuse to see you.'

Paniatowski stopped and turned around. 'He'll see me,' she said confidently. 'He needs to know if I've found out his secret.'

Paniatowski was met in the vestibule of the suite by a short, broad man with a shaved head.

'I'm going to have to search you,' he said.

'You do know who I am?' Paniatowski asked.

'Yes,' the man replied. 'That's why I need to search you.'

Paniatowski spread her arms. 'Then let's get it over with.'

The process was slow, thorough – and as asexual as if the man had been searching a wardrobe. When he'd completed it, he said, 'Follow me,' and led her into the lounge.

Forsyth was sitting behind the desk, and an upright chair had been positioned on the other side of it, facing him.

'Ah, my dear Monika, what a pleasure to see you again,' he said. 'I take it that Symons has introduced himself.'

'In a manner of speaking,' Paniatowski said.

Forsyth gave the other man a disapproving look. 'You really don't have any concept of the social niceties, do you, Clive?' he asked. He turned back to Paniatowski. 'Symons is my valet,' he said.

'Symons is your bodyguard,' Paniatowski countered.

Forsyth nodded. 'He's that, too. You're not going to cause him any trouble, are you, Monika?'

'No,' Paniatowski replied. 'It's already been pointed out to me, by my sergeant, that there are some battles I simply can't win.'

'Excellent. My respect for Sergeant Meadows – who is not quite who you think she is – increases daily,' Forsyth said. He gestured to the chair. 'Do take a seat, Monika. Can I offer you a glass of vodka?'

'No,' Paniatowski said, sitting down.

Forsyth looked hurt. 'But it's Zubrowka – your favourite. I ordered it specially.'

'Still no,' Paniatowski said, sitting down.

Forsyth sighed. 'I do wish you'd try to be more civilized during these meetings of ours, Monika,' he said.

'I want to know why you had to have my daughter abducted,' Paniatowski told him.

'We'll come to that later,' Forsyth promised. 'Before that, I'd like to know how things are in Bellingsworth. What have you been doing since you made your arrest?'

She could argue – could say that she wouldn't answer any of his questions before he answered the one that was truly important to her – but she knew that there would be no point.

'I got our technical boys to check out a few of the buildings in the village,' Paniatowski said.

'Oh yes?'

'They found listening devices in the Miners' Institute and Tommy Sanders' house. There weren't any bugs in Len Hopkins' home, but that, I assume, is because they were removed on Sunday night.'

'You surely don't expect me to either deny or confirm that, do you?' Forsyth asked.

'How long have you had an interest in the village?' Paniatowski asked.

'For months,' Forsyth replied. 'We moved in soon after the Yom Kippur War, which was long before most of the miners even realized there was the possibility of a strike.'

'And your aim was to influence the strike ballot when it was eventually called?'

'It was.'

'You won't win, you know.'

'On the contrary, I expect the Bellingsworth miners to vote massively against the strike.'

'But most of the other pits won't. There *will be* a strike.'

'I think you rather misunderstand our purpose in Bellingsworth,' Forsyth said. 'We regard it as a laboratory, in which we can try out various strategies and analyse their effectiveness.'

'And why would you want to do that?'

'The miners must be crushed – and crushed decisively. If Britain is to survive as a world class nation, there is simply no choice in the matter. But they won't be crushed this time, because our current prime minister, Mr Heath, hasn't got the stomach for a long and bitter fight. However, we will eventually have a prime minister with more spirit, and when she takes on the miners—'

'She?' Paniatowski interrupted.

Forsyth smiled like a mischievous schoolboy.

'Did I say *she*?' he asked. 'I meant, of course, *he*. I wouldn't want you to think, when the Conservatives get rid of Heath and elect a new leader, that I've had anything to do with it. Oh no, that would never do at all.'

'You're full of shit,' Paniatowski said.

'At any rate,' Forsyth continued, ignoring the comment, 'when a prime minister comes along who *does* have the stomach for a fight, we will give *him* all our support, and it is then that the lessons we have learned in Bellingsworth will be invaluable.'

'You fixed the brass band competition in Accrington, didn't you?' Paniatowski asked.

'We had a quiet word with two or three of the judges, and pointed out there are certain things about their private lives they might not care to become public knowledge, if that's what you mean,' Forsyth said.

'That is what I mean,' Paniatowski agreed. 'What was the point in fixing the competition?'

'We come back to our laboratory idea again,' Forsyth said. 'Harold Wilson – who has twice been elected prime minister, and will be again – has a theory that when people feel happy, they tend to opt for the status quo. Thus, he has always tried to schedule elections at a time when the weather is pleasant, or when England is basking in the glow of a sporting triumph.'

'So you thought that if the miners won the brass band competition, they'd be less inclined to vote for a strike?'

'Exactly.'

'And has it worked?'

Forsyth looked slightly uncomfortable. 'Events have moved on since the competition, so we have no real way of assessing its impact,' he said.

'Events have moved on,' Paniatowski repeated. 'Is that another way of saying that Len Hopkins was killed?'

'It is.'

'Len's letter never got as far as the Department of Education and Science, did it?' Paniatowski asked.

'It did not. We intercepted it before it had even left the village.'

'And you wrote back to him on DES notepaper.'

'Or a reasonable facsimile thereof.'

'What was point of Gary's visiting him?'

'Gary?'

'That was the name by which your agent was known to Becky Sanders.'

'Ah, indeed. The purpose of his visit was to give Len Hopkins quite a large amount of money.'

'But the money was not intended to finance his research into his ancestry, was it?'

'No, it was to be used as a cash incentive for miners who were still not sure which way to vote in the forthcoming ballot.'

'It was to be used to bribe them, you mean.'

'If you choose to look at it that way.'

'That doesn't sound like one of *your* schemes, at all,' Paniatowski said. 'It seems far too crude.'

'It is crude, when stated as baldly as that,' Forsyth agreed. 'But if it had been handled correctly, Len Hopkins would have been left with the impression that he'd been co-opted by the DES, as part of a general scheme to widen workers' educational opportunities.'

'But it wasn't handled correctly?'

'Unfortunately, it was not. The boy . . . did you say Becky called him Gary . . .?'

'Yes.'

'Gary is one of our less experienced operatives, and the only result of the conversation was that Hopkins was left with the unfortunate idea that we were trying to recruit him as a secret agent.'

'Which you were.'

'Of course.'

'Was that when you decided to kill him?' Paniatowski asked.

A single snowflake fluttered gently through the air, and landed on Meadows' sleeve. She looked down at it, and shivered. The snowflake melted, but another quickly took its place. And then another. The snow storm, which had been threatened for so long, had finally arrived.

Meadows stamped her feet, rubbed her hands together, and looked up at the suite on the top floor of the Royal Victoria.

'How long has the boss been in there now?' asked a voice to her left.

'About half an hour, sir,' Meadows replied, keeping her gaze fixed on the window.

'I'm sorry,' Beresford said.

'Forget it,' Meadows replied.

'No, I can't do that,' Beresford told her. 'I've been an arsehole to you and everybody connected with this investigation.'

'Especially the boss,' Meadows said.

'Especially the boss,' Beresford agreed. 'She says things are fine between us again, but I don't know if she'll ever *really* forgive me.'

'She'll forgive you,' Meadows said confidently.

'How can you be so sure?'

'She'll forgive you because she loves you,' Meadows said. She paused. 'Don't get me wrong – I don't mean she loves Rock-hard Colin, the Ram of Whitebridge. He's a bit crude for her taste.'

'I'm starting to think he's a bit crude for mine,' Beresford said.

'But you are a big part of her life, and she doesn't want to lose you,' Meadows continued.

'What about you?' Beresford asked. 'How do you feel?'

'Well, for a start, I *don't* love you.'

'I know that,' Beresford said. 'But do you forgive me?'

Meadows turned to face him. 'If I was the inspector and you were the sergeant, I'd tell you that I might eventually forgive you, but that for the moment, you were on probation.'

'Tell me anyway,' Beresford said.

'You're on probation,' Meadows said.

Beresford grinned. 'So I'll have to watch my step, won't I?'

'It would seem like a good idea.'

The snow was more heavy now, landing on their hair, melting on the sleeves of their coats.

'How long are you going to stay here?' Beresford asked.

'Until she comes out again,' Meadows told him. 'You, too?'

'Me, too,' Beresford agreed.

He looked up at the suite on the top of floor of the Royal Victoria, and wondered just how well – or how badly – things were going up there.

'Do you think Monika will get her deal?' he asked.

'I don't know,' Meadows admitted. 'It depends on how much Forsyth wants to guard his secret.'

'Assuming he *has got* a secret to hide,' Beresford pointed out.

'Yes, assuming that,' Meadows agreed.

TWENTY-EIGHT

'We did *not* kill Len Hopkins,' Forsyth told Paniatowski firmly. 'I want to be quite clear on that point. We are strictly prohibited, within our remit, from taking life unless it is a case of self-protection.'

'So you used poor little Becky Sanders to do your killing, instead,' Paniatowski said in disgust. 'You scrambled her brain up so much that on Monday morning, her main concern was not that she had taken a life but that she had a history test.'

'She places great importance on her education – and that is just as it should be,' Forsyth said.

'So if you didn't have Len killed because he refused to handle your bribes for you, why did you have him killed? Even without working for you directly, he was still an asset, wasn't he?'

'Yes, but he was a greater asset dead than alive.'

'I don't understand.'

'If you kill a man, you make him a martyr. The death of Thomas à Becket meant that it was nearly four hundred years before the English crown felt really confident about clashing with the Catholic Church again. John F. Kennedy's legislative programme would never have been passed by Congress while he was alive, but in the wake of his assassination, it was swept through. Those are only two cases, but I could provide you with countless other examples of men who did more for their causes by dying than they could ever have done by continuing to live.'

'So if Tommy Sanders had died, it would have strengthened the will to strike, but Len Hopkins' death turned the wavering miners against it?'

'Exactly.'

'You wanted the right kind of reporter covering the story for Northern Television – one who would really stir things up – and that's why you put pressure on the management to assign it to Lynda Jenkins.'

'Ah, yes, dear Lynda. The woman may have impressively large breasts, but their size is as nothing when compared to the size of her mouth and her willingness to do whatever it takes to get on.'

'And, of course, things were only made worse by what Ed Thomas said at the meeting on Monday night.'

'Who?'

'Ed Thomas. He brought fraternal greetings from the Kent branch of the National Union of Mineworkers. Then he gave a speech in which he said that Len was a traitor to his class who had deserved to be killed, and that if a hundred more traitors were murdered, that could only be a good thing. By the time those Special Branch officers – who you'd conveniently arranged to be there – hustled him out of the building, the pro-strike and anti-strike miners were at each others' throats, and those men who were undecided were tilting towards the anti-strike side.'

'From which it would appear that if he really did want a strike, he should have moderated his words a little,' Forsyth said.

'He was a plant.'

'Are you sure of that?'

'I rang the Kent NUM.'

'And they said they'd never heard of him, I suppose.'

'Oh no, they'd heard of him. They even put him on the phone to me. He's a real firebrand.'

'Well, there you are, then.'

'He's also sixty-two years old, and lost his right arm in a mining accident twenty years ago. The "other" Ed Thomas was one of your people, wasn't he?'

'There'd be no point in denying it, because you simply wouldn't believe me,' Forsyth said.

'And anyway, it's true,' Paniatowski countered.

'And anyway, it's true,' Forsyth agreed. 'Have you worked out yet why, with great regret, I considered it necessary to abduct your daughter?'

'It was a way of removing me from the investigation.'

'Precisely. Suspicion can sometimes be a much more powerful force than certainty, and is undoubtedly more effective in dividing communities. So I didn't want *anyone* arrested for Hopkins' murder – and I certainly didn't want you to arrest the person who had *actually* carried it out, because that would have defeated the whole object of the exercise.'

'And you thought that Colin Beresford would make a worse job of handling the investigation than I would have done?'

'Just so – which is, when you think about it, quite a compliment to you.'

'I still don't understand why you went to such elaborate lengths to snatch Louisa,' Paniatowski confessed. 'You could have just had her grabbed off the street.'

'I did it the way I did to protect Louisa,' Forsyth said. 'If Gary had grabbed her off the street, she would have struggled and might well have got hurt, whereas, arranged the way it was, she had no suspicion that anything was wrong until she was too doped to care.'

'There's more to it than that,' Paniatowski said. 'There has to be.'

'It would also have been putting my operative – Gary – at more risk. There might have been witnesses. A police car might have arrived on the scene.' Forsyth paused. 'Besides, by using Dr Sutton, I was killing two birds with one stone.'

'I don't understand.'

'Sutton has grown into something of a force in left-wing politics in this area. He was starting to be annoying, and needed knocking off his perch. I thought that his being charged with child neglect would achieve that aim. If he'd just kept his mouth shut and taken his medicine, he would probably have got away with no more than a fine and a stern talking to, but it would have ruined his credibility in the namby-pamby left-wing circles. It never occurred to me that he would be foolish enough to break down and confess that he'd been working for me – so kudos to Sergeant Meadows for forcing that out of him.'

'So it was a mistake to use Sutton,' Paniatowski said, almost gleefully. 'You made a mistake!'

Forsyth bridled. 'I'd much prefer to call it a minor misjudgement,' he said.

'I'm sure you would – but you'd be wrong. If you hadn't used Sutton, I'd *never* have seen your hand at work in Bellingsworth,' Paniatowski insisted. 'I would have known about Gary, of course – but I'd never have connected him to you. Let's face facts, handling things the way you did was the sort of blunder an amateur would make.'

Forsyth had begun to redden. 'I made a hurried decision, in the early hours of the morning, and anyone else who found himself in my position would have acted in just the way I did.'

The words echoed around Paniatowski's brain.

I made a hurried decision, in the early hours of the morning.

And what was it Forsyth had said earlier?

Events have moved on since the competition, so we have no real way of assessing its impact.

She needed time to weigh those two statements – to work out exactly what they meant.

'I will arrest Gary, you know,' she said, buying herself that time. 'You need have no doubts about that.'

Forsyth's annoyance drained away, and was replaced by a glow of complacency.

'He boarded a plane in the early hours of Tuesday morning, and now he's far away from here, with a new identity,' he told Paniatowski. 'Now, no doubt when I say "far away", you think I am referring to Australia, and that may well be the case, but it could equally be Canada, the United States, New Zealand, South Africa, or anywhere else in the English-speaking world. You'll never find him, Monika.'

'Then let's forget him,' Paniatowski said easily. 'Let's talk about you, instead.'

'Me?'

'I know you. You plan everything out long in advance – you consider every little detail – so what were you doing making a hurried decision in the early hours of Monday morning?'

'There are many things you don't understand, my dear Monika . . .' Forsyth began.

'And what would have been the point of fixing the brass band competition – of creating a feeling of well-being in the village – when you intended to shatter that feeling, only hours later, with a murder?'

'I don't know what you mean,' Forsyth said.

But he did.

'Once Len Hopkins was dead, you accepted it as a fact, and milked it for all it was worth, but it was never part of *your* plan to have him killed. That decision was Gary's – and it took you completely by surprise.'

'Nonsense,' Forsyth said. 'You surely know me well enough by now to realize that I keep a very tight grip on my operatives.'

'I'm sure you do – *normally*,' Paniatowski agreed. 'But Gary's not a *normal* agent, is he?'

'I have no idea what you mean,' Forsyth said.

'Here are my demands,' Paniatowski told him abruptly.

'Your *demands*!' Forsyth repeated incredulously.

'My demands,' Paniatowski said. 'Firstly, I want Tommy Sanders admitted to the best – and most expensive – sanatorium you can find.'

'And who'll pay the bill?'

'You will.'

'That's an outlandish suggestion.'

'Secondly, I want Becky Sanders kept out of prison until her grandfather dies, so that she can be with him to the end.'

'But it could take him months to die – especially if he's receiving expensive care.'

'I know.'

'And how do you expect me to keep the entire judicial system at bay all that time?'

'You'll find a way. Thirdly, once she's in gaol, I want her given the best psychiatric help available, and once she's stabilized, she's to be immediately released into the care of good well-trained foster parents. I also want her to be given a new identity.'

'And would you perhaps like me to throw in the kitchen sink as well?' Forsyth asked.

'No, that won't be necessary,' Paniatowski told him. 'But I would like you to set up a trust fund for her, one that will ensure that she never has to worry about money again for the rest of her life.'

'All that would cost an absolute fortune,' Forsyth said.

'Yes, it will,' Paniatowski agreed.

'And why would you think, even for a moment, that I'd agree to any of those demands?'

'You've already pointed out that we'll never catch Gary, and I accept that,' Paniatowski said.

'Good,' Forsyth replied, though he was clearly puzzled at why she was going off at such an apparent tangent.

'But if you don't give me what I want for Becky, I'll pretend that there's a real possibility that we *could* catch him,' Paniatowski continued. 'I'll organize a huge nationwide manhunt, and I'll have the artist's impression of him on the front page of every daily newspaper. We'll get a lot of crank calls – we always do – but eventually we'll get one from someone who really *does* know him.'

'And a lot of good that will do you,' Forsyth said, though he was starting to sound concerned.

'That's when things will really start hotting up,' Paniatowski continued. 'I'll pull in all his family – and all their friends – for questioning. They'll say they don't know where he is . . .'

'They *won't* know where he is.'

'. . . but I'll pretend I don't believe them. I'll turn their homes – and their lives – inside out. By the time I've finished, they'll be nervous wrecks, and none of their friends will want to have anything to do with them ever again.'

'Why should I care what happens to Gary's family?' Forsyth asked, uneasily.

'Because it's *your* family,' Paniatowski said.

'Rubbish! Pure fantasy!' Forsyth told her.

But there was the faintest flickering of an eyelid which told her that what had been a strong suspicion was now a stone-cold fact.

'I thought he reminded me of someone – someone unsettling – when I first saw the sketch, but it wasn't until I was sitting down here that I was sure it was you. He's your grandson, isn't he?'

'No, of course not,' Forsyth said weakly.

'Then why have you kept referring to him as "the boy"?'

'It's a figure of speech.'

'The fact that he's your grandson explains a great deal,' Paniatowski continued. 'I'm guessing that, much as you wanted him to, your son flatly refused to follow in your footsteps. What is he now? A stockbroker? A merchant banker?'

Forsyth's eyelid flickered again.

'No comment,' he said.

'No comment!' Paniatowski repeated. 'That's the last refuge of the trapped and harried. You must have been so sorely disappointed in your son, but then your grandson came along, and he wanted to be a spy – just like you. You were over the moon about it, and *because* you were over the moon, you made the mistake of handling him yourself, instead of letting some other controller do it. Not only that, but you were so keen that he should succeed that you gave him far too much responsibility, far too soon. And he screwed up. He mishandled his attempt to bribe Len Hopkins, and he came up with the crazy idea – which you would never have sanctioned in a million years – of turning Len into a martyr. He also – and you probably don't know this – got Becky pregnant.'

'The stupid little shit,' Forsyth scowled. 'The stupid, *stupid* little shit.'

'From the moment you learned that Len was dead, you've been doing little more than cleaning up your grandson's mess,' Paniatowski continued. 'But he'd never have got in the mess if it hadn't been for your ambitions for him. In some ways, he was as much a lamb being led to the slaughter as Louisa and Becky were. This whole thing only happened because you *allowed* it to happen, so it's at least as much your responsibility as it is his.'

Forsyth sighed. 'We all make mistakes when we're dealing with the ones we love,' he said.

'Even if that someone is a stupid little shit,' Paniatowski replied.

'I can stop you doing what you've just threatened, you know,' Forsyth said. 'I can nip it in the bud.'

'You're wrong,' Paniatowski told him. 'I'll have the support of my chief constable – who hates your guts – and he'll have the support of all the other chief constables around the country, who are sick of people like you getting in the way of honest decent policing.'

'They can be dealt with,' Forsyth said grimly. 'They can all be dealt with.'

'Yes, they can – in time,' Paniatowski agreed. 'But not before I've had the opportunity to make your family aware of just what a monster you've turned Gary into – not before they've started to *hate* you for it.'

Forsyth fell silent, but Paniatowski knew what was going on in his mind.

He was picturing himself walking through rose gardens, hand-in-hand with his granddaughters, and playing happy, noisy games of cricket with his grandsons. He was remembering happy family parties, at which he sat at the head of the table. And he was realizing that she was right – and that he could lose it all.

'If I give you all that you ask for, Monika, you must promise that you'll never mention it to me again,' he said finally.

He was looking into her eyes, and she read the hatred in his. She knew the feeling wouldn't last, and that by morning his mind would have written a different version of this encounter – a version he could live with. But for moment he *did* hate her – hated her for outmanoeuvring him, hated her for refusing to be intimidated by him. She experienced a sense of triumph which was almost joyous. She knew *that* wouldn't last either, but while she had it, she was determined to savour it.

'Well?' Forsyth demanded.

'The best way to ensure I never mention it again is to make certain that we never *meet* again,' she said.

Forsyth shook his head, impatient at what he saw as her stupidity.

'Make certain that we never meet again,' he repeated. 'Oh, please, Monika, don't be so naïve.'

AUTHOR'S NOTE

In March 1984, the British government, headed by Prime Minister Margaret Thatcher, announced that the agreement reached with the miners at the end of the 1974 industrial action was no longer relevant, and would therefore be revoked. It added that twenty mines would be closed down, with the loss of 20,000 jobs.

The strike which inevitably followed was a bitter and divisive one. It tore the union apart, and engendered a distrust of the police which still exists in many ex-mining communities.

The role played by the security forces in the strike is – as it was bound to be – far from clear. It is certain that the F2 branch of MI5 (under Stella Rimington, who would later become the organization's director) used the government communications centre in Cheltenham to tap the phones and bug the offices of miners' union officials. It has never been really denied that MI5 had moles in the NUM, who kept it appraised of both the miners' tactics and the private lives of some of their leaders. And there is a clear link between Rimington and David Hart, a millionaire friend of the prime minister's who pumped a considerable amount of money into the dissident back-to-work movement.

Beyond that, there is only speculation.

Did MI5 use covert and dubious strike-breaking tactics, while keeping the police, who were nominally in charge, completely in the dark? There is at least one senior police officer, Donald McKinnon, who is down on record as claiming this was most certainly the case.

Did the security services deliberately set out to smear the miners' leader, Arthur Scargill? A number of well-informed people – including members of parliament – think that they did.

But though we may never know the full extent of the activities, we now have a clear picture of the consequences. In 1983, there were 174 mines operating in the UK – by 2009, there were six.

It is likely that despite whatever else had happened, the development of alternative sources of energy and globalization had already sent the coal mining industry into terminal decline, but it is doubtful that the decline would have been quite so rapid without the political will of Margaret Thatcher and the support given to her by MI5.